Praise for
The First to Tell

"Another great comedy from a master storyteller, this time a somewhat dark comedy. First off, this is NOT a book for youngsters – it is strictly adults-only. Second, if you don't get dark or black humor, this isn't for you. If you do, be prepared to laugh your socks off. This is black comedy at its finest from a multi-talented author who, it would seem, can turn his hand to just about any genre."

—Anne-Marie Reynolds for *Readers' Favorite*

"The First to Tell is a complete package filled with humor, an impressive plot, vivid characters, and an exciting story - all signatures of Milan Sergent!"

—Rabia Tanveer for *Readers' Favorite*

"This is the third book I've read by Milan Sergent, and it feels like he's only gotten better with each outing. The First To Tell resembles a Coen Brothers screenplay in a novelized format. Simultaneously appalling and hilarious. Immensely satisfying to read. If you're a fan of dark comedies, you don't want to miss out on The First To Tell."

—Pikasho Deka for *Readers' Favorite*

"A captivating novel that navigated a brilliant plot and brought the story to a satisfying end. Milan used dark humor to tell a fantastic and realistic story that taught me many lessons. Allow no one to become a custodian of your secrets or have power over you. This book was wholesome."

—Jennifer Ibiam for *Readers' Favorite*

"With his unique style of writing and ingenious syntax, Milan Sergent effortlessly tells a tale so dark and serious with humor that lightens the mood at just the right moment. This story has some of the most interesting and well-spun characters that I have ever come across in a novel. An absolutely exciting and intriguing story that will catch you off guard at almost every turn! I highly recommend this book for anyone who wants an outside-the-box experience. I can't wait to read the rest of his work."

—Anne-Marie Ledo for *Readers' Favorite*

MILAN SERGENT

THE FIRST TO TELL

Cryptic Quill Publishing LLC.

PANTS ON FIRE

Liar, liar, refocus your vision.
Your veneer of indifference, once dewdrops dripping,
Has now become a torrential flood of recognition.

"Outsiders and Apparitions:
Possessed Poems and Art for Family Picnics"

Milan Sergent

To my beautiful and talented wife,
Multi-Award-Winning Author Beatrice H. Crew.

Cover design and all text
copyright © 2022 by Milan Sergent.

All Rights Reserved.

Published by Cryptic Quill Publishing LLC.

ISBN 13: 978-1-954430-11-2
Library of Congress Control Number: 2022900304

TABLE OF CONTENTS

GUILT TRIP

Many eyes were on Cooper Pearmain as he placed the photo of his dead wife, posing in a bejeweled frame, on the table beside her empty plate. It sparkled from the flickering candle inches away in its frosted container. He gritted his teeth and focused on what he was doing as he unfolded the pressed napkin from the extra silverware and spread the cloth underneath her as she would have done—if her lap wasn't in a coffin six feet underneath Hollywood soil. Despite the whispers from nosy patrons, he had to place her napkin though he wondered why; it would never make up for the past. This European trip was the main thing his wife had planned after Cooper's retirement, so he sat alone at his table for two in an upscale Parisian restaurant, a special place his wife would have enjoyed above all others.

Cooper's flesh was still itching under his suit from the full body wax he suffered through two days earlier in the Swiss Alps. His wife wouldn't have wanted him to be "unhygienic" or "look like a gorilla" for his twenty-four-karat gold body wrap he had endured with great humiliation.

"You look like the Oscar I should've won," Cooper had imagined his dead wife saying from the spa bed beside him.

Cooper leaned over the restaurant table and wiped off a smudge of gold, which the esthetician had forgotten to remove from the glass on the photo frame. He couldn't believe he had to pay for a full-priced body wrap for his wife when she was only eight inches now—framed in her cell of rhinestones that the store thought were priceless gems when she had bought the gaudy thing. And from the look she was still giving him in the photo, he dared not complain about the cost. That had only ever made matters worse, for the only thing that had ever *mattered* was her, and she had made damn sure he knew it, too.

"Would Monsieur Pearmain prefer a drink before ze lovely lady arrives? A glass of our finest champagne, perhaps?" asked the waiter in his best English, after he rushed over from another table.

"Oh, the lovely lady is here, and she hates to be ignored, just so you know." Cooper lifted his hand to bring the waiter's attention to the photo frame. "It's best to ask Lilibet."

The waiter lowered his rectangular-framed eyeglasses and gaped at the picture of Lilibet.

"Yes, go ahead; she hates to be kept waiting, don't you, sassy muffin?"

The waiter cleared his throat. "Would Madame Lilibeth prefer—"

"'Lilibet.' Her name is Lilibet—no H. And you had better *bet* she'll let you know if you mispronounce it," said Cooper.

"*Ahem.* Would Madame Lilibet prefer a drink? How

about a glass of our finest champagne?" asked the waiter, cutting his eyes back at Cooper for approval.

"She would like the whole bottle of champagne, please. This is particularly important: Make sure the bottle is chilled in an equal mixture of ice, water, and salt; too much ice and Lilibet can't drink it. And she would like it served with her foie gras, but only if it's from the male mulard ducks. I'll have a glass of brandy while I look over the menu."

"As you—sorry—as *madame* wishes."

"Oh, and one more thing," said Cooper, grabbing the waiter's tuxedo sleeve near the elbow. "If you will . . . turn around, please."

"Turn around?" the waiter asked, with his back now to the table.

"Yes, now lift the tails of your tuxedo, please."

"Excusez-moi?" A slice of the waiter's dark fringe fell across his forehead when it had been so high on his stiff pompadour earlier—"an ass bang," Cooper's brother had called the hairstyle when Lilibet had tried to get Cooper to look like a greaser dude, going as far as standing beside the barber's chair with a photo of John Travolta from the film *Grease*.

Cooper tried to think of the correct French translation of his request. "Um, soulevez les queues de votre smoking."

"Hmm, you are ze naughty one, no?" The waiter raised one eyebrow at Cooper and, with a sigh, eased up the tails of his coat.

"Good. Now, if you will, bend over just a little more so Lilibet can have a good look at your buns."

"Bend over?" The waiter sucked in his lips and

glanced sideways at Cooper as he leaned forward.

"Yes. Lilibet always likes to inspect the waiters' buns. If she's impressed, she always leaves a huge tip."

"From the madame, of course," the waiter said with a wink before leaving the table.

Cooper whispered to Lilibet's photo, "I know I wasn't able to get you all the specifics you wanted, honey dumplings. But I gave up my yacht to give you the six-month European vacation."

He nearly choked on a piece of bread when his dead wife's eyes seemed to harden on him.

"Don't look at me like that. I know you're still mad at me about missing the Bond film re-enactment. But you see, Lilibet, deep down most men—most healthy men—have a bit of pride after a certain point."

Lilibet's eyebrow seemed to raise even sharper, as it often did when she was bitter. And how could she be, with the French folk music ebbing and flowing in the background, the male crooner plucking a daisy, whispering, and moaning with calculated panache into the microphone? Cooper suspected the singer was putting everyone in a trance in French code, brainwashing the diners to donate their wallets, estates, and firstborn children to the restaurant, but not for financial gain, no, *pas du tout*! So they could give everyone else fashion and etiquette lessons.

"Oh, come on! I would've looked like a fool doing the tango with you—with a picture frame—in that casino, and you know it." Cooper lowered his voice even more and leaned closer to her photo. "Did you want them to lock me up, huh? Is that what you wanted? I'm sorry, okay? I'm sorry for what happened."

This was only part of the truth. Lilibet knew Cooper had become paranoid about dancing ever since July 12, 1979, when Major League Baseball hosted the Disco Demolition Night at Comiskey Park in Chicago, Illinois. All the white rock-n-rollers were admitted practically for free if they brought any disco records they could find and blow them all up on live television between the infamous doubleheader. Enraged rioters flung records, fireworks, golf balls, and insults, endangering even the players. All because they eventually figured out that disco was the preferred music of gay, Black, and Latin people at the time, and it was giving them a voice. The protestors had grown scared after seeing their esteemed rock-n-roll heroes cutting disco singles and shaking their butts in tight spandex and polyester. Disco "officially" died not long after this, as well as any dancing that didn't involve merely nodding your head like you were having an angry seizure.

The waiter brought out Lilibet's food. "Excusez-moi," he said, trying to slip away discreetly.

"You didn't interrupt anything. Lilibet is giving me the silent treatment."

"I imagine she is quite good at that, no?" The waiter uncorked the champagne and poured some in a crystal glass for Lilibet before easing the bottle back into the ice bucket at the end of the table.

Cooper placed his order and took a sip of his brandy. The truth was, he would've relished any damned moment of silent treatment he could've gotten if Lilibet would've blessed him with it. The only times she refused to flap her gums was when Cooper tried to bring up the past—the vile skeleton that needed to be released from their unfinished closet. Perhaps if things hadn't turned so toxic between the two of them shortly after they had married, he would've kept his sanity, and she wouldn't be dead. Still, there was no escaping her. He could see the final days leading up to Lilibet's death everywhere. Even the brandy in the bottom of his glass, with its golden-amber color, reminded him of that time, the catalyst, when he was in the shower and had become so terrified that he lost control of his bladder function.

1

RETIREMENT FARCE

Cooper eased the door closed to the bathroom and placed his clean and folded underclothes on the marble sink. He grabbed a premium blend cotton washcloth from the linen closet and his wicker tray of designer soap, body lotion, shaving cream, and deodorant and placed the items on the edge of the tub. He checked to see if his bottle of sulfate-free shampoo and conditioner, the latest award-winning products for the remaining hair clinging for dear life to his scalp, was still in the basket hanging under the showerhead. He made a mental checklist of anything missing that needed to be done for the party in an hour. Everything needed to be as pleasing as possible for his guests tonight. Cooper couldn't help it; he always had to go the extra hundred miles to make up for Lilibet's refusal to budge.

"It takes a lot of seasoning to make tripe edible," his innovative mother used to say. In fact, it was her last words to Cooper before he married Lilibet—his mother's last words before she died soon afterward. There were too many come-to-think-of-it moments in Cooper's later years. Sex Ed teachers should definitely teach boys the dangerously thin line between lust and love in school.

You should probably lock the door, the thought occurred to Cooper, after stripping off his clothes and stepping in the tub. He had to quit being so paranoid and focus on positivity for the evening. Positive and cognitive. He slid the plastic shower curtain closed. The water pelting his bare skin was always too hot or cold at first, but soon he relaxed and washed away the residue of his last interaction with Lilibet. The soap slipped out of his hand, and he reached down to retrieve it near the drain when a shadow inched close to the white shower curtain, now beaded with steamy water. He bolted upright and reached for the end of the curtain to peel it back and see if the maid would dare enter without knocking. Lilibet had her own bathroom and was so germophobic she wouldn't dare enter Cooper's—that and the steam would ruin her hair. There was always a "love spittoon" near the bed because she forced him to gargle with mouthwash between every kiss he had to schedule with her, and don't even ask why she made him keep a hot water bottle with an attached hose on hand.

"Lilibet, is that you, dear?"

Before Cooper's hand reached the flap, a long chef's knife began slicing and slicing through the curtain. Between the rips in the plastic, he could see Lilibet in her shower robe and cap, a mud mask smeared over her face with only her bulging eyes and gnashing teeth peeking through the sick pea-green goop. The tenth slice grazed the tip of his lonely willy, and the yellow splatter it caused made Cooper realize he had just pissed in the shower.

"Lilibet, stop! What are you doing? You nearly castrated me-he-hee," he said with something between a nervous laugh and a childlike sob, backing against the farthest corner of the shower where he instinctively covered his privates.

"Oh, stop being such a whiny baby, and guess who I am? Guess what movie this is from?" she replied, still hacking at the curtain while frigid air gushed through what now looked like soggy party streamers hanging from the rod overhead.

After Cooper slid down the wall to the bottom of the tub, getting a nose and mouthful of jet spray, Lilibet threw the knife on the floor with a huff.

"It was the shower scene from *Psycho*, only I did it way better; you just don't want to admit it." Her eyes settled on his shriveled privates, where she pointed and laughed. "Cooper, you really are a drooper, you know that? Which reminds me: I need to see how the noodles are coming along in the kitchen."

Minutes after she left, he was still too stunned to stand up and turn the water off. The bathroom floor was soaked. For now, it was only water, but one day it would probably be his blood. Why wasn't he prepared this time? He supposed because, for once, it was his most special day. Often his wife had awoken Cooper or caught

him by surprise, standing behind him with a gun or knife in her hand or a heavy object over his head, only for him to figure out that it wasn't his time to die, that he was supposed to guess what scene from a movie she was re-enacting. But this was the final straw. He was going to demand she stop the re-enactments.

Forget pee-shy; he doubted he would ever feel safe enough to even shower in his own home again.

* * *

Cooper dried off, dressed, and swallowed the lump of dread in his throat as he approached Lilibet in the kitchen. She was standing under a pink neon sign, which took up half a wall above the custom Bocote wood cabinets: *Lilibet's Kitchen.* This seedy announcement didn't mean she was the cook by any gourmet definition. It meant she got first dibs and "samplings" on whatever the cook prepared for them. Guests were soon to arrive at the Pearmain Mansion in the Garden District of New Orleans, where Lily-Butt insisted on living—the main drag to be seen—Avenue Saint-Charles. She always had to be center stage and wouldn't have their historical home named after the original owners as was tradition.

"Honey dumplings, I think we both owe it to ourselves to have, you know, have that talk. It's just, well, you and I both know we've been ignoring the elephant in the room for many years and—"

"The elephant wasn't in the bathroom minutes ago. More like a mouse tail," she said between snickers and fingers held two inches apart.

Cooper ignored her insults and pressed on. "It's just, well, tonight means so much to me and, and I don't want anything to go wrong."

Lilibet spun around from the dessert tray she was hovering over. With her lips clenched, her eyes fixed twice their normal size on Cooper.

"I don't know why you are making such a fuss," she said. "Hardly anyone is coming to your party. The Bloombergs didn't even respond to your invitation."

"They aren't responding because that loose tongue of yours has cost me client after client, which is part of the reason I'm retiring from my law practice. And don't even try to deny it this time. The Bloombergs told me so themselves—told me they didn't appreciate you spreading gossip about them and that they were changing law firms."

"Well, how dare they try to make me look like the bad guy here? It's no loss. You don't want to represent them anyway." Lilibet flipped her wrist while puffing her lips into a snarl.

Cooper stiffened and squeezed his ticking eyelids shut. "See? See there what you do? You said the same thing about the Waltons and Musk family, the Rothschilds, the, um, Kennedys, and, and—anyway, the point is, can you please not destroy every last relationship in my life?"

Oh, hell, he realized his last few words had been too much—too truthful. No telling what she would do now.

Lilibet elbowed him in the stomach and ran toward

the back door on the other side of the counter, but Cooper tripped her and reached the door before she did. She grabbed at his ankles while he made damn sure she was watching as he locked the back door to their sprawling 1850s home.

"There!" Cooper said with a sneer, displaying the key before putting it in his pocket. "My guests, my retirement party—MINE—will be starting in a few minutes, and I'll not have you pretending to drown yourself in the pool this time, so you can change out of that thin white dress."

Lilibet climbed to her feet. "Go right ahead. Lock every goddamned drawer and door in the house. You're like the crypt keeper with all your keys; you know that?" She grimaced hideously, which was so easy for her these days. She lurched around the kitchen, hunched over, and rattling a pretend set of keys, before standing upright and putting her hands on her lily-white hips squeezed in as far as they could go under her heavy-duty girdle. "Besides, I can fill up the hot tub faster than you can brag about your last court case. Hell, I can drown myself with a bottle of cheap champagne if I need to."

"*Hmph.* Well, doesn't the entire country know that!" hissed Cooper.

At least five times since his marriage to Lilibet, he had read hair-raising stories in various gossip papers and magazines about their public fights and the drunken scenes Lilibet had made. And over time, the reports were that Cooper was a lush, as well, thanks to his wife's behavior. He was beginning to wonder if her actions were a desperate grab to remain relevant. He knew there were washed-up celebrities like that—willing to become infamous just to be "in" and famous. And if those types had to share a prison cell with the likes of Charles Manson, then so be it; they would do anything. Something in Cooper's gut seemed to be warning him that his wife's antics were going to lead them down yet another dark and dangerous dead end. "Dead" being the word that would finally be illuminated in lights. Only this time, it wouldn't be on a theater marquee announcing some flop of a film starring Lilibet. This film would be a documentary of the Pearmains—a shock doc. Had Lilibet acted in so many films about death that she was indifferent to the matter? Or worse, perhaps the boundaries between movies and the real world were blurred to her.

"Ahhh, yes, death by champagne; that would be the way to go, let me tell ya." Lilibet reached in her newest designer "bag" and pulled out her over-teased blonde wiglet.

"And you! You won't be able to snatch this off my head and tell everyone I have to wear a wiglet. Not tonight, you won't." She forced the hairpiece down the garbage disposal while Cooper dove after her to stop it. He wasn't going to pay for a third garbage disposal in two years.

With a sinister grin, Lilibet flipped the switch activating the disposal, which made awful grinding and coughing sounds as it tried to shred the hideous creature. She seemed to take the greatest delight in shredding

things as if it were their marriage that she was ripping into tiny, anguished pieces.

"Of course, you don't need a wig now—after you blew my African safari allowance on two hair transplants. I know where that new hair came from, and you still expect me to believe you got a Brazilian wax," said Cooper, while the maid trembled past them to place the last few hot plates on the sideboard in the formal dining room.

Lilibet checked her makeup, her warpaint, in the silvery reflection of the toaster while sampling her fifth hors d'oeuvre. ". . . And for the last time, Cooper: my hair's not Marilyn Monroe blonde; it's Scandinavian blonde."

Cooper opened the liquor cabinet and added extra tequila to his drink. "Oh, how could I forget? How. Could. I? You would never dream of admitting you copied yourself after Marilyn or any actress. You— Lilibet Bathroy Pearmain—you were *original*," Cooper said with a long and breathy ending, as he bowed before an invisible audience, taunting her. Tonight, only Lilibet's audience would be imaginary. Cooper had already had a retirement party at the law firm where he worked as their top intellectual property lawyer for twenty-two years. This party was for *his* friends and family.

"Careful, you retired old fart. You're leaving alcohol fumes all over my clean kitchen. We're not close enough to the French Quarter to use that as an excuse." Lilibet fanned the air with an unused silver platter.

"Like you've ever cleaned a kitchen."

"I would," said Lilibet, "but none of these old fuddy-duddies are worth the effort. I don't know why you think they are our friends. They don't ever invite us to their houses. They're all take and no give. Especially that weaselly brother of yours. I can't believe you invited him and his daughter to the party."

"Our relationship has been a little strained lately. I doubt he'll even show up." Cooper hated confessing that to Lilibet. The last thing she needed was more ammunition to fire in her guns.

"Well, if Stan does show up, I don't want that brat of his snooping anywhere around my house. He had better keep a watch on her the entire time. If I catch Farrah opening another drawer or cabinet again, I'll bite her monkey paws off and glue them over those inquisitive little eyes of hers. Do you understand me?" Lilibet jabbed her finger toward Cooper while one eyebrow pointed sharper at the arch.

She laughed softly as if they had been having a most lovely evening already. Then she turned to the kitchen table and began squishing and tugging at an already perfectly prepared floral arrangement until it was off balance and shedding petals. Lilibet always insisted on fresh flowers throughout the house, even if she had to steal them from the local cemeteries. "The dead don't need flowers," she always said, unless, of course, when planning her funeral. Cooper had begged her to stop doing it. Surely it was bad karma if anything were.

"Now, Hollywood," she continued, "that's where my

true friends were until I lost my career and moved to this, this swamp."

Lilibet shut up after she seemed to notice Cooper's head drop.

The doorbell rang.

"Look at us, huh? Here it is your special night, and everyone will think we were fussing," said Lilibet, wiping a tear of laughter from her cheek.

"Us two? *Nah.*"

Forget and move on with their lives had been the goal. But Cooper couldn't help but rightfully expect a locked door to open someday and find a hideous monster of certain death ready to pounce on them. They doubled over with laughter. An unnatural remedy that developed over time because of their relentless fighting. But the laughter was only a facade—a front to make everyone think they were a somewhat normal couple. Cooper would give anything to be free of Lilibet, be free of guilt, and live a peaceful life in his final years. The truth was they both detested each other since the deadly day in their early marriage. So, here they were, bound together in unholy matrimony by the secrets they had on one another—a perverse way of keeping one's enemies closer.

Cooper grabbed Lilibet's cold claw of a hand and went to the front door to greet the guests. He could also swallow a mouthful of raw liver with a convincing smile of savory delight. Wasn't that what adults learn to do? Wasn't that what life fed you after the few seconds of good things in youth?

"Welcome to our humble home just a short sashay

from the Vieux Carré!" sang Lilibet, squeezing in front of her husband. She draped her arms on either side of the doorframe as though she were still a dancer in a chorus-line film, knocking Cooper hard in the nose. "Why, the humid Creole air here leaves a lady's bosoms all moist and glistening, unlike the dry Hollywood air I was used to for years. But never mind my fans; my husband always comes first. And he loves it here, don't you, my little sugar booger?" she cooed in her newfound Southern accent before pinching his aching nose.

"Oh, yes, Cooper always comes first. That's why you constantly beat me to the door, honey dumplings." Cooper checked his nose to see if it was bleeding before shaking his first guests' hands and inviting them into the formal living room. Among the men and women were two of the Pearmains' new best friends, a married couple from Denver named Donald and Linda Hargraves. Donald was the CEO of the CPA firm that managed the Pearmains' taxes. Linda ran a fashion blog for plus-sized women called *Double-Plus Gorgeous*. Besides Cooper's only brother, Stan, and his niece, Farrah, the other guests included A.J. and Philip, a couple of married men who bought a home on Bourbon Street near Esplanade in the French Quarter. They ran an antique furniture store Lilibet frequented on Royal Street.

"Tell me again now; who is the top and who is the bottom?" Lilibet asked the gay couple in a loud, drunken voice while other guests shuttled past them as if to avoid their answers.

The couple's eyes met with a familiar weary roll while

the maid served them their choice of drinks.

"Ignore my wife," said Cooper, feeling sorry for the two men. "She judges everyone by who is on top."

"Well, that certainly isn't *you*, is it, sugar booger?" Lilibet cackled, swirling the ice cubes around in her drink with a sassy smirk. Everybody searched the guests' faces before something close to a smile formed on their sunken expressions. Cooper knew trying to have the party was a bad idea, but he just couldn't stand to be stuck at home with Lilibet and her constant nagging, and more than anything, he feared leaving her alone just so he could have a bit of fun for once. He was terrified of what would happen to him, period, if he made Lily-Butt really mad.

"Oh, everybody needs to lighten up. It's only sex, for God's sake. Is this a party or a funeral, huh? Oh, I forgot; it's the latter." She lifted her glass toward Cooper. "Once you retire, you kick the bucket. Well, this old gal is gonna get her kicks before she kicks the bucket, I'll tell ya."

Lilibet slammed her drink down on the antique end table and grabbed the white Pomeranian from A.J.'s arms. She tossed the dog up and down in the air while its beady eyes bulged in terror. "Momma could just eat you up, yes she could," she baby-talked the dog, who grunted and sneezed with frustration with each toss.

A.J. and Philip snatched their white cloud of fluffiness away from Lilibet and cuddled the dog close between them. The last guests to arrive were a young married couple from the Garden District: John Henry Mayfield, a college student of law, and his wife, Ami, who was getting her degree in psychology. John Henry and Ami approached Lilibet with a gift bottle of wine, which she took from Ami's hands like a trophy.

"Now here's a couple who aren't afraid of sex," Lilibet turned John Henry around in front of the other guests. "Look at those buns, would you—all round and firm from humping your little bride every chance you get, I'll bet. Do you see his buns, Cooper?" Lilibet snatched Cooper closer by his suit lapel.

"Yes, Lilibet. I'm not blind, remember?" sighed Cooper, wondering when she would make him squeeze them.

"That, Cooper, that is what a real man's ass is supposed to look like—so tight I could open this bottle of wine between those melons—just pop that cork. I'll bet he'd be a real danger in a bouncy house those sugared-up kids love to jump around in these days."

Cooper stole the bottle from Lilibet before she ended up raping John Henry with the vintage merlot. Ami Mayfield visibly stiffened and shrank an inch, while A.J. turned his partner's head away from John Henry's buns, which he had been straining his neck to see.

"I, uh, think now's a good time to get that autograph you've been wanting, Ami," said John Henry through his teeth vanishing behind a fading smile.

"Oh . . . right," squeaked Ami. With shaking hands, she fumbled through her purse and removed an old nude photo of Lilibet, which she flashed to the guests. She then handed Lilibet a black marker to sign it.

Lilibet's penciled eyebrows rose an inch, and she feigned embarrassment better than a vestal virgin.

"What? Where did you ever find that? I don't remember authorizing anyone to take nude pictures of me. Those greedy, perverted paparazzi think nothing of violating beautiful actresses."

"Yeah, you do remember, Lilibet. That was a movie still for that underground horror flick you did, *Libertine's Day Mascara*. Oh, relax; it's only sex, you said." Cooper sucked in his cheeks and smacked Lilibet on her rear end so hard she spilled her drink, and he was certain one of the hooks came loose in her girdle.

Lilibet began smearing her name all over the photo. "Why, of course, I'll autograph her little picture. It's just, I didn't realize Ami Cable here was such a fan of my work."

"It's Ami Mayfield—Ami with a lowercase *i*—just so no one thinks I come off as a narcissist. Though, as we learn in psychology, one should come to accept herself as an uppercase *i*—or himself—sorry." Ami jumped as if she had a hiccup and clasped the arms of A.J. and Philip, who were nearest her. "We must all consider ourselves powerful and deserving," Ami said in a much higher and sillier tone.

"Oh, so you're majoring in child psychology," said A.J., kissing his Pomeranian's head.

"No. I want to help women . . . grown women," Ami replied. With her plastered smile crumbling, she backed away from the boys. Her husband, John Henry, kept sneaking curious glances at the gay couple before quickly looking away. Ami grabbed his arm and pulled him to a distant spot in the room.

Cooper knew Lilibet had done another snide play on words. Behind Ami's back, she was always calling her "Ami Cable" because she was so damn *amicable* toward her husband, a kindness she obviously loathed to offer Cooper. He lifted his crystal glass to make an announcement before Ami had time to figure out the insult.

"Thank you all for gracing us with your presence—"

"Well, they certainly didn't with any presents . . . cheapskates," mumbled Lilibet.

"As you all know," continued Cooper, positive that he was blushing, "I officially retired this week, and the—"

Cooper waited for the guests to stop applauding and congratulating him.

"Yeah, but I still get to keep spending as usual," shot Lilibet, stroking her new custom-designed necklace that eclipsed the moles, wrinkles, and sunspots flecking her upper chest.

Cooper snorted bitterly. And when the next party came along, Lily-Butt would have the jewelers melt it all down and recast the golden calf into a new conversation piece, because in her mind, she was saving money and the planet by "recycling."

"Ya need some more write-offs on next year's taxes, Cooper. Time for that long vacay—the harem of women with big bazookas we talked about," said Donald, the tax CEO, raising his glass as he huddled in the crowd against the wall. Linda elbowed him and turned red. Lilibet gave a pissy grinding of her jaws and pumped out her breasts as though she was serving the hors d'oeuvre crumbs off them.

Cooper downed his refill of tequila to prepare for Lily-Butt's wrath. "Well now, *you* are the tax genius, Don. To launch my retirement, I was thinking of buying a yacht and spending a few months at sea."

"Hmm, what do you know?" said Cooper's brother, Stan Pearmain. "You told me you were going to have to hunker down and cut out all the spending once you retired." With a shifted grin, Stan rubbed the top of Farrah's head as though she were a pedigree dog that had just won *Best in Show*.

Lilibet's nostrils flared so big, Cooper could see straight up to her alcohol-shriveled brain cells. "You bastard! You promised me a six-month European vacation. Remember the twenty-four-karat gold body wraps in the Swiss Alps to restore our youthful glows?"

Cooper was sure he was blushing as the room grew sickeningly silent, and Lilibet swaggered closer and closer to him, spouting off all the things they had planned.

". . . Tea with Maggie Smith at Buckingham Palace. She'll be devastated; she's a dame now, you know? The Bond film casino re-enactment we planned for *Never Say Never Again*. Ha! You swore you could never say 'no' to that! The one thing that you know damn well would reignite my career! I even took refresher lessons on the tango for that."

Cooper held his hands out, trying to calm his wife. "Honey dumplings, think of the hotel money we'll save having our own yacht. Once the European trip is done, you'll forget all about it after one big hangover. But a boat is an investment that lasts."

"We could've had both if you hadn't been in such a goddamn hurry to retire and surround yourself with bazookas!" A shower of alcohol splattered the guests around Lilibet.

Just before Lilibet sloshed her drink on Cooper, the maid cleared her throat nervously and announced that the food was ready in the dining room. The guests nearly toppled over one another to escape the formal living room.

"Oh, now it couldn't be your washed-up acting career that keeps you from owning the world now, could it?" asked Cooper, wondering how he always managed to fall into this vicious trap that Lilibet lived to drag him into.

She sloshed her booze on him and began hitting and slapping him as he backed into the dining room.

"You two-faced bastard! I am anything but washed up, and you know it. I sacrificed my entire career to move to this gumbo swamp for you. That alone should be a major write-off. But oh, no, you've been giving over half of your income to dozens of college scholarship programs—just handing it out like it was some damned Halloween candy." Lilibet's lips warped into a grimace. "Didn't think I knew about that, did ya?"

"Aw, that is so nice of you, Cooper," said one of the guests, while a few clapped nervously. "Think of how many kids you'll help get into college who can't afford

it."

"Yes, think about it, Brother of mine," said Stan Pearmain. "Always considering others." With a toothy smile, he placed his hand on his daughter's upper back while she inspected the china cabinet.

"Nice, my ass," hissed Lilibet. "Should I tell our guests why you've been giving away my European vacation money behind my back? Should I tell them why our financial security doesn't matter, Cooper?"

Thinking of the one thing that could possibly stop Lily-Butt, before she ruined what little reputation she had left, Cooper grabbed her *Underground Film Critics Society Award* off the marble mantel and threatened to throw it into the burning fireplace.

"You wouldn't dare!" Lilibet growled. Ami cut her eyes at John Henry as though waiting for his signal to run for their lives.

"Honey dumplings, just calm down now," whispered Cooper. "I think you've had a little too much sippy-sippy." He eased his arm up and made a drinking motion with his free hand. The maid tried to distract Lilibet by offering her a trembling plate of food, but she hurled it at Cooper's feet. Lilibet stormed out of the room and returned two minutes later with disheveled hair and a wild expression on her face, panting through her gaping mouth. Cooper feared he was seeing what he thought he was in her clenched fist as the guests cleared toward the far side of the dining room.

"Look here what I found in your underwear." Lilibet unrolled the red fishnet bikini briefs and held the horrid object up for all to view. "You see, Ladies and Gentlemen, my husband, Cooper, is a drooper." Lilibet held her finger erect and then let it droop in front of her smirking lips. "That's why he needs his prostate orgasm assister. That's why his buns are flat, unlike John Henry's there." She turned Cooper's underwear around and displayed the rip in the seat. "But now this hole— this hole is because he eats all that damn spicy food here."

Certain his spirit had left his body, Cooper returned Lilibet's trophy to the shelf. He lowered his chin to the collar of his suitcoat and felt as though he was trudging through quicksand before he finally reached the door leading out of the room. He could never show his face to his guests again. The crowd began to dwindle, and others returned their half-eaten plates of food to the dining table. Cooper retreated to the closest guest bathroom and locked himself inside.

"What's a prostate?" asked young Farrah, loud enough for everyone to hear. "Oh, I know; it's like in that song we sing sometimes in church: '*Let angel's prostate fall,*'" she sang loudly.

"Um, yeah, sweetheart. That's what it means," lied Stan Pearmain.

Seconds later, the nerve-grating sound of fingernails scratching the bathroom door outside alarmed Cooper's ears. What character role was Lilibet playing now? Was there a *Psycho 2* movie, or had she finally snapped?

"Oh, Coopie, come out, come out wherever you are. *Coooopieeee* . . .," Lilibet's breathy voice called creepily

through the door. He could almost see and smell her boozed-up breath seeping through the doorframe.

Cooper's heart seemed to expand into his esophagus. As much as he never wanted to see the inside of a shower again, he eased the white lace shower curtain back and prepared to hide in the bathtub when Lilibet let out an eardrum-shattering growl.

"Open the goddamn door, you spineless toad!" She began rattling the door so hard a fleck of peeling white paint came loose and flung three feet away from the toilet bowl. "Is Cooper drooper afraid of wittle ol' Wiwibet?" she asked in a baby voice that was anything but little. "What's a-matter? Can't handle a woman who is no longer afraid of you—who's no longer willing to let you abuse her?"

The doorframe began to split near the locked knob, so Cooper removed his left foot from the bathtub and dove against the door, leaning against it with all his strength.

"That's a damn lie. I never abused you," yelled Cooper, hoping any remaining guests could hear him and stop believing Lilibet's drunken games—her lies for attention and sympathy.

"Not between the sheets anyway. Did you hear that, guests? Coopie droopy here only abuses himself between the sheets." Lilibet began to cackle in the hall outside, and then Cooper heard a deep and dull scraping noise that grew louder as it approached the door. His teeth ached from clenching his jaws. Surely, Lilibet wasn't trying to barricade the door with the antique hall cabinet, was she? Had she finally gone completely mad?

"Please, Lilibet, will you please stop this and just calm down?"

"Calm down? That's your answer to everything, isn't it, you worm?" Lilibet started rocking the hall cabinet, which kept slamming against the door. The hinges began to groan and buckle. Pressing hard against the door with his back, Cooper fumbled for his cellphone in his pocket. He needed to call the police before she demolished the entire house—or worse.

Before Cooper could dial the last number, an explosion flung him headfirst into the toilet bowl. He quickly lifted his head, and water streamed down his face. He looked up at Lilibet, who snarled at him over the toppled wardrobe halfway inside the bathroom. He had reached the bottom with her and couldn't think of a single thing to say in his defense, couldn't think of any way to reason with the demon in heels.

"Wait! Don't leave," Lilibet shouted over her shoulder at the guests. "I—we were only acting. Cooper was just going along with all of this to show everyone I still had the old acting gift in me. Weren't you, Cooper? Cooper!" Lilibet's voice sounded desperate. "And if you couldn't tell what movie that was from, then to hell with you all. Just climb back in your station wagons and drive back home to Dullsville."

Again, this wasn't to be his last day on the planet, unfortunately. Just when his long, tumultuous marriage seemed to reach a deserved resolution, with an audience as witnesses, Cooper found himself on the endless

loop—saved by another last-second breath, another last-second rabbit Lilibet pulled out of a hat. He sidestepped back into the room, pretending he was Fred Astaire swishing an umbrella. And he, too, would sing in the damn rain.

"We really convinced 'em, didn't we, honey dumplings?" said Cooper, convinced by the traumatized expressions of the remaining guests that they hated horror movies.

2

FAN ANTICS

Two days later, Cooper checked in the dresser mirror to
see if his buns were as flat as Lilibet claimed before he
emerged like a groundhog from his bedroom across the
hall from her "queen's chamber." Either the booze and
isolation had done their job to calm the tension between
Lilibet and him, or they hadn't. He stepped over the
toppled wardrobe, passed the dining room, grabbed the
newspapers off the front driveway, before heading into
the kitchen. Mist from the nearby Mississippi River had
left the newspapers soggy. Mist depressed Cooper more
than anything now. The house was still a mess. He didn't
blame the maid for quitting. After Lilibet's performance,
he had never been so humiliated, not even when he had
wet the bed at summer camp as a boy. He blamed himself
for entertaining the foolish thought that Lilibet would
feel guilty enough to clean the mess herself while Cooper
had sulked in his darkened bedroom—another futile
expectation on the endless loop.

He placed the papers on the kitchen table to dry and began gathering the dirty plates and glasses from the dining room, and he loaded them into the dishwasher. The dried food left a spicy stench in the air that needed exorcising. Johnny-come-lately Lilibet shuffled into the kitchen, grabbed her orange juice from the refrigerator, and rummaged through her medication drawer near the sink. All the pill rattling sounded like a band of maraca players before she found the right bottle scattered among some jewelry she had left there because her jewelry box was too far a walk. Every room in the house had its own makeshift jewelry box, whether a table, display bowl, or even one of her shoes.

She swallowed one capsule, dropped the other, and gazed hypnotically at the remaining dishes on the kitchen table. Cooper knew her method by now: a premature hello from her after awaking would mean she had enough energy to help him with the dishes. But he sure as hell wasn't going to speak first as long as he could resist her.

"Ow-ow-ow!" she groaned so loud Cooper nearly dropped the silver service he was hand polishing. This was his cue to acknowledge her first or at least look at her, but he refused.

"I just had a twinge in my back," she finally responded, while gazing at the red button on the dishwasher.

"Yeah, from lying on it for two whole days," Cooper wanted to say. But he had other issues he couldn't let her get away with this time. "Why did you have to humiliate

me like you did? I never dreamed you'd go that low."

Lilibet put her dirty glass back in the refrigerator. "You were going to throw my best acting award in the fire—okay, my *only* award. There, I admit it; are you happy? Besides, you should've gone ahead and done it. That's the way this game works. When I say I'm going to do something, I do it! I can't help it if you're a chicken—a chicken with a broken pecker. Anyway, we're going to have to hire another maid; all of this cleaning biz is killing my back."

While Cooper finished cleaning the house, Lilibet arranged for an interview with a new maid and then tried phoning a few of the guests who had fled before her explanation for the fight.

"No one is answering your calls. What do you know about that, huh?" Cooper said, after storing the silver service in the china cabinet and singing the main chorus of "Karma Chameleon" to remind Lilibet of her actions.

"You are always so paranoid." Lilibet snarled and unrolled one of the newspapers, *The Big Easy Journal*, and searched for her favorite section: the society page.

"Of all the nerve!" she sputtered and shook the paper.

"A problem, honey dumplings?" asked Cooper, running a mop over the kitchen floor. Lilibet lifted her feather house slippers so the mop could reach under her feet, and she nearly fell off the barstool.

"*The Big Easy* printed an article about the two of us having another one of our public antics. Lies. Glittery dollar-store garbage!" she hissed. "That wasn't a public antic. It was a—a skit at our private party—our own home, for heaven's sake. Wasn't it, Cooper drooper?" Lilibet pinched his groin with her claws. "I warned you. You can't trust those friends of yours. One of them even sneaked photos of us."

"Now who's being paranoid? Who took the pictures?" groaned Cooper, looking at the photo of Lilibet holding up his underwear while he was about to hurl her trophy into the fireplace. They both looked intoxicated or drugged. A bitter fire in their eyes few actors could mimic.

"They didn't publish their name. The cowards!"

"Will you please stop calling your antics 'a skit'?" said Cooper, freeing his aching groin. "You're starting to believe your explanations. Honey dumplings, I think we are long overdue for a talk."

Lilibet finally started helping Cooper unload the dishwasher. She dumped the silverware on the table with a clatter and pretended she had injured her finger.

"New Orleanians are starting to talk. We moved from California to get away from gossip, remember?" said Cooper, grabbing a plate before she broke it.

"Aah, let those coonasses talk," said Lilibet. "They live such dull lives. They're desperate for entertainment."

Cooper stored the serving platter in the overhead cabinet. "What are they saying about us?"

"Nothing of importance." Lilibet crumpled the paper and started to toss it in the trashcan, but he ripped it from her hands and smoothed out the news article on the clean table.

"No wonder you didn't want me to see this. They say I'm impotent and henpecked—that we don't have any money and we're both alcoholics, which is the reason I was forced to retire."

Lilibet plopped her left leg on the barstool and, with both hands, smoothed out the purple and green veins bulging up and down her leg. "What about me, huh? They implied that I'm some sort of animal abusing nymphomaniac, just because I would like my sorry husband to hump me once in a while."

Lilibet jumped when her cellphone went off to the tune "One Way or Another" by Blondie, announcing she had just received a text. She grabbed the phone from her robe pocket and read the text.

"I cannot believe this! Those sorry-ass fuckers!"

"Whom would that be this time?" asked Cooper, dreading her response.

"The garden club. They sent me a text saying they have dropped me as a member. That the recent article about us was the final straw. They don't want to risk getting a bad reputation because of my—our—recent behavior."

"Don't worry about it. You don't do the gardening anyway. Jorge does it all."

"Oh please! None of the members do their own damned gardening, Cooper. It's always been about who has the sexiest gardener. They are all just jealous because the hottest young man in New Orleans chose to work for me, Cooper, for me! Oh, I've seen them all drooling when he's out there, all hot and sweaty, wearing nothing

but his little blue-jean shorts. They all find excuses to go for walks when he's working. Hell, it's like a neighborhood Easter egg hunt. They just pray they'll find the prized eggs when Jorge bends over." With her teeth flashing, Lilibet curled her fingers in the air like she was plucking large grapes.

She threw her cellphone across the kitchen, shattering a seventeenth-century serving plate on a display stand in the corner hutch. "Well, they're not going to get away with this. We're hiring *two* sexy gardeners, Cooper. One who can pole dance down our topiaries while he's trimming them."

With scheming eyes that blackened to resemble obsidian, she lifted the bottom of her leopard-print house robe and began moving from room to room. Was she looking for the heaviest antique vase, the right piece of furniture, to take out the gossips, give them a concussion? Cooper shuffled behind her shadow. She pursed her lips and rubbed essential oils deeper and deeper into her arms, while she gazed at everything and nothing.

"Look, honey dumplings, I don't know what you're plotting, but I don't feel up to any more trouble. We've got to learn to start ignoring all the gossip. I'm old now and tired of moving. We're starting to look like that nomad family, you know, like in that film you were in *The Untraceable Undertakers from Red Horizon*." Cooper kept an arm's distance behind her, knowing he should offer a calming embrace, a tender touch to her stiffened shoulder at a minimum but couldn't chance the

claws again, not today. He was beginning to believe her big plan might be too devious for even Satan to handle.

In her possessed path through the parlor, Lilibet stopped to pour some brandy from a crystal decanter into a glass before downing the drink in one swoop. She slid her fingertips across the length of the red-marble mantel over the fireplace like she was smearing streams of blood. Her posture relaxed, signaling that she had released her inner demons perhaps. A good sign Cooper took this to be. But in a move that made his heart skip a beat, she grabbed the cast-iron candlestick holder off the end and shook it inches from his face.

Cooper couldn't believe the horrid thoughts were reoccurring more often now. And no wonder. Would he ever be able to kill her before she managed to finish him off first? A self-defense killing, a killing for the restoration of sanity and country, for the new life he had hoped for but was fated never to have. He sighed and squeezed his eyelids shut. She would just have to kill him. Sacrificial lambs were becoming too common in his family.

"I say we should really give these coonasses something to print in their rubbish tabloids and then prove 'em wrong—make fools out of those dirty little gossips." Lilibet snarled, as a bit of brandy dripped down the corner of her lips.

Cooper tried to ease the candlestick from her grip, but she started prodding him in the chest with the thing, forcing him backward inch by inch while she panted through her jutting bottom teeth.

"When I was in my prime, that's the way we Hollywood celebrities shut down the paparazzi. You play to the rumors, Cooper. You play to them and then shatter their goddamned preconceptions!" Lilibet tossed the candleholder against the mirror above the mantel and broke it until it resembled a spiderweb. In the dozens of segmented pieces, Lilibet's ratted-out blonde hair looked like countless white widow spiders trapping him in their deadly nest.

Taking a deep breath, Cooper turned his back from his once beautiful antique fireplace and fled to the parlor window. He buried his face in the lace sheers where, behind them, the formal garden beckoned to him, sprawling so serenely, so regally under the patches of sunlight that occasionally managed to break through the towering canopy of live oaks. In the dull breeze, the Spanish moss that shrouded the trees tickled the tops of the boxwood hedges and azaleas before eventually breaking off and enshrouding the lower bushes, choking out the flowers. Jorge had no doubt caused them to bloom by grazing his famous ass against the leaves.

"I suppose it's pointless to—" Cooper turned around and saw the gorilla face Lilibet was making, and he lost his nerve.

"Pointless to do what?" Lilibet huffed. She kicked the candlestick out of the way before collapsing onto the delicate fainting couch, causing the old springs to grind flat. There she reclined on her right elbow with a sassy rocking of her head as though she had just shown the world the error of its ways.

Cooper wanted to say, "Pointless to continue begging you to stop taking out your anger on the furniture and appliances I worked for years to pay for." But seeing that a few of the springs under the couch had just pierced through the fabric, he knew Lilibet would only accuse him of calling her fat. And then she would go on another long tirade about how antique furniture was meant for an era when people didn't grow as big because the toxic fumes from the oil lanterns they used poisoned them and stunted their growth.

"I don't see how you—sorry—how *we*—"

"How we what?" asked Lilibet. Her eyelids twitched neurotically.

Again, Cooper realized he was about to say the wrong thing. But how could she expect them to shatter any preconceptions when most all the rumors about them were true? At least about Lilibet anyway.

"I just don't see how this plan to prove the rumors false will work," he said, stepping over shards of mirror to place the candleholder back on the mantel.

"It was the Mayfields who sold the story to the papers. I'd be willing to sacrifice my only child."

Cooper cut his finger on a glass shard he tried to knock off the mantel. He couldn't believe his wife had said what she just did. His own blood came to the surface, and here she was becoming more and more callous as if the past had only been a rumor as well.

"Oh now, Lilibet. You have no proof they sold any stories. You seem so jealous of Ami Mayfield. Is this some paranoia you have against psychologists? You

stopped seeing Dr. Houston and Dr. Collier years ago. Always you find something wrong with them—always an excuse—and always you claim some conspiracy against you."

"Oh, you think so, do you? Well, we had better squash these new rumors before the lies from years ago resurface." Lilibet smirked and pointed to the phone on the table beside the rosewood couch. "Go ahead." She snapped her fingers. "You give Buns Henry and Ami Cable a call and invite them to go on a two-week trip to Vegas with us. That alone will crush their lies about us having no money. You do that, and I'll guarantee the guilt will ooze off 'em. They'll feel so bad they'll decline your offer. And then we will know who sold the story about us."

How could Lilibet live with herself? Cooper felt as if a grave had just opened. "The lies" she relabeled so easily. Lies from years ago that Cooper had to pretend weren't true—the lies that nearly cost them everything, and perhaps it already had.

"You are being ridiculous. I can't do such a thing. They will probably ignore our call like all the others you've driven away. They are probably thanking their lucky stars they have caller ID."

"Do it, you spineless old goat, or I'll go straight to plan B. And you know what B stands for." Lilibet raised forward on the couch and gnashed her teeth. "Do it, and maybe little sugar booger can have some dessert later." Lilibet lifted her robe while cooing in her sweetest voice. Cooper was sure she meant the area now hidden by

rumples of cottage cheese thighs, an area just south of her sunken belly button, now invaded by little gray hairs on a ring of stretch marks. One day, without her knowing, he wondered if he could count her real age like one does the rings of a hewn redwood tree.

Cooper felt Lilibet's harsh glare compelling him to dial the number he found for the young college couple in his address book, which was hard to flip through because every page remained as smooth and fitted together as on the day he bought it. He prayed to every celestial deity that one of the Mayfields would answer so Lilibet wouldn't have to resort to "plan bitch."

After seven heart-stopping rings, John Henry answered.

"John, my friend. This is Cooper Pearmain. Lilibet and I wondered if you and your young bride would like to go with us on a two-week trip to Vegas. We're leaving tomorrow morning—leaving bright and early. I know it is awfully late notice."

"Ami isn't here at the moment, but we were just saying we should take a trip during spring break," said John Henry. "Yeah, sure. Count us in."

Cooper put his hand over the mouthpiece. "John Henry said 'yes,'" he whispered to Lilibet.

"Oh, he did, did he? Well, tell them to leave their wallets and credit cards at home. We'll pay for everything. That will guilt him into changing his mind," Lilibet whispered in return.

". . . We have been a bit stretched for money lately, to be honest," said John Henry, after Cooper's new offer.

"He said 'yes,'" Cooper whispered to Lilibet, raising his eyebrows in satisfaction. With a pursed scowl on her face, she jumped up from the fainting couch and jerked the receiver out of Cooper's hand.

"John Henry, this is Lilibet. And there will be none of this you two 'meeting us there' nonsense. We are all going together in one vehicle—together for the *whole* trip."

A minute later, Lilibet placed the phone receiver back on the base. Her expression appeared dizzy and pale.

"He accepted the offer, didn't he?" asked Cooper, crossing his fingers that they hadn't. "I guess there wasn't much 'oozing guilt' to turn down a free two-week vacation to Vegas after all. There goes my yacht and your trip to Europe."

"Oh, Cooper. We're going to have to rent a stretch limo for the trip, I'm afraid," muttered Lilibet with glazed eyes. "John Henry's only concern was there being enough room for all of their luggage in our little car."

"Well, of course. The lad needs more legroom after all of that praising you gave him about his buns. He can't have any luggage cramping his prized tush-tush. He might get a bruise or something." Cooper stood with his arms folded and smirked at Lilibet. He hated to spend money on a vacation he never wanted to take, but part of him was glad the Mayfields had accepted—if only to teach Lilibet a lesson for once.

3

Junk In The Trunk

Cooper was later arriving to pick up the Mayfields than the "bright and early" he had sworn they were leaving. It took extra time to rent a stretch limo to accommodate all Lilibet's cosmetics and clothes, which Cooper called her "costume changes."

"Don't you blame the cost of this limo on me, Cooper Pearmain. You heard John Henry; he said they have a lot of luggage."

"Maybe they gave up waiting for us and won't be home," said Cooper. "Anyway, if they are, you make sure you give him lots of elbow room for those pristine ass cheeks of his, now Lilibet." He released the steering wheel and stretched each arm wide, losing control of the limo, which nearly swerved into the St. Charles Avenue streetcar.

"Will you stop with that? They need room for their

luggage, Cooper, *luggage!* We aren't pigs like you. We don't wear the same boxer shorts and stretchy pants all week."

"I'm not the one who needs to watch what I say around them. The Mayfields are religious." Cooper made the sign of the cross as best as he could remember from his youth. "They probably packed a ton of Bibles to try to save you."

"Who told you that?"

"Linda across the street. She said they want to have twin boys as soon as they finish college. And get this: they want to name them Deuteronomy and Leviticus because all the other biblical names have been used so much they're old school now." Cooper tried not to laugh. He knew this would hit a nerve with Lilibet.

"So, they're going with something from the *Old* Testament. Makes about as much sense as them collecting nude studio photos of me. I suppose you're going to say they're using the photos as bookmarks for their Bibles. That just proves my suspicion about them. They are snakes who are obsessed with me . . . but they're snakes nonetheless."

Cooper was glad he was wearing his tinted shades so his wife couldn't see him rolling his eyes. He would have an ocular migraine before reaching Texas at this rate.

"Oh, now, Lilibet, I hardly think that *proves* anything except your own paranoia. You know how it is today: There's a church for absolutely anything and anyone somewhere as long as you pay the membership fee. Hell, even the paranormal research groups and Satanists are

Christian in the South."

"Apparently horny, dull-as-oatmeal psychologists, too." Lilibet sneered and shimmied lower in her bucket seat like a pissed and battered boxer leaning into the corner ropes to save energy for a planned knock-out blow.

"It's either conform or starve. Burning sage only drives dead Aunt Betties out of houses north of the Mason-Dixon line. Down here, it's holy water, crucifixes, and an assembly line of local priests, baby. Anyway, I don't know what we're supposed to talk about for the whole trip. I don't know anything about kids today. I'm sure they think we're old school, too."

"Just use a little of the slang words you've heard lately," said Lilibet. "We'll show them old school. When I get through with them, they won't ever open their traps again."

"But I don't know what most of their slang words mean."

"I don't think they do either, truth be known. They just say stuff to sound cool—'rapping,' they call it, I think. Oh, and they tend to call each other Karen and Felicia these days."

"Even to other men?" asked Cooper, feeling like he was on another planet suddenly.

"Oh, yes. I've been called Karen many times, especially when I have to report someone for their poor work ethic. It's usually 'Felicia' when I'm leaving. But I think the word 'bruh' is used for men mostly."

"Bruh? As in one of those pig-tailed macaques in the

East Indies?" Cooper would have to be pretty pissed at someone to use that word. He was a bit concerned about miscommunication. He remembered a time when LOL meant "lots of love" instead of "laugh out loud." This caused an issue when he got a letter from his niece informing him that her puppy had died after her dad accidentally ran over it. Cooper ended a sympathy card with LOL, and she wouldn't speak to him for six months.

Not long after turning on 4th Street in the Garden District, Cooper found the young couple's house sitting atop a hill from the quiet street: a beige two-story home with rectangular columns, shutterless windows, and simple lines and trim work all around to the parking garage in the back.

"Oh hell. So much for giving up on us; they're waiting in the driveway. Bibles packed." Cooper jumped out of the car to help John Henry load the luggage in the trunk, while Ami pointed out certain features of their home's exterior and landscaping to Lilibet.

"John Henry and I didn't want anything too fussy. We're all about simple but dignified lines, you know, function over form. We were immediately drawn to the positive light we felt here. This home originally belonged to a local parishioner—a rebel in his day. They say before the Civil War, he stopped some slave traders from selling slaves in front of St. Louis Cathedral and told them to conduct their business behind the church in St. Anthony's Garden instead."

"Probably because of all the sweet-smelling flowers in the church garden and nothing more," said Lilibet,

with a satisfied grin. "Back then, residents of the French Quarter complained about the odor on the sidewalks, you know, from the terribly unsanitary pens they kept the poor slaves in before they sold them to help build your 'light and functional' home here."

Noticing the deadlock developing between the two women after such a brief greeting, Cooper decided to break the silence and break it fast.

"My-my, you are really packing there—lots of junk in the trunk," panted Cooper, trying to sound cool after loading two more heavy cases into the trunk. He eyed Lilibet sideways to see her reaction. He planned to never let her live down making such a spectacle of herself over John Henry's buns.

The boy wrinkled his forehead confusedly at Cooper, then he bent way over the bumper to squeeze one last piece of luggage inside the trunk. "Yeah, I, uh, like to be prepared for anything, Cooper. Who knows where we might end up? I'll bet you're one of those fellahs who changes lanes without giving a signal."

"Well, you know what it's like to be down low on those dirty back roads. Ya gotta get your lean on and just go for it? But don't look at me, I've gotten a little fat, and that's spelled with a P.H. You know what I'm sayin', Felicia?" asked Cooper. He rubbed his belly, unsure if he got the lingo correct. John Henry's expression morphed between a wink, raised eyebrows, and a creased brow ridge.

They all climbed in the spacious limo, and Lilibet saw the bed of purple flowers near the garage and nearly fell backward onto the brick driveway. "Ohhh, look at that, won't you? Are those daylilies?"

"They are. Imported from France and nearly impossible to cultivate," replied Ami.

"I can't even!" said Cooper, conjuring a strange pause in the conversation. "I, uh, mean we're all woke A.F. here, um, saving the planet, going green and all. But let's *turnt* this ship around and hit the streets, bitches," he continued, trying to sound young and hip until Lilibet reached her umbrella across the seat and stabbed him in the only hip that hadn't been replaced yet.

"Oh now, Ami Cable, you've been holding out on me. You know I love lilies. I simply must have one for the trip."

"Why certainly," said Ami.

No sooner had she agreed, Lilibet trudged through the middle of the flowerbed, breaking off a handful of the daylilies she hadn't crushed. Ami's mouth dropped.

"For God's sake, Lilibet; Ami said one flower, not the whole garden," yelled Cooper through the window, while his wife wobbled back to the car as though she had stolen a Ming Dynasty vase.

"Oh, shut up, you old bore. It'll sweeten the air in the car." Lilibet looked over her shoulder at Ami and John Henry, sitting with wide eyes in the back seat. "Trust me, fifty or more miles down the road, Cooper's feet will choke the breath clean outta ya." She ripped off the leaves and wedged three purple flowers in her teased hair, then she shoved the rest of the flowers in the air vents.

Long after Cooper backed out of the driveway and began steering the limo out of the Garden District, Lilibet seemed to break from the silent treatment the Mayfields were giving her.

"Anyway, you know why my daddy named me Lilibet? He said, when I was born, all the other babies in the delivery room were so ugly I was a lily among the thorns—you know, from the Song of Solomon." Lilibet plucked one of the daylilies out of her hair and gazed at it as she rolled the stem between her fingers. She sniffed the flower and wrinkled her nose. "He named me after the true lily, not these cheap imitations they call daylilies." She snatched the other flowers from the vents and her hair, unrolled her window, and tossed them at a street prophet's feet on Canal Street. The prophet nearly dropped his sign warning everyone that they were going to Hell soon.

"Hey, Elijah, I think you're lost today. The Lavender Line is on lower Bourbon!" Lilibet yelled at the man. Seemingly proud of her wit, she slapped Cooper's right arm and snorted. "Sugar booger, you and I are quite a pair in this arrangement, aren't we?"

John Henry whispered something in Ami's ear, most likely explaining about the Lavender Line to his young bride, Cooper imagined. With John Henry's buns, he probably always knew just when he had gone one block too far into the gay section of the French Quarter, or perhaps the boy liked adventure. He had certainly crossed another line of demarcation by getting in the limo.

"I'm not falling for it this time," Cooper mumbled to Lilibet, following the navigational system to get them onto the highway toward Las Vegas. "I'm sure you were going to try to impress our guests by referring to yourself as a lily and me a blooming idiot. Is that the 'arrangement' you were referring to, honey dumplings?"

Lilibet's lips formed a sinister smile. "Just remember, Cooper, a lily has the longest lifespan of any other flower in an arrangement."

"Ah, are we to hear the merits of a lily all the way to Sin City? They're also known to be very toxic to humans," sighed Cooper, realizing it was going to be a long trip, and he was all out of slang words.

"Excuse me for trying to get this shitty party started. The stock market—is that what you want to discuss with our guests?" Lilibet looked over her headrest at the Mayfields. "The last trip we took, from the snow-capped mountain of Colorado to the swamps of Lake Pontchartrain, I had to hear Cooper go on and on about the best fiber laxatives for his bowel irregularity. We got stuck in traffic on the causeway, and guess what happened to poor Cooper drooper?"

Lilibet gave up on a response from Ami and John, who sat stiffer and paler than when she had trampled their garden earlier. Ami busied herself with texting.

"You'd better just hope we don't get stuck on a bridge this trip, or you'll wish we had a car full of lilies," said Lilibet.

"I got that issue treated by a doctor. *Stress*, dear. Remember? I'm. Not. Supposed. To. Stress," Cooper

growled through clenched teeth. "Why don't we let our young guests do a little of the talking for a change?" He smiled at them through the rearview mirror.

"Yes, do tell us all about yourselves—every sordid, sexy little detail," said Lilibet. She applied a fifth layer of red apocalipstick to her pucker and propped her bare, stubby little feet on the dashboard as though she was fourteen and starring in *Lolita*. Cooper fought the temptation to speed up and then slam on brakes.

"Well, there's not much to tell, really," said John Henry, studying Ami's reaction first.

Lilibet fluffed her blonde hair and stretched her calloused toes on the dashboard. "Oh, don't feed us that bullshit. I'm sure you and Ami Cable are pros at telling. Why I bet you could sell your stories to every publication in the country."

"I, uh, grew up one of three children in Monroe, Louisiana. My parents said I always made excuses for everything they hated, so I would make a good attorney. So here I am—in my last year of college. And I was hoping you might give me a few pointers on passing the bar and corporate attorney stuff, Cooper," John Henry said.

Perhaps Cooper had forgotten what kids were like in college. Hungover, hormonal, uncertain about their expensive futures. When Cooper was in college, he was all of that and worse. About the only thing he could afford eating every day was a dozen cigarettes, and stuff squished between two stale buns. But there seemed to be something else with John Henry; he reminded Cooper of a lost boy abandoned in the wilderness, like he was a shell of a person, smiling on cue, going through the motions of communication, but his head was somewhere nobody else could see; Neverland perhaps? And it could be as Lilibet had said of the Mayfields before they left to get the limo. "Don't worry about dehumanizing them, Cooper. We're not taking humans on vacation; we're going to be chauffeuring four parents' opinions."

"Ami is from Nebraska," John Henry continued dutifully. "And after one semester in California, she moved to New Orleans to study psychology, wasn't it, Ami?"

"Yeah. I'm now in my third year. John Henry and I were married a year ago. My parents helped us buy a home and expect us to pay them back with grandchildren." A little color began to return to Ami's cheeks, and she relaxed in her seat.

Lilibet cupped her hands in the air. "So that's how you've been building up those juicy melons of yours, is it, John Henry? Been practicing having the old in-laws lots of grandchildren. Practicing, practicing." She jerked her head over the seat and gawked at him with dancing eyes. John Henry smiled sheepishly and looked out his side of the window while Ami dug her fingernails into his hand she had been holding.

"Well tell us how many, huh?" asked Lilibet. Her tongue wagged this time.

"At least once a day," John Henry mumbled with a blush.

Ami swatted John's leg. "She meant children—not

how many times we've been *practicing.*"

"You dirty little boy," said Lilibet with a smirk enlivening her face. "Careful; people will think you're a—oh, what's the word for a male nymphomaniac, Cooper?"

"According to you, every other male except *moi.*" Cooper wanted to also blame the press, which usually pointed back to Lilibet's big mouth. But he knew what Lilibet was really doing, and he didn't want to be a pawn in her game of getting the Mayfields to confess.

"The word you are looking for is satyromaniac," said Ami, leaning forward in her seat. "Despite what some think, it's not necessarily an abnormal condition unless there is failure to control it. Some psychologists suggest men suffering from satyromania perform mental exercises to harness their sex drives toward more creative and not procreative activities. But my husband is healthy and normal, Lilibet. No need to worry."

"Yes," said Cooper, already feeling a knot of tension tightening in his abdomen, especially with the gravel truck doing its best to pass him but failing at every highway incline. "I think we should change the subject."

"Oh, Ami Cable, you might be learning psychology at your little university, but save yourself some trouble and go ahead and add this to your list of psychoses: All men are incurable sex maniacs. If they aren't getting it from you, they're screwing around in some barn somewhere." Lilibet's black-lined eyes hardened on Cooper and then on the Mayfields. "I can't tell you how many men I've had to fight off of me over the years—

married, widowers, boys I've babysat—hell, even a dead man once tried to rape me."

"Oh, now, Lilibet. You've gone way too far this time. There is no way a dead man tried to rape you," said Cooper, sure he was blushing enough for the two of them. The gravel truck driver finally managed to pass Cooper and do what he had been desperate to do for miles: fling gravel all over the limo windshield.

"Yes, he did," swore Lilibet. "It was one of the actors when we were filming *Fast Ticket to Seedyville* out in the middle of the Maze District in Canyonlands National Park. We had been filming under this towering rock formation, and old Jim died of a heat stroke and hit his head on the sacrificial altar prop—took an hour for a medical helicopter to get there. We had to pull him in the shadow of the rock, and I leaned over him, trying one last time to force water down his stiff lips, and his hand grabbed my crotch, and the sicko moaned. Naturally, I fell backward from the horror of it all, and everyone saw it. Jim had an erection so big you couldn't tell if the towering shadow being cast was from him or the stone pillar behind him."

"If I may? What you described isn't all that uncommon," said Ami.

John Henry's head snapped around to face his wife.

"Corpses have been known to move involuntarily for months postmortem," continued Ami. "Air gets trapped in the lungs, which can cause moaning sounds. And the erection, in that case, is known as postmortem priapism and was especially common with people who died from

crucifixions or by hangings. Only the uneducated and superstitious in those days assumed the postmortem arousal stemmed from lusting after the angels who supposedly came to escort the dead into the afterlife."

Lilibet sucked in her cheeks and raised one eyebrow defiantly at Ami. The gravel truck was finally successful; three big rocks shimmed loose over the tailgate and smashed the limo's front windshield like bullet holes.

"Goddamnit . . . that son of a bitch! If they're going to have those stupid 'Stay back one hundred feet' signs on their shitty trucks, they shouldn't always be killing themselves and everyone else to pull in front of cars. Ride the frontage road, at least. Oh no, no, no, that would be inconvenient." Cooper looked over his shoulder at his guests. "You know what I'm going to do? I'm going to get me a sign that says, 'Keep back sixty-point-ninety-six meters. Not responsible for broken gravel trucks.'"

"You see, Ami?" continued Lilibet. "The only hope to cool men off is by chopping off their golden nuggets. Chop 'em right off." Lilibet's fists collided, simulating the closing motion of a pair of hedge clippers.

Cooper drew his knees in closer together and noticed in the rearview mirror that John Henry had done the same.

Cooper became distracted by visions of gravel trucks burying him under a pile of stones and Lilibet wielding sharp hedge clippers, chopping at anything that dangled freely. How had his life come to this? *New* was the key word; after the disaster that their lives had become in California, he had hoped to finally make a clean start and

new friends in New Orleans, anything to get a little time away from his insufferable cancer brandishing garden tools. He snapped out of his nightmare when blue lights flashed behind him on the interstate. He pulled over between the orange construction barrels that had been there collecting dust for four years, barrels he called the newest tourist trap.

"The cops have to make money somehow since they're too lazy to catch criminals these days."

"License and registration," said the police officer, before handing Cooper a ticket for speeding through a construction zone.

"What you need to do is ticket that gravel truck that just flew past me and destroyed my car. But oh no, you and the glass-repair companies are getting kickbacks from the gravel industry; don't think I'm not on to you," hissed Cooper, tapping the side of his head.

"There's no need for this, officer. Perhaps you didn't realize who I am," cooed Lilibet, leaning over Cooper's lap so the officer could see her cleavage better through the driver's window. "Does queen of the underground film industry ring any bells?" She shook her breasts for effect.

"Well, I'll be." The officer lowered his sunshades as if in shock. His grin flattened, and he handed her the notepad and pen, which Lilibet said she would be happy to autograph. Cooper removed his seatbelt and reached for the door handle.

"Wait," Lilibet gasped. "This is a ticket? Why are you giving *me* a ticket?"

"For trying to bribe a police officer," said the man, before turning his back.

"Officer, wait," shouted Cooper, breaking into a sweat as if something were controlling him, compelling him to surrender. He held his wrists out the window, so the cop could easily handcuff him.

The officer turned around with his hand on his pistol. "What?" he huffed.

"What the hell are you doing, Cooper?" asked Lilibet. Her eyelashes twisted.

Cooper's tongue went numb and his throat, dry. Was he losing his mind? He wanted to confess to a murder so the police officer would arrest him, and he would be free of Lilibet, free of the secrets that were knitting their burial shrouds with toothpicks.

The officer snorted before jumping back on his motorcycle and speeding off through the heavy traffic like a rocket.

"Do you see that?" hissed Cooper, pointing between the windshield dings at the speck in the distance that was the police officer. "He's going to get the gravel truck driver some donuts before they get stale, and then he's taking his kids to Disney."

4

ROUGHING IT

After several hours of driving and pausing for Ami's restroom breaks, Lilibet insisted they stop in San Antonio, Texas, and have lunch at a saloon-style steakhouse beside the Alamo. She was strangely quiet for the first time that Cooper could remember in years. Did she suspect that he had a moment of weakness with the police officer?

"Table for three, please. Last name is Pearmain," said Lilibet, as if it were code to bypass security.

"She means a table for four," said Cooper, to the hostess in the saloon-girl costume. "All the dust out here gives my wife a bit of brain fog."

Lilibet brushed the hostess's feathered headdress out of her face as the girl leaned over the desk to add their names to the guest list. "Oh, you *are* still with us, I see," Lilibet said, coldly cutting her eyes at Cooper.

She strutted so tall she looked like she would fall over backward as the hostess led them to the next greasy

wooden table available. With her chin and brows lifted in a well-rehearsed look of bliss, Lilibet paused as if being photographed by fans while Cooper pulled her wood-pegged chair out for her under the mounted buffalo skull overhead.

"Isn't this just sooo . . . *rustic*? It's like we're really roughing it," said Lilibet. "They might have us go out back and kill our own dinner. Isn't that what . . . *manly* men like? Don't you imagine, Coopie?" She pulled a bottle of disinfectant spray from her purse and sprayed the entire table, her chair, and the laminated menu before sitting down and using a sanitary wipe on her silverware as though sanding ten years of rust off the utensils. Cooper was convinced this was why they had banned indoor smoking in restaurants, because of the fire hazard Lilibet would create from her fear of germs.

"It's great here, actually." John Henry's eyes settled on the television screen at the bar where a baseball game was in full swing.

"I'm hungry. I hope they have a vegetarian option here." Ami frowned at all the animal heads on the walls.

"Don't be ridiculous," said Lilibet, burying her head behind a greasy menu. "Your hair will fall out, and you'll end up looking like Cooper drooper there if you don't get enough protein."

"Or claim you never have an appetite after indulging in too many liquid suppers. Then raid the refrigerator for the cheesecake at midnight, and you'll end up looking like my honey dumplings here." Cooper patted Lilibet's knee, and she jerked sideways in her chair.

The waiter took everyone's orders. Cooper and John Henry ordered steak, trying to out-man one another as to which one liked his steak the rarest. Ami ordered the three-bean veggie casserole, a salad, and sparkling water.

Lilibet snarled. "I certainly don't want to shatter anyone's expectations of me. I'll just have a triple gin martini. Perfect, like my life was before I met Cooper; dirty, like those nosy informants for the gossip magazines; and stirred, like a real man is supposed to be when he sees his wife peel off her negligee in the bedroom."

With an awkward pause, the waiter nodded knowingly and left to place their orders and probably place a call for security backup.

"Honey cakes, it's a long way to our next stop," Cooper whispered. He grabbed her frozen claw that was her hand and massaged the 18-carat emerald-cut diamond on her wedding ring, hoping to remind her to be nice and sober. "I think you need to eat something."

"What you need to worry about is why John Henry there didn't order milk and cookies from the bar. That's the big shock here." Lilibet gripped the edge of the table defiantly and tilted her head back.

John Henry began drinking his beer while the food was being prepared. "So, Cooper, where are ya from, and how did you and Lilibet meet?"

"I came from a middle-income family in a nice neighborhood in Downers Grove, Illinois. We probably had more money before my dad became severely injured in an elevator accident. He tried to stop the elevator

before it reached the thirteenth floor and ended up pounding on the elevator buttons, causing it to short out and plummet ten floors. Just as he was beginning to move around a bit, he became impatient and didn't want to wait on the nurses to help him to the restroom, so he fell and broke both hips."

"That's where the Pearmain hot-headedness comes from. Hot-headed until they hit rock bottom," said Lilibet, halfway through her triple martini.

Cooper decided to ignore Lilibet and continue a real conversation. "I remember slowly watching my mother sell over half of our furnishings to pay the bills to help put me through college. As a young teen working two jobs, I found it wickedly hard to save money for college when I was always seeing so many cool things I wanted to spend my savings on."

"Blind hookers," said Lilibet flatly.

"That is not even close to the truth, and you know it," Cooper sighed, wishing he had some great sexual exploits to shove in her arrogant face.

Lilibet chomped on her olive garnish. "Oh, Cooper, don't bore these kids with your child-labor stories. I'll bet neither one of 'em have had to work a job to pay for college."

Just as Cooper was about to apologize for his wife's rudeness, John Henry and Ami nodded their heads. "Neither one of us has had to work while in school, thankfully," said Ami.

John Henry lifted his mug of beer in a toast. "So, you got where you are by pulling yourself up by your own

bootstraps, as the saying goes."

"Not entirely. I had some lucky breaks," added Cooper, bumping his brandy glass against the mug. "After becoming an intellectual property attorney, I got a great referral, which landed me a job at a law office in Los Angeles, where I primarily worked to license and protect copyrighted movies, books, and music for the entertainment industry."

Lilibet puffed on an invisible cigarette and stared at Cooper. He knew she wanted to bask in his discomfort, knew she was dying to discredit him. That bull had been restrained behind the rodeo starting gate for too long. A clown needed to get the horns.

"Wow," said John Henry. "I bet you got to meet a lot of big-name celebrities—um, besides Lilibet, that is."

"Cooper occasionally received invitations to attend private parties in the Hollywood Hills where he met his first wife, didn't you, sugar booger? She soon wised up, though." Lilibet licked her lips with delight.

"I suppose so. She left me for the first movie director I introduced her to," confessed Cooper, gnawing the tender flesh of his inner lip. "But then came Lilibet." He patted her claw, offering as much of a smile as he could force. "I don't remember at which movie star's party I first met her. The drugs and alcohol were passed around like business cards and handshakes in those days." Cooper would never forget seeing her desperate grab for attention that night—a chandelier arm.

"Never until that moment had I ever dreamed I would see a woman in a beaded black gown run to the

top of a curved stone staircase, take off her high heels, and teeter barefoot atop the handrail so she could reach the chandelier." Cooper continued to pat Lilibet's hand, calming the savage beast.

"The chandelier?" asked Ami, with wide eyes. Her veneer of maturity seemed to shed a stiff layer or two. Her bare leg oscillated to the Southwestern music, and both competed for attention from the rowdy patrons.

"That's the only stir I ever gave old Cooper when I began swinging from the light fixture high over the crowd's heads," said Lilibet, before ordering a second martini when the waiter began placing the food on the table.

"Should I tell them what you said, honey dumplings? Should I?" asked Cooper.

Lilibet's pupils vibrated. "Don't you dare!"

John Henry sawed halfway through his steak and paused. "Wait. So, you mean she was actually swinging from the chandelier at a Hollywood party? You hafta tell us what she said."

"Lilibet said, 'How dare you bunch of snots treat me like I'm not a movie star. Look at me goddamnit! I'm such a star I fell out of heaven. Wooo! *See-me-fly-so-high*,' she yelled, speaking in what she later called tongues. At least two guests had crystal prisms plop into their wine glasses. Elizabeth thought one of the diamonds in her rings had fallen out. In her fake but famous Romanian accent, Cloris cheered on Lilibet's aerial stunt. Brando, whose attention Lilibet had tried to attract all night, ordered several men to help him carry a heavy sofa from the living room into the foyer to catch her before she could break her neck or short out the electricity."

Cooper imagined that if Lilibet had been as big then as she was now, she would've probably caused a blackout in the whole neighborhood. "After landing, Lilibet thought she was giving Brando a big wet congratulatory kiss on the sofa, but it was me instead. She ensnared me at that moment when she ran her hand up my chest to the side of my head, lingering on my ear. I never knew the human ear was that sensitive until I felt the tickle of her fingertips."

"It was all the well-rehearsed hand of an actress and nothing more," said Lilibet, sipping bitterly on her martini. "I thought my lusty lips were parting in their hungered, drunken passion for hunky Brando. But then I saw him behind Cooper's big old head, gazing longingly at me on the sofa."

"And you are oh so certain Brando wasn't gazing at me, huh? He later came out as bi, you know." Cooper downed his brandy and slammed his glass down in front of Lilibet as if the glass were the winning queen in a chess game.

"Wait! Are you serious? Brando was bi?" John Henry slowly stroked his chin once while staring at his half-empty mug.

Lilibet's eyes seemed to fix on a distant memory that proved Cooper was right. With a long face, she pushed gently away from the table and stood up. She turned her back to everyone and began walking to the restaurant's door.

"Where are you going?" asked Cooper, chasing behind her.

"I won't be long. I want to go make a wish at the old mission well at the Alamo."

"Wait for everyone to finish lunch, and I will drive you," said Cooper, worrying she would fake another suicide attempt for attention.

Lilibet jerked her arm free. "The well isn't far from here under the oak tree in the courtyard. It's important that I go alone. You can meet me there when you all are finished with lunch. Look, it's not like I can jump in the goddamned well. It has an iron grate covering the damned thing, all right?"

People waiting to be seated near the door began to watch Cooper and Lilibet, so to avoid looking like an abusive husband or something, he let her go.

After everyone finished their lunch, Cooper paid for everything, and they walked over to the Alamo. No one was screaming near the courtyard, so this was a good sign his wife hadn't pulled another stunt. In fact, when they rounded the corner, she was sitting on the stones that surround the top of the water well, and she was reapplying another coat of lipstick. When she spotted Cooper, she wadded up an empty pastry wrapper and thumped it to the side. She jumped up from the well and met them halfway.

"Did you make a wish?" asked Ami.

Gazing right through them, Lilibet eased her hands up to her face and pressed her fingers to her cheeks as if something awful had happened. "Yes," she mumbled.

Cooper at once noticed her diamond wedding ring was missing on her finger. Or perhaps this was only the well-rehearsed hand of an actress and nothing more, as Lilibet had bragged about earlier.

"Honey dumplings, what happened to your wedding ring? Did someone mug you?" Cooper began looking around for anyone who appeared to look like a thief.

"It's all my fault. I made a wish and then shoved a twenty-dollar bill through the iron grate over the top of the well, and the money became stuck, so I poked my ring finger in the opening, and my ring came off.

"Are you serious? That ring—" Cooper realized he was yelling. He paced in circles. "That ring cost a fortune. I don't understand. You couldn't even take it off with a tub of cooking grease, a bottle of diuretics, and an icepack. We have to find someone with management right away."

Lilibet placed her hand on Cooper's arm. "There is no need to make a fuss. What's done is done. The management said they send a special crew down in the well once a year to clean it out. And they will contact me if they find it."

"Once a year, my ass! I could purchase a small country with that ring, and I'll be damned if I leave here without it." He stomped over to the well and tried to pry the protective grate off the top, but it was screwed on tight. He made Lilibet, Ami, and John Henry form a wall in front of him as he removed his pocketknife, which had a built-in screwdriver. The *Mission Impossible* theme

song began to play in his head.

"I don't know, Cooper. This is a national historic landmark. You could get in serious trouble if you get caught," said John Henry.

"That's why you and the girls are going to distract everyone while I get to work on these screws. Flex those buns of yours if you have to."

John Henry pretended he was taking pictures of the women with his cellphone, trying to get the perfect shot. Lilibet struck every pose in the book that her old limbs could bend. Ami mostly turned left, then right, then back left like a rotating Christmas toy soldier.

The screws were on tight, but Cooper was slowly making progress, one scraped knuckle at a time. "Oh, for God's sake. It's only a little water in the bottom of this damned well, not the Ark of the Covenant. I need to get the Alamo to install security gates in my neighborhood, and we wouldn't have to bolt our porch furniture to the floors to keep it from being carted off in the night," he muttered and grunted. He hated that he had become so grumpy and cynical over the years; it wasn't really him, but whenever he vowed to stop, Lilibet would inevitably do something else to ruin his intentions.

"Oh gosh, oh gosh; people are looking over here, Cooper. Are you done yet?" asked Ami, through a clenched smile, while he continued to huff, breaking his screwdriver and two knife blades before loosening the fourth and final screw.

"Yes," he puffed and collapsed against the stone edge of the well. Three of his fingers were bleeding and twitching uncontrollably.

"It's too deep," said John Henry, leaning carefully over the edge. "Even if you climb down, we can't lift you out of there."

Cooper spotted a kid who appeared to be about twelve, and he was wandering by himself near the edge of the courtyard, stomping on occasional ants like he was King Kong. The boy was chubby, "table muscle or belly brawn" Cooper learned to call such boys growing up, especially the ones who thought they could intimidate others because they had an extra six notches in their belts. The kid would be perfectly strong enough for the task, right? Cooper ran over to the kid, and the boy's boot came down hard on Cooper's right toe. He hopped around on one foot until the pain subsided, and he could speak in a normal octave.

"Whoa there, big, tough fellah. You're really wiping out those ants down there, aren't ya? Say, how would you like to make fifty whole dollars, huh?" Cooper dangled a wad of cash in front of him like it was a cream-filled pastry.

"Mmm-kay. Wut I gotta do?" the boy asked, grabbing for the cash with sticky fingers, but Cooper raised his arm over his head, preventing him.

"Nuh-uh-uh. First, you have to agree to go down in that old water well over there and get my wife's ring for her. You see, she accidentally dropped it."

The boy's eyes sparkled. "Is it a diamond ring?"

You thieving little shit, Cooper thought. *I'm sure you'd just love to hide that ring under your boy boobs and claim you couldn't find it, wouldn't you?*

"A real diamond? Are you serious, kid?" Cooper lied. "No, it's a white rhinestone—cheap costume—but you know how sentimental women get over things."

"Mmm-kay, I'll do it," the kid said, taking the cash before Cooper led him over to the well.

"Don't tell me you are up to what I think you are, Cooper Pearmain?" asked Lilibet.

"The kid agreed to help, Lilibet. He agreed to get the ring for fifty bucks."

The boy held out his hand again before Cooper returned his wallet to his pants pocket. "All right, all right. For one hundred bucks," Cooper added, while a bead of sweat rolled down his spine. The little stinker had better get that ring back, or Cooper was going to leave him in the well and screw the grate back on top with his brittle fingernails if he had to.

"He's just a child, Cooper. Children think they are superheroes sometimes, too," said Ami, bracing her trembling hand over her forehead.

"Bah! I used to climb trees taller than this whole courtyard. He's small enough that I can let him down into the well with the rope and bucket hanging over it." Cooper motioned for them to stand guard. "If anyone comes near the well, tell them it's closed because dangerous gasses have been leaking out, and we're the gas experts."

"I can't do this. I don't like to lie," said Ami, fidgeting, while Cooper began unwinding the wooden bucket low enough for the boy to climb into.

"Oh, I'm sure you always tell the truth . . . no matter how much it hurts," Lilibet said to Ami. "Trust me, dangerous gasses leaking won't be impossible—not after that steak dinner Cooper just ate at the Greasy Cantina over there."

"I'm going to lose my master's degree over this," mumbled Ami. She pulled out her phone to take a quick call under the shade of the oak tree overhead.

"Bah, you'll find another career. Hurry up, will ya, kid? Get inside. It's like those little car rides at the fair. You know? *Vroom, vroom, weee!*" Cooper said playfully to the strange boy. For once, he didn't care how this scheme of a vacation might compromise the young college couple, not with a fortune lost in the well. He worked too hard to pay for that ring, which millions of girls could only imagine wearing on their finger.

The more Ami began to protest, Lilibet did a little dance where she squatted, holding a pretend shovel to her right, and then she threw her hands up to her left. "Dig a Little Deeper in the Well," she sang.

Cooper snapped his twitching and bloody fingers, and John Henry started turning the crank to the old water well. After the bucket lowered a few inches, Lilibet's face popped over the edge of the well, where she peered down at the boy with her penciled brows now up to her hairline.

"You better watch out," she said to the boy in a spooky voice. "The well monster is gonna eat you!"

What had Lilibet done? Cooper could see the warning signs coming like a volcano about to spew. The

he-man ant-stomper's face screwed up and turned purple. He started to wail. The bucket creaked and swung when he tugged at the rope and tried to climb up it. John Henry chickened out and stopped lowering the crank.

"No, the ring is down there, remember? *Vroom, vroom, weee!*" said Cooper. He pushed down on the boy's shoulders to get the bucket to lower again.

"*Eeek*, Momma, Momma, Momma!" the boy screeched.

When a crowd of people began heading toward the well, Cooper grabbed the boy out of the bucket and lowered him safely to the ground, pulling a muscle in his back in the process. Lilibet doubled over with laughter. If Cooper could get away with it (or even lift her), he would grab his wife by her fake eyelashes and toss her into the well right about now. Why would she deliberately sabotage his efforts to find her wedding ring? Unless her so-called losing it wasn't an accident. Did Lilibet wish to appear single and available on her vacation in Las Vegas? Did she really think some young man with a body like John Henry's would fall for her?

"*Ugh!* Did that dirty old man touch your wittle goo-goos, my Toby-wobie munchkins?" asked a woman, plowing out of a gift store with seven garish sombreros squished under her flabby arms. She dropped a bag full of maracas that spilled at Cooper's feet, sounding like a nest of rattlesnakes, which would be much more inviting than the crowd of angry tourists now swarming around him.

"*Uh-huh,*" little Toby whimpered. He buried himself in the sweaty folds of his mother's belly, which muffled his fake sobs. With a demonic scowl, the little he-man emerged from her navel, reared back, and kicked Cooper in the shin while a shower of icy fruit drinks from paper cups and lumps of triple-scoop ice cream pelted him. A man, built like the back end of an eighteen-wheeler, drew back his chubby fist and aimed it at Cooper's nose.

"There he is, officer," munchkins' momma bellowed, with her finger stabbing at Cooper. "There's the pervert who had his way with my son . . . here in broad daylight."

Hours earlier, Cooper would have welcomed a life sentence in jail away from Lilibet, but not now. He had heard what inmates do to suspected child molesters. And murderers, in particular, loved it when the law allowed them to do whatever they wanted as if it somehow redeemed them of all their other crimes. Free admission into Heaven for you, my child. The Eleventh Commandment: Thou shalt take an eye for an eye and rape the accused rapist. TWELVE MONTHS TO A LIFETIME OFFER. Group discounts.

"And all of you were witnesses to the molestation?" the security guard asked the gathering crowd, who all agreed that they had.

"Yeah, uh did. Most disgustin' thang I ever see'd," said a woman, with a middle-parted mullet and teeth. She pointed at Cooper, and her frayed bra strap, which was held together by a safety pin, slipped and lodged on the hairy mole growing from one of the tattooed Confederate-flag stars on her shoulder.

The security guard aimed his pistol at Cooper. "I need you to git on the ground, face down, and put yer hands behind yer back."

"You've got this all wrong. I didn't touch Toby—well, not like that. You see, my wife, Lilibet, there, lost her diamond wedding ring down the well, and Toby agreed to let me pay him to go down in the water bucket to get the ring. He wasn't cheap; he insisted on a hundred of my hard-earned bucks. If anything, I'm the victim here."

Cooper, who had only raised his hands in the air, jumped when the guard fired a bullet, which penetrated a fold in his pants near his knee.

"I said git on the ground, ya pervert, or you're gonna be doing the Mexican hat dance." The guard waved his pistol around.

"Go ahead and shoot 'im. Save us taxpayers another mouth to feed," said the man who tried to punch Cooper earlier.

"Tell them, John Henry," said Cooper, after lying down on the ground. When his friend remained silent, Cooper strained his neck over the cobblestone to look for John Henry, but he and Ami had abandoned the scene.

"Tell them, Lilibet," said Cooper, turning his head to see his wife sitting on the edge of the well, painting her fingernails.

"Tell them what, Cooper? Tell them how you bribed a little child and put him in danger over a stupid ring the management promised they would look for later? Tell them how you vandalized a national monument because

of your greed? Or tell them the dark secret you've been hiding for years . . . the secret you seem to want to get arrested for?"

"I paid the boy to help because, because that ring—that ring that symbolizes our love and commitment—obviously means more to me than it does yooou!" spat Cooper over his shoulder, while the guard locked handcuffs on his wrists.

As the guard placed him in the back of his car, Cooper saw Lilibet waving at him. Nah, what was he thinking? She couldn't even offer him a last goodbye; she was merely fanning her nails dry.

5

NOOBS IN THE CAGE

After giving his fingerprints, Cooper did as he was told and sat on the stool to have his picture taken for police records in some godforsaken penitentiary on the outskirts of San Antonio. The seat wobbled like a salad plate balancing on a soda straw.

"I can't sit on this stool; it's wobbly. Ah, I see what's going on here. You want me to look drunk; is that it—drunk and pervy for the photo—so you all can prove to the judge that I belong in this criminal cage; is that it? Well, you all will be hearing from my attorney," said Cooper, after hopping back upright.

"There's nothing wrong with that stool. Now sit, or you'll get an extra ten for insubordination," huffed the officer, grimacing down at him.

Cooper squared his legs and eased down on the seat as evenly as he could. Immediately the seat began to wobble worse than a deep-sea fishing trip he got stuck on during a tropical storm. When the camera flashed, Cooper was sliding off the seat at a forty-five-degree angle, and his eyeballs were bulging. After stripping naked and having his buttocks probed entirely longer than necessary, Cooper snatched on his orange coveralls and entered the holding cell. Rough-looking inmates all around the perimeter of the cell glared at him as the cell door slammed shut and locked.

Swallowing hard, Cooper turned around and grabbed the iron bars. "I know my rights, damn it. I'm allowed one phone call," he yelled, trying not to show any fear. He had to pee badly but realized the only toilet in the packed cell was a hole in the floor. How long can a man survive without passing urine? He wondered.

"Looks like we got us a noobs in the cage, fellahs. You got your black and white?" asked a man. His oily skin shimmered while he gnawed on a toothpick.

"I'm okay with all races," said Cooper, realizing he was among the minority in the cell.

"Ain't talkin' 'bout no race. I'm talkin' about your papers so we can see what you are in here for."

"They didn't give me any papers." Cooper backed against the cell bars when the men began to surround him.

A man, the size of a refrigerator, pushed through the crowd, rubbing his knuckles. "Yo, man, the only noobs who ain't got no papers are rapists and child molesters."

"We ain't gonna have no chomos sharing no cell with us," said an inmate, with a shaved head and face tattoos.

Cooper held out his arms in a calming gesture. The stench of testosterone was in such overdrive, the communication deteriorated to little more than a bunch of grunts, catcalls, and crotch grabbing. *Ah, the joys of education and enlightenment since the caveman days*, he thought sarcastically.

"Look, fellahs, I don't know what you're thinking." Or *if you can*, he wondered in all earnestness. "The only reason the police put me in here is for trying to get a diamond ring that got lost down the Alamo water well."

"Didja hear that, boys? The fresh meat here lost his jewelry. Yep, I bet it was real purty on your fanger," said the man with facial tattoos. "Ya didn't have no plans to git engaged with one of my boys here, didja?"

Cooper had never been so afraid, well, except for the bathroom stunt Lilibet had pulled on him with the knife. He was unable to move or speak now. He felt a warm dampness trickling down the leg of his prison uniform when the gang grabbed him. He had pissed his pants. This would surely add more torment than he was already receiving.

"Please j-just kill me. M-make it swift. Get all that hatred out," he stuttered, squeezing his eyelids as tightly as possible, prepared to suffer excruciating pain and then go to blessed eternal rest, eternal nothingness. No memories. No more regrets. No letting Lilibet beat him to life's exit first.

As soon as the inmates' pants began to unzip, an officer slung open the cell door, and they released their grips on him and stepped back several feet.

"Cooper Pearmain?" the officer called out. "You are being released on bond. You're free to go until the trial."

In disbelief at all that had happened, Cooper staggered out of the cell and changed out of his soiled uniform and back into his clothes before returning to the front desk.

John Henry, who had been waiting nervously at the desk, put his hand on Cooper's back.

"And just who the hell are you?" Cooper hissed, pulling away from the boy.

"Sorry I vanished on you. I had the staff at the Alamo check all of their security cameras, Cooper. It proves you didn't touch the kid inappropriately, but his mom is still planning on suing you for kidnapping, child endangerment, and a list of other charges."

"Yippee," Cooper said snidely, circling his finger in the air in a puny gesture of celebration. "Maybe they can deduct the hundred bucks I already paid them and for nothing . . . except the body massage I just got by a bunch of knuckle draggers."

"Did you enjoy it? I won't tell Lilibet," whispered John Henry, with a twitch of his brow. He craned his neck to see inside the cell Cooper had occupied earlier. Someone whistled at him.

"No, Johnny boy. No, I didn't enjoy it. Geez, did they get the ring or not?" he asked, after he signed some papers and staggered out of the police station where the limo was waiting for them in the parking lot. Cooper was never happier to see the sunlight and breathe fresh but dusty air. Lilibet was sitting in the front passenger's seat with her head buried in her cellphone while Ami sat in the back seat with her head pressed against the window. Her eyes open but lifeless.

"No, they said it wasn't time to do the well inspection yet. Look, Cooper, Lilibet paid the Alamo a thousand bucks for the damage, and they agreed to drop any charges."

"For the damage?" Cooper yelled. "All I did was remove four screws. That's the trouble in this life when it comes to screwing; you end up paying for dear life."

John Henry paused with a look of dread distorting his face. He started to brace his hands on Cooper's arms but stopped within inches of doing so. "And there's one more thing: we have all been banned from ever setting foot near the Alamo ever again."

Cooper spun around and wagged his finger in John's face. "Ah, of course, they have. That's so they can keep that ring after they find it. Ugh, just brilliant. Well, they aren't going to get away with this, even if I have to resurrect from my grave to get that ring back."

After collapsing in the driver's seat and slamming the limo door, Cooper looked over at Lily-Butt, who still had not acknowledged him since she had just sat there and let him get arrested at the well. She appeared to be adding a twentieth item to her shopping cart on her phone.

"Your nails are finally dry, I see," said Cooper.

"What. Is. That. Ungodly. Smell?" Lilibet hissed. She snatched a travel-sized bottle of fragrance from her leather bag and sprayed ten swirls of vanilla fog around

Cooper.

"Oh, we wanna know what that smell is, do we? Well, let me take you to meet my lovely cellmates—whom I narrowly escaped, mind you—and you'll think Bourbon Street at the end of spring break smells like a bouquet of fresh roses." Cooper opened the limo door and jumped out. "Come on, then. Maybe you'd like to spend a couple of nights with the boys now that you look all single and on the prowl."

Lilibet applied another coat of mascara. "Don't be ridiculous. Get in the car, you big baby. You've wasted enough time. We could be in Vegas by now, enjoying the show and the big wheel."

"If you two don't mind, I think I would rather just go back home instead. I mean, I appreciate the offer and all, but I think I've had enough excitement," said Ami, after Cooper crawled back inside the car.

"What? We just got started," squawked Lilibet. "Don't be such a killjoy. Start the car, Cooper. We've come too far. I'm not going to spoil my vacation because old-fogey Ami Cable back there doesn't know how to have a good time."

Ami looked over at John Henry for backup but only received a bashful smile for her effort. "They did rent this limo for us," he whispered and held her hand. "Maybe we're just a little stressed. Things'll get better once we're in Vegas."

"Okay," mumbled Ami, rolling her eyes with one cheek dimpling regretfully after Cooper merged back onto the highway toward Las Vegas.

"I've never seen anyone so tense. Have you, Cooper?" asked Lilibet, popping her head over the seat like a meerkat out of its hole to smirk at Ami. "You know what you need? A good stiff drink. Of course, I hardly ever touch the stuff, but some people would live far longer as drunkards than having a damn stroke over a silly little incident like we had at the Alamo, for God's sake." Lilibet snapped her fingers. "Cooper, pull over at the nearest booze joint and get poor Ami some liquid courage."

Ami cleared her throat. "No, really; I don't need a drink."

"Of course, you need a drink," snapped Lilibet. "We all will if we're going to have to smell Cooper all across this godforsaken desert."

"She said she was good, honey dumplings," Cooper droned through clenched teeth. Already he decided he should've taken his chances and refused bail.

As soon as Lilibet saw what she assumed to be a booze joint, she reached over Cooper's right arm, grabbed the steering wheel, and forced the limo to make a sudden right turn off the highway, through sand and gravel, over the tire rail, and into the crumbling parking lot.

6

LOCKING HORNS

The moment the ice started melting in Ami's margarita, Lilibet reached across the table, downed the girl's drink, and licked the ring of salt off the rim in one swoop.

"If there's one thing I can't stand—if there's one thing—it's watching someone waste a good drink," she said, putting the empty glass down before finishing her own drink. "I'll tell you where the good drinks were . . . at all the opening receptions I was invited to in Hollywood, and I was invited to all the best—me!" Lilibet sloshed a few ice cubes against her breasts, trying to get the last drop of alcohol.

"Yes, and you would attend the opening of a pregnant woman's belly if there was plenty of booze and a camera nearby. You've had enough, honey dumplings," Cooper said, paying the bill and helping Lilibet out of her seat.

The bar was so dark it was hard to see. The neon beer signs on the walls flickered from a short in the wiring.

Cooper's shoes kept sticking to the floor with every step.

"Rat! There's a rat?"

"Where?" asked Ami, spinning around on her tiptoes.

"I think it scurried under the tables." Cooper pointed toward the table near theirs. "That must be why someone keeps yelling and throwing or banging pots and pans in the kitchen."

"Either that or it's some type of stupid foreign religious ceremony," said Lilibet.

"No, I think they're Christians. They always have big smiles on their faces," said John Henry.

Lilibet rolled her eyes. "If so, the waitstaff must be doing some Old Testament smoke offerings because every time that kitchen door opens, there's a fog in here."

"I think we should leave before we get bit by a rat," said Cooper.

"Okay, okay, but I need one more drinky-poo to go." Lilibet jabbed one finger in Cooper's eye.

"You don't need one more. You hardly ever drink, remember?" Cooper pulled at Lilibet's arm, guiding her toward the door before everyone thought they were having their own religious ceremony.

Lilibet leaned back on her heels and shook her head like a wet dog. "We're practically in margarita country, and it's only respectful to the locals."

"Respectful? You're damn near worshipping them at this point," huffed Cooper.

"Besides, Cooper drooper, besides, you all can be boring as hell, except for Buns Henry here," Lilibet slurred, and slapped the boy on the rear with a feisty grin on her face. She clung to John Henry, who helped her back to the limo while Cooper paid for a "respectful" margarita to go. Too bad he didn't have any sleeping pills or respectful arsenic to slip inside her drink. He was worried about her drinking so much again. The last time she did, Cooper's life was ripped apart. Destroyed. What was his wife up to now?

Just as Cooper was about to leave the business with a tall plastic cup in his hand and feeling guilty for his terrible thoughts, Ami came back inside and bumped into Cooper.

"Lilibet said, 'don't forget to get four orders of tacos to go—oh, and some key-lime pies.'"

"She did, did she? And a bag of biscuits de Reims and an authentic New York pizza while I'm at it?" Cooper handed Ami the drink and returned to the counter for the fourth time.

Miles down the highway, with food crumbs all over themselves, John Henry leaned forward on the back seat. "So, how long did you guys wait to get married?"

"We dated about a year," said Cooper. They didn't wait nearly enough centuries; he was desperate to say.

"Cooper wanted me a hell of a lot sooner. Only I was busy filming three movies on location."

"And, like everything else honey dumplings ever had her way with, the wedding ceremony proved to be an underground movie production unlike any she had been cast in before."

"It's a good thing, too, mister tightwad," Lilibet

snapped at Cooper. "Because of my Hollywood connections, I worked out a deal with the leading movie-production company, and they let me borrow a humongous plaster sphinx and other magnificent Egyptian movie props used in the filming of *The Ten Commandments*. I had them placed on the Nipomo Sand Dunes in California. So, naturally, I had to dress as Queen Nefertiti."

"Who did you dress as, Cooper?" asked John Henry, wiping pie crumbs off his shirt with a paper napkin.

"Rameses the Great. Lilibet made me get waxed and spray-tanned and don next to nothing. I didn't want to, but she can be quite the tyrant if you haven't learned by now. Don't argue with me, Lilibet; it was well noted by the crowd and tabloids how you made your grand entry at the wedding."

"I was not a tyrant. I can't help that I commanded attention. Oh, you should've been there, Ami and John Henry." With wild eyes, Lilibet slapped the top of the leather seat. "I arrived in a horse-drawn chariot, which took me and Cooper all the way through the desert to the officiant, who waited at the base of a pyramid where slaves fanned him with palm leaves. It was magical until Cooper had to ruin the whole event as usual." She scowled at him.

"I didn't have time to ruin anything. I was holding onto the carriage for dear life. You should have known the dunes were unstable." Cooper's voice rose two octaves.

"What happened?" asked Ami, picking the lettuce

out of her taco and eating the green shreds.

"I think we should change the subject. I know . . . how about a little relaxing music?" Cooper turned on the limo radio to a heavy-metal song to drown out Lilibet. Some guy growling to war drums about beautiful people and their large steeples. Lilibet started hitting him to make him move his hand so she could turn off the noise.

"One of the damned carriage wheels broke off, and the whole thing toppled over right in front of all the guests; that's what," laughed Lilibet.

"Don't start with that 'Cooper caused the guests to sweat' mess. It was scorching hot, remember?" said Cooper, preparing to lose what little pride he had left.

"Everyone, including the media, got an eyeful. Cooper here was freeballing under his half-pleated kilt."

"There was a heatwave, remember?" said Cooper, realizing he was speeding again.

Lilibet was practically drooling over the back of the car seat. "And then, and then the stunned guests began laughing and singing that *wholesome* fifties song 'Great Balls of Fire,' right as I landed on top of Cooper, ripping my blue gown, and everyone got an eyeful of my right breast. It was so awful, the officiant said, 'Since the honeymoon consummation has already begun, I guess I'll skip the preliminaries and go ahead and pronounce you husband and wife.'"

"The poor guy was mortified. But you had to make an entry," said Cooper.

"Mortified, my ass," hissed Lilibet. "The press got a picture of the officiant swatting a palm leaf away from his face because it was blocking his view of the orgy." Lilibet put on her actress voice as if she were under the fading spotlight before the final curtain closure. "There was nothing left to do. There in the hot sand, Cooper and I went with the comedic tragedy and kissed. The sacred serpents, jutting like solo horns on our headdresses, accidentally interlocked. It could've been great—the only redeeming part of our wedding—except old Cooper here was more worried about getting loose and covering his sweating balls."

"How could I? Your cackling lips kept smearing pomegranate red all over my face. Every damn photo looked like I had a penchant for rosy blush," said Cooper. "It went well with my kohl-blackened eyelids you paid the makeup team to overdo."

"I was trying to make you look like a proper pharaoh, Cooper Pearmain! And trust me, you needed all the help you could get."

Cooper exhaled a soul of regret. If only he had known he would become eternally trapped in a mortifying "Till death, do you part," locking horns with Lily-Butt, he would have added a little makeup to his enhance his balls before they, too, became immortalized along with the nutty mess she had made of his life.

7

SHITTY PICTURE
GANG BANG

Nearing El Paso, Texas, late that afternoon, Cooper pulled over to fill the limo with gas. While Ami and John Henry went in the station to use the restrooms, Lilibet shuffled slowly up to Cooper at the pump. Her hands on her hips signaled that she was livid about something.

"Do you have to be so softhearted toward the Mayfields? They are obviously trying to get more dirt on us to sell to the tabloids. Their parents may have bought them that big old home in the Garden District, but they still have college to pay for." She came to a stop and pressed one high heel down on the gas hose on the ground, causing the gas to gurgle and sputter in the tank.

"What do you suggest I do, Lilibet; make 'em confess at gunpoint—tie them up to the bumper and drag them down the highway or something? I know you don't want to hear this, but it's long past time we had a talk about that night when—"

"It's time we shake the Mayfields up—have a bit of fun." She hip-butted Cooper so hard, she knocked him against the car.

"Oh, no, no, no. Your idea of fun is absolutely terrifying; need I remind you? Remember what happened when you—"

"You are such a killjoy." Lilibet snatched the receipt from the gas pump and shoved it in Cooper's pocket. She held her claws in front of his face. "Now give me those car keys. It's time someone took control here. We are going to teach the Mayfields a lesson by lying like hell."

Ami and John Henry paused in the parking lot when they noticed Lilibet behind the wheel. She bore down on the horn. "What are ya waiting for, ya decrepit old sloths? Get in. This vacation is just getting started," she yelled out the window while revving the engine.

Cooper started to let the front passenger's seat back and rest for a change but sat back up when he remembered one of the last times Lilibet had driven: He had just had outpatient surgery at the hospital—a cyst removal on his back near his spine. The doctor wanted the cyst to continue draining, so he left a bit of gauze hanging out of the incision. By the time Lilibet took several wrong turns outside the French Quarter in their new car, the anesthesia had worn off, and it felt like a cigarette searing into Cooper's spine when she hit every damned pothole. They ended up on a street with gang members shooting at anything that moved, and Cooper yelled out in pain. Lilibet swore Cooper had been shot, so she rolled down the car window. And with Minnie Riperton's song "Lovin' You," complete with its chirping birds and its joyous squeals blasting, she yelled at the gangs that she was calling the police on their asses. In doing so, she hit another crater that broke off their hubcap, which went flying and hit the closest shooter in the head and knocked him unconscious. Needless to say, they got another new car the next day, so the gangs couldn't trace them. Lilibet claimed, of course, that it was all Cooper's fault for being such a whiny baby.

"What's the matter with you two? Are you afraid of my driving? You look like an opossum has run across your graves. Isn't that the saying you people use in the South? I'm gonna fix y'all sum opossum pie, I do declare," Lilibet said in her cheesiest drawl. The car swerved between both lanes while she checked her lipstick in the rearview mirror as the sunset heated the endlessly flat horizon.

"Uh, no, your driving is, uh, fine," said John Henry, gripping the seat. "Ami and I are still a little shaken. We, uh, had a run-in with a couple of shady characters in the store who cornered us like they were going to rob us."

"That's nothing. You wanna hear about shady? You should live in LA. Cooper took me to this seedy bar there one afternoon, and someone kept sending me free drinks. Cooper got so jealous he refused for me to accept them.

"Don't confuse concern over your drunkenness for jealousy," said Cooper.

"You were jealous. Anyway, the bartender said the

man who was paying for my drinks was the head of the mafia, and he didn't stand for women refusing his generous offers. So, you wanna know what old Cooper did?"

"What did I do, honey dumplings? Run to the little boys' room and cry in the sink?" Cooper didn't like where this lie was going. He would probably have to change his name after she got finished.

"Oh, you know what you did! Stop trying to make the Mayfields think you're some angel."

The Mayfields looked too uncomfortable to ask, so Lilibet continued anyway.

"Cooper said to the bartender, 'now, you tell that son of a bitch that I'm with the FBI and that backup is on the way.' Then he dragged me out of the bar, threw me in the car, and took off down the highway. The minute I heard Cooper cursing, I knew the mafia head was chasing us, and that was seconds before the bullets started hitting our car. When one of the tires blew, Cooper turned into a raging demon and drove off the highway into the Joshua Tree desert and slumped over the steering wheel and pretended he had been shot. The mafia head came to the window and leaned over to make sure he was dead. Naturally, I was preparing to be taken as his love slave and endure his big sweaty body ravaging me day and night." Lilibet rubbed her breasts, and her head rolled on the headrest, flattening her platinum rats.

"Oh, you poor thing," whined Ami. "That must've been traumatizing."

Cooper accidentally let out of snort of squelched

laughter. The Mayfields apparently didn't know the depths of Lilibet's fantasies. She shot him a lethal glare and slapped his left thigh far too close to his tender region.

"But do you wanna know what old Cooper did? He kicked open the door. It knocked the mafia chief out cold. While he lay unconscious in the sand, Cooper took the man's gun and dragged him atop this rocky outcropping—isn't that what they call it? Anyway, Cooper dropped him in a rattlesnake pit; I could hear them suckers rattling thirty yards away. He came running back as white as a noontime snow, threw the spare tire on the car, and got the hell out of town."

"You mean you left the man to die?" asked John Henry. His neck swelled with revulsion.

"I don't know if he died or not. I would imagine so," said Cooper, playing along with the story for fear of something worse from Lilibet.

"That's awful. You should've at least reported it to the police." John Henry crossed his arms, and a crease formed between his eyebrows.

"He tried to kill us and ravage Lilibet; you heard her," Cooper raised his voice to impress his wife.

"Oh, I suspect they are just having fun—getting a rise out of us," said Ami. "Cooper wouldn't do such a thing."

"You think so, do you? Let him drop your unconscious body in a nest of a hundred angry rattlesnakes in the middle of the desert and see how you come out. Don't believe the gossip rags that claim Cooper is henpecked. He's just being polite because you two are a couple of snowflakes . . . snowflakes melting in the back seat. Don't ever doubt; Cooper is capable of the cruelest of actions. I learned over the years never to cross him." Lilibet's head jerked back when she floored the gas pedal, dangerously passing other vehicles until they were speeding down the interstate toward Las Vegas. After fifteen minutes, Ami patted the back of Lilibet's headrest.

"Slow down, Lilibet; there is something in the road up ahead."

As soon as Ami called everyone's attention to the danger, Cooper spotted it, a gray wolf, standing defiantly in the middle of the highway. Its eyes glowed white in the headlights.

"What does that mangy mutt think it's doing, calling my bluff? Well, this mama ain't afraid, let me tell you."

With both elbows rising like vulture wings, Lilibet gripped the steering wheel. Her eyes hardened on the wolf as she drove the limo square into the creature, which let out an awful howl as it flew into the air and crashed into the windshield, splattering gray fur and blood all over the hood and glass. Its front paw wedged into the recess between the hood and windshield wiper where the beast remained, howling like some living police siren. Lilibet turned on the radio and cranked up the volume. A classical song that made Cooper feel like they were driving to Dracula's Castle in some horror movie.

"You have to pull over. It's trapped on the hood," yelled Ami, covering her face with her hands.

"Are you crazy? It might have rabies. I'll get it off the

hood. I did my own stunts in *Hotrod Outta Hell's Kitchen*, you should know." Lilibet began oscillating the steering wheel sharply, making the limo swerve through both lanes of the highway. After nearly clipping a church bus full of bouncing children, which was trying to pass her on the left, the howling wolf slid off the hood, leaving a splattered reminder of death all down the side of the kiddie bus. The children's faces pressed against the long row of windows left imprints of horror on the glass. Lilibet turned on the windshield wipers, only smearing the sticky fur and blood worse than it was.

Ami slumped down in the back seat and tried to catch her breath while the lingering aroma of burned rubber filled Cooper's nostrils, and the howls of agony still lingered in his ears. John Henry took Ami's hand to comfort her. Lilibet turned her headlights on bright to better see through the lumpy streaks of red on the glass. With a nervous rattle in his throat, John Henry leaned his head between the front headrests.

"I couldn't help but notice that you referred to yourself as 'mama.' Did you and Cooper ever have any children? Ami wants to have children after we both finish college." He patted her knee, and a thin smile formed on her pasty face.

After uncomfortable silence from Lilibet, Cooper knew he had better speak up to avoid her wrath later. "We never wanted children. Look, John Henry, if you want this life, you have to make sacrifices."

"My husband is just trying to be modest," said Lilibet, turning the music down. "The problem is he becomes a horny beast in bed. And with a penis as enormous as his, well, it disfigured the living hell out of my lady parts. And when, by some miracle, I managed to get pregnant, his battering ram made minced meat out of our unborn bundle of joy. I warned Cooper; I warned him: God never intended a baby to be that close to its father's erect penis constantly torpedoing toward it. Would you all? I mean, it's so unfair to a tiny child who can't say 'no,' for nine solid months of bang, grunt, bang, grunt, bang! I mean, where are you pro-lifers on that one, huh?"

Cooper froze with horror. He caught a glance of the Mayfields' faces in the rearview mirror. The whites of their eyes now rivaled the overhead moon over the border of New Mexico where they had crossed. Lilibet had gone way too far this time.

"You wanna know why I started drinking and putting on weight? Well, now you do," added Lilibet, speeding again. "Cooper had gained weight as well, but he didn't receive warnings from movie studios to keep his figure camera ready."

"No, after I tucked away my battering ram for good, I was busy suing film and music studios for copyright infringements," Cooper hissed to the Mayfields. "When the movie offers began to dwindle for Lilibet, she pressured me to use my own money to buy her parts in one failed film after another until she was soon labeled box-office poison."

Fresh burned rubber billowed behind the car, and Lilibet's bottom lip protruded. "It's not because I wasn't a better actress than all of the others put together; it's because I couldn't get over the depression you caused me."

"Shall I tell the Mayfields what really caused your depression?" Cooper bravely made direct eye contact with his wife.

Lilibet's eyelids ticked, and her bottom lip rose at the corners to resemble fangs. She swerved and hit something the size of a rabbit.

Cooper looked behind his seat. "You see that, Mayfields? Lilibet Bathroy is always like that, overly theatrical with every damned detail in her life. She can't even use the toilet in the privacy of her own bathroom without acting like some studio was filming her. That's what cost her the title role of the last movie she auditioned for."

"How dare they reject me to star in that film!" huffed Lilibet. "They didn't have one single lead actor in that shitty picture. They just grabbed people off the streets and handed them a script. Argh, you . . . you were such a coward, Cooper. You could've at least threatened to sue the producers; they stole plot ideas from at least half a dozen other films. I can name them all in two seconds."

"I gave the third degree to the last dozen film executives who turned you down, honey dumplings. I couldn't risk losing my job as well; someone had to make the bribe money to get Hollywood to hire you. They sure as hell aren't going to settle for your body at this point."

Lilibet caused the limo tires to squeal. "Who the fuck do you think you're talking to like that—some old biddy in a nursing home? I still get fan mail from men asking to see more of my body. I just didn't want to rub your nose in it. I try to be respectful of other people's feelings."

Ami slid down in the back seat and began hyperventilating. John Henry looked drugged like someone had beat him over the head with a befuddling stick.

"I'll tell you who you are talking to: a man you nagged until he threatened to sue the wrong movie studio and ended up losing the case and his job. A man who moved from Hollywood to New Orleans after his wife's career ended and after she—"

Cooper bit his tongue when Lilibet's right fist smacked him in the nose, and warm blood dribbled down his chin and shirt.

"Lilibet! Now I am sorry, but violence is never acceptable," panted Ami, holding her skirt tight over her thighs. "You two really need to see a marriage counselor."

"You know what else is not acceptable?" Lilibet screamed. "Telling on people who are supposed to be your goddamned friend, that's what." Her coiffed hair came unraveled, and her fingers flexed and released on the steering wheel.

"Cooper is bleeding, and we are all tired. Perhaps we should stop somewhere for the night," said John Henry, while Ami fished through a wadded-up fast-food bag, removed the unused paper napkins, and handed them to Cooper, who kept his head tilted back against the

headrest. Each passing day, his life seemed to be spiraling out of control, and he feared what he might do or what literal dead end his wife's rage would bring them down again.

"You all have no idea of the hell that I have been through," said Lilibet as black streaks of eyeliner ran down her cheek.

"No, we wouldn't," whined Cooper through his pinched nose. "Not if you keep attacking anyone who tries to talk to you about it."

What had Cooper agreed to? For once, he had an undergraduate of psychology on his side, admonishing them to seek help for their marriage, and Lilibet wanted to destroy her. Lilibet pulled into the parking lot of the first luxury hotel she could find along the highway. The young valet looked on in terror as Cooper stepped out of the vehicle with as much blood on him as had dried on the front of the limo.

"If you value your life at all, don't even ask," Cooper said, handing the keys to the valet after Lilibet had knocked the whole set out of his hand, plowing between them in her path toward the hotel.

8

FLEA MARKET FILM STAR

Lilibet refused to say a word to Cooper from the second they entered their luxury suite. She let him recline on the sofa. Like a beached jellyfish, he raised a limp tentacle up to nurse his nose with a washcloth full of ice he borrowed from the champagne bucket, courtesy of his hard-earned money and not the management, he reminded her between groans of exaggerated agony.

She finished spraying and wiping everything, including Cooper, with disinfectant. Then, with a large magnifying glass and a lint brush, she checked the bed linens and every surface in the suite for body hairs before refreshing herself in the bathroom, which had a glass peacock mural standing proudly over the gold pedestal sink. When she couldn't find another inch of exposed skin to enhance with makeup, she took her contour brush and made a few skillful swipes of deep bronzer to

enhance her cleavage spilling out of her white evening dress. She then backcombed her bangs with her eyelash comb, sealed her makeup with hairspray, and rubbed petroleum jelly on her teeth to make it easier to smile. And heaven knows it was hard to smile with a no-good husband who never took her side like any decent husband would.

She didn't mean to draw blood tonight, but she would be damned if she were going to let Cooper reveal their darkest secret to the likes of the Mayfields or anyone if she could help it. Old Cooper drooper would just love to have her locked away and be done with her, and she knew it. Besides, he wouldn't dare talk, not with the incriminating evidence she had on him, and she realized it was the only reason he wouldn't leave her. A tear formed in each eye, so she shoved away from the sink and then tugged at her eyelashes to see if the super-glue was holding out before reapplying another coat of mascara.

Be damned she would before she'd apologize to her lousy husband or anyone for that matter. Forgiveness was never gifted to her, oh no. All through her youth, her parents lurked outside her bedroom and bathroom doors, waiting for her to do or say one little thing that offended their self-righteous principles, and then they made beelines for the switches and leather belts. Then they made her bend over her bed like a hotel whore where they would smack her bottom until her last tear moistened the bedspread.

Thinking back, Lilibet couldn't remember anything

she had done that was worthy of that much pain and humiliation. Unless it was when she had watched *Sonny and Cher* as well as *Laugh-In* on television at a friend's house at a time when hippies were slapping their own hips with their hands or tambourines. Lilibet had been dancing in her room to one of the few records her parents had approved—some song from *Mary Poppins*. She had ironed her long hair and had worn a Pocahontas-style headband. Somewhere during the kiddie record, the Devil must've gotten hold of her, and she began slapping her right hip rhythmically, and she dared to sing, "Sock it to me!" a common saying for that era.

The door swung open like Heaven's Gates, and needless to say, her mother did sock it to her, but not as bad as when young Lilibet tried to follow the braless trend of the women's liberation movement. Who knew to be a godly girl, your tits had to be nicely lifted to their fullest potential? While boys got to show off their bare chests playing crucified Jesus in a loincloth in the church plays.

"Please, just for once, forgive me and don't beat me. I will wear my bra from now on." Lilibet wept as her father hovered over her like the grim reaper ready to send her to Heaven with the first chop of his belt.

"Your mother and I always forgive just as Jesus forgives us, but you still must be punished, Lilibet. The Bible says parents must not spare the rod of punishment," he said, around the time she had just about had enough and decided her bottom, her pride, and her life belonged to her.

"Who gets to beat you and Mommy when you sin?" Lilibet had dared to ask her parents one day while the stinging welts on her bottom healed. "Shouldn't I get to do it? Isn't it always good to lead by example? Or do grownups' sins only require forgiveness . . . and a few glasses of wine during Communion?"

Lilibet shoved her makeup case and those memories out of her mind for now. It was time to join the Mayfields for dinner. Of course, Cooper wanted her to remind him when it was time to leave so she would have to feel sorry for his lack of recuperation from the little bump he got on the nose. But she wasn't going to baby him. She grabbed her purse, slipped into the hall, and made her way to the formal dining room of the hotel where Ami and John Henry were waiting just outside the entry, looking over brochures of things to do in the area as well as in Las Vegas. A band played softly behind a dance floor, and the lighting was dim except for the blue spotlights and backlit walls showcasing the contemporary sculptures.

"Where's Cooper? Is he not feeling well still?" asked John Henry, looking worried.

"Haaa, Cooper, Cooper, Cooper," droned Lilibet, lifting her two-inch lashes to the ceiling. "What? Afraid you won't have fun with just Lilibet? Well, I have news for you: I was the hit of every celebrity party until I married Cooper-the-party-pooper and moved to Dullsville." Lilibet glanced around the dining room and then back at the Mayfields. "Ugh, literally nobody is here."

Leaving them standing there, Lilibet lifted her chin and stormed off to find the table of her choice. To hell with waiting for the hostess to seat her. She found a spot with a window view of the city lights across the highway. She scanned the room, hoping some good-looking man would notice her and think she was single while there was time. A minute later, John Henry and Ami rounded the corner and found her, and of course, Cooper was trailing behind them like the needy puppy dog he was—broken nose as good as new.

After a quiet dinner and a few drinks, Lilibet shoved away from the table. "I am about to die of boredom. Come on, Ami, and dance with me. Cooper thinks he's too manly to dance."

"Oh, I don't know. I have two left feet," said Ami. Her lips tightened into an exaggerated frown, and her eyes darted around as if the patrons were actually looking at her nerdy ass. The girl was young, though, and this charged Lilibet with hopes that everyone would, by association, see her as younger than she was—just one of the girls out partying during spring break. *Don't you wish you had a piece of this, fellahs? Well, come closer and drop dead.*

"You know you can't refuse Lilibet," said Cooper.

"I tend to cry hysterically if I don't get my way, and if that happens, Cooper turns into a drooling beast." Lilibet pulled Ami out of her chair by the back of her navy-blue polyester dress. She practically had to drag the girl all the way to the dance floor where only an old man and his wife were dancing arm in arm. The sleepy music had to go, though, so Lilibet requested the piano player and singer perform one of her favorite dance songs: "Hot Child in the City" by Nick Gilder. As soon as the sultry drum and bass line started, Lilibet began prowling and gyrating around the dance floor. Danger ahead. She was a hot child in front of a lusty audience. But Ami (poor, pitiful Ami) shuffled her feet and arms left and right with a goofy smile until Lilibet began shimmying against her to test her response, loosen her up, or something. Was the girl just a nosy fan of hers, a fan who collected naked studio images, or did Ami fancy her? Not that Lilibet was into women, but she would love to have bragging rights.

When Lilibet pressed against her, Ami squeezed her eyes shut as if she were about to be executed. Her smile and chin tightened, and she stretched her neck back until she looked like a turtle emerging from its shell. The other couple shook their heads and hobbled off the dance floor. "Oooo-ahhh," Lilibet called out and hip-bumped the old man, and he stumbled forward several inches in his escape. She then spun Ami around and locked eyes with her.

"You know, Ami, Cooper didn't really want to retire. He just couldn't take his law firm any longer. It was so toxic and corrupt; I was afraid he'd start becoming aggressive again, or worse, start drinking."

"But he already drinks," said Ami, snapping her fingers and bobbing her head off the beat as though, in her head, she was listening to some slapdash oom-pah band in lederhosen and felt hats.

Lilibet hiked up her skirt over one leg and shook her

breasts. "Oh no, Ami Cable; that isn't drinking. Cooper's not really drinking until he passes out before lunch. And he hasn't done that in many months."

The band started playing sleepy music again, so Lilibet fussed at the band. "Don't you old codgers know any more decent songs? No wonder nobody is here." She left Ami standing on the dance floor and returned to the table. Ami soon followed and slumped down in her chair and exhaled as if she had been jogging.

"What were you boys up to while us girls were on the dance floor, eliciting unwanted lascivious attention? Were you measuring your unleashed cocks to see who has the biggest?" asked Lilibet, with practiced lips that once exhaled puffs of smoke from an opera-length cigarette holder she had used in a period film. To make the boys jealous, she swiped her fingers over her upper chest. "Ugh, I feel like I'm just covered in testosterone. It was just oozing from that gang of manly admirers near the dance floor."

"We didn't see any men go near the dance floor," said Cooper.

"Well, they were just ogling us from a distance; trust me. They were just too reserved to make a move with the puritan music. Who owns this place, some monastery?"

"We like it here, don't we, John Henry?" Ami reached across the table and held her husband's hand.

John Henry nodded while he finished chewing a piece of ice. "Cooper and I were just discussing business stuff. He was telling me what a great company he worked for. He said I should look into working there once I graduate."

Lilibet wanted to crawl under the table. Of course, he would say such a thing. Her husband had just contradicted everything she had told Ami.

"Oh, Cooper, come off of it. You hated it there, and you know it. You only liked your company in LA. You are such a liar. All you do is lie, lie, lie."

Cooper gritted his teeth and shoved his finger in Lilibet's face. "Shut up, you old cow. I'd probably like anything until you get your meddling little claws in all my business."

Lilibet sloshed her fourth martini all over Cooper, which splashed Ami as well. At the same time, she and Cooper dove at each other with their hands aiming for the other's throat.

John Henry jumped up from his seat and put his arms between them before pulling them apart. Lilibet placed her hand over her breasts, and her mouth gaped. How dare John Henry treat her like she was the problem.

"Watch where you put your paws on my wife, buddy," Cooper said to John Henry, shoving his shoulders.

"I didn't touch your wife—not like *that* anyway." John Henry backed up several feet. His nose wrinkled, and he shivered. "God, you guys, come on!"

Lilibet lowered her head and gazed into her empty cocktail glass. She rolled her thumb and index finger over the stem. "How do you like that? Now he's insulting my appearance." She grabbed her used napkin and dabbed the corners of her eyes. "I never realized I was so unattractive."

"No, I did not—I didn't say you were unattractive," whispered John Henry. "Is she, Ami?"

Ami shook her head robotically while Lilibet and Cooper briefly held hands. Lilibet was impressed that Cooper finally had some balls.

John Henry began hammering his arms in the air. "I'm sure every straight man in this room would be willing to grope you. Hell, all they'd need to do is have one look at all those nudie pics you had made . . . I mean . . . if that's their thing."

"My wife did NOT do porn if that's what you are insinuating!" said Cooper, rubbing Lilibet's back.

"They were artful still shots from a few movies I did and nothing more." Lilibet sucked in her cheeks, hoping that John Henry would confess to getting off on the photo. Just once, she would kill to make Cooper jealous. "How your wife got a hold of one of them, that's what I would like to know."

"Oh that," said Ami, blushing. "I studied movie production in college my first year in LA before moving to New Orleans. The students had to do a report on an underground movie actor and provide at least two props. So, in my research, I found a photo of you at a flea market, and it was well within my budget, which was great since my parents wanted me to get a real education, and they stopped funding my movie-production dreams."

Lilibet wished she had never asked. Her photo—her glorious photo in a musty, blue-collar flea market filled with crocheted toilet-seat covers, dented furniture crawling with bed bugs, and ten-year-old dried floral arrangements in mason jars. Ami was just trying to tarnish the star she was. Or better yet, Ami was covering up that she was one of the informants for the gossip papers. Or perhaps the girl did fancy her. Understandable, but Lilibet had best be diligent: The poor girl would probably even try to collect her toenail clippings or, hell, perhaps even a stool sample. One thing for sure, Lilibet was going to have to turn up the heat with her tests on the Mayfields, with or without her sorry husband's help.

"Well, missy, you hit the jackpot then. Photos of me usually end up in the finest of galleries. Collectors refuse to part with them even at top auction prices. You probably got a counterfeit, like I have here." Lilibet lifted her hand toward Cooper, flashing the massive emerald ring on her right index finger and knocking over John Henry's wine glass.

"That can't be a counterfeit. It's gorgeous," said Ami, soaking up the spill with her napkin.

Lilibet puckered her lips bitterly. "No, I meant my husband. I had to get this baby for myself. Last Christmas, I dragged Cooper to the jewelers and showed him exactly what I wanted—exactly. I even made him take a photo of it with his cellphone, and do you know what I ended up with under the tree? A damned ruby bracelet. I even had to climb up in my own attic with my leg in a cast to get the ornaments for the tree because he was too damn lazy to do it."

"A compression sock, Lilibet; hardly a cast. You wear compression socks to help with your varicose veins because the doctor said you were obese," Cooper sighed, and paid the waiter a fortune for the dinner that would never digest thanks to all the insults Lilibet had received.

"HOW. DARE. YOU?" Lilibet took her martini glass, smashed it on the edge of the table, and shook the jagged remains in Cooper's face. "Shall I tell your little kiss-ass friends here just what you are, huh? I'll do it this time, and you'd be finished if I did—FINISHED."

Cooper swallowed like the coward he was. His eyes crossed as he stared at the edge of the sharp glass three small inches from his tender eyeballs. For once, Lilibet could see herself actually doing it, actually slicing up her husband's face, maybe cutting out that insulting tongue of his—or better yet, blinding those eyes that beheld the beauty in everyone else but her.

A shock of reality traveled through every nerve and node in her body. She lowered the glass. The Mayfields' faces had never been more drained of color, more frozen with fear, the way she imagined her fans looked when they viewed a few of her films where she had to pretend to kill someone. The awful memory slammed her in the gut—the memory that dared not surface. It wasn't true. She wasn't crossing over into a blurred boundary of reality and acting.

You have never been a good actress, Lilibet. It takes no talent to play the bad girl when you are naturally evil and shallow. You have no ability to care for anyone but yourself and your own fame, the voices in her head returned.

She could see her church members from her childhood at Christmas around the beginning of an era of fearmongering and hysteria called the "Satanic Panic," where society, once again, proved they could be easily swayed to mania. Everyone from country music sweethearts to daycare workers was being accused of blood-drinking, organ harvesting, and being part of some diabolical Satanic agenda to rape and sacrifice children and turn every one to the darkest side of paganism, forcing Christians to take the Mark of the Beast, and eventually beheading them until God grew tired of watching the shitshow and came for them on his white horse in the clouds.

But the only "forcing" Lilibet remembered was done by her church and parents instead. It culminated most disturbingly at the church's annual record and book-burning event held in an open field behind the Almighty House of God. They had joyfully built a huge bonfire with flames rising over ten feet. Pastor Booth and Lilibet's parents were standing at the head of the group near the makeshift cross they had embedded in the winter ground, so in case anyone's conscious bothered them, they could be reminded that Christ suffered worse. All the other members, especially the children, had thrown their Satanic books, tapes, and records onto the inferno, creating a toxic fog and squeal that caused their faces to become charged with righteous zeal as if they were assisting the Salem Witch Burnings.

"That's it, my children," the pastor shouted over the roar of the flames. "Those records are chockfull of evil, backward masking that is turning our boys into queers and our girls into sluts. The secular musicians worship goats and perform their wicked music with the rhythms cleverly striking on the second and fourth beats instead of the first and third beats, the way the Good Lord intended."

Lilibet was hesitant to throw her music records and books on the bonfire. What few she was permitted to have anyway.

"Everyone, pull in close and form a prayer circle around young Lilibet here. May the circle be unbroken, be unbroken. She has a spirit of dissension. I need you to reach out your right hands, reach them out. We must pray. The world and all its foul influences have gotten a stranglehold on her," the pastor spoke in his most strained and wounded voice. A voice that made it seem like he was watching the flames of Hell devouring his disobedient flock, and he would beg one more time for God to spare them. A voice destined to induce a pricking of the heart.

Then it was just as Lilibet had feared. Her mother returned to the circle with a handful of celebrity gossip and fashion magazines that Lilibet thought she had expertly hidden under her mattress at home. Mother slammed them down into Lilibet's hands in front of everyone as if she had caught her with a sack of stolen bank money.

Lilibet's Sunday-school mate Lynn Snodgrass smirked in the circle. The bonfire flames exposed the wicked delight on her devious face. Lynn had told Lilibet earlier that she wouldn't make it as an actress even if her parents let her. ". . . You could put all the lipstick in the world on a hog, but it would still end up wallowing in its own poo," she had said.

"As a sign unto God that you are renouncing your wicked ways and dedicating yourself unto Him, you must confess your sins openly and according to the Book of Acts chapter nineteen, verse nineteen and twenty, we are admonished to burn this vomit of Satan in the fire," her mother had said, wiping tears from her eyes. Her breath, snakelike in the winter air, had looked like the Holy Ghost escaping her lips to possess Lilibet instead.

Looking down at the magazines in her quivering hands, Lilibet had felt a rage building inside her as she inched toward the flames of the bonfire. She knew deep down that there wasn't anything demonic about the periodicals or wanting to be a film actress. Acting was just pretending like everyone in the circle was doing. And though they couldn't shake a mere headache without pain meds, much less put hospitals out of business, they pretended they had some holy power radiating from their bodies that, by encircling her with their sacred temples, little red imps with pitchforks would purge from her bowels and run, screaming into the flames, to rescue the latest tribute to Marilyn Monroe and a dog-eared page featuring navy-and-white polyester jackets and checked bell bottoms.

"Lilibet, please put the glass down. Your hand is bleeding," said John Henry. With a drooping smile, he handed her his napkin to wrap around the wound.

"Oh, no worries there. The cut can't be too deep . . . not when you're as obese as I am." Lilibet stormed out of the restaurant and back to her bedroom suite, where she locked the door and deadbolt. Cooper could go sleep under a bridge somewhere for all she cared.

Ten minutes later, he tapped on the door gently at first, calling to her in his stupid baby talk, which made her want to vomit. Then the part she had been relishing to hear: his phony cloy voice dissolved into a growl between the hammering of his fist on the door. She could just see his red face pressed against the last thing she hoped he would forever see in his desperation to get back inside her life . . . the cold door locked.

Kiss it, Cooper Pearmain; Lilibet chuckled inside as she spread her limbs across the entire king-sized bed. *Kiss it and tongue the doorknob while you're at it.*

9

BOTCH-HAIRED
BANDIT

Cooper gave up on Lilibet opening the door. He couldn't yell. Shouting might cause more of a disturbance than he already had. He didn't want to pay for another hotel room, not when he was also paying for the Mayfields' suite as well. He thought of his options. At least he still had the keys to the limo. Lilibet would probably drive off without him otherwise. But he didn't want to sleep in the car—not with his bad back. He started to knock on the young couple's door and ask to sleep in their suite, but he and Lilibet had surely already worn on them worse than cheap wool underwear in a heatwave marathon.

There was only one choice that wouldn't cost him more than he ever wanted to spend on this ridiculous test of Lilibet's: The limo. Cooper made his way to the parking garage and searched until he found the vehicle.

He opened the door to the back seat, crawled inside, and reclined on his left side. A half-hour later, he was burning up, so he sat up to remove his dinner jacket when the silhouette at the window startled him. Although the garage was dimly lit, he could tell it was an ugly undeveloped girl. Cooper's pupils focused harder. He was wrong; he had assumed the earrings sparkling like bullets wedged in the flesh to be the masochistic trophies of a girl, but it wasn't. There was also a desperate-to-grow boomerang of hair on the sad upper lip and bangs so high and jagged, they looked as if they were cut while horseback riding during an earthquake.

Cooper got chills. The man was pressing the tip of a pistol against the glass, speaking in Spanish. Cooper didn't understand a word of what he was saying, but he didn't need to. He knew if he didn't open the car door, the man would shoot him.

Cooper unlocked the door on his side, swung his legs out of the car, and tried to run, but the man darted around to the other side of the limo and shoved his gun against his chest.

"Dame tu dinero!" the man yelled between breaths.

"Did I have dinner?" asked Cooper, trying to understand what he was asking. "Yes, I already ate."

"Dame tu dinero!" the man said more forcefully, shoving him with the pistol, which Cooper expected to go off at any second.

"Damn it to De Niro? You mean Robert De Niro? I don't understand, but YES, 'damn it.' Damn everything." Cooper could tell this wasn't appeasing the gunman as he backed into his car, where the man had now cornered him.

He started groping Cooper's chest before shoving him around and bending him over the car seat behind the open door. He then began squeezing Cooper's butt cheeks. Oh, bloody hell, he feared; he had escaped a near prison gang bang only to be sexually assaulted in a parking garage. His fear eased when the man slipped Cooper's wallet from his back pocket.

"Don't take my wallet, please, please," Cooper begged; before the butt of the gun came down on the back of his head so hard, Cooper saw a flash of light and then everything went black.

Something was pulling at his leather shoes when he regained consciousness, dragging, and jerking his legs to the left. His toes were becoming unusually hot from the friction. A misting of cold sweat covered Cooper's body. He realized he was still face down on the back seat, and his legs were hanging out of the limo. The wind and whooshing sounds of passing cars signaled that the gunman had carjacked him and was now speeding down the highway. The flashing lights weren't in Cooper's head now; it was the passing headlights. Would he be better off letting himself fall out of the car onto the highway and risk getting hit by oncoming traffic? Cooper would rather take a bullet instead. Gripping the seatbelt, he used all his strength to pull himself inside the back seat, where he closed the door.

The gunman, who had taken his car keys, rattled off something in Spanish and began swerving the car when he tried to aim his pistol at Cooper over the top of the seat. Cooper had a slight advantage, realizing that the man couldn't aim backward and drive. But if he tried to attack or choke the carjacker, they could both die in a crash. Thanks to the brief light of a streetlamp, they had whisked past, Cooper spotted his dinner jacket, which had fallen on the car floor. He eased his hand down beside his leg and lifted it up before searching the inside pocket. Luckily, he was able to retrieve his cellphone. While the driver continued to yell and look in the rearview mirror, Cooper held the phone low behind the seat and texted John Henry:

> *Call police. I've been carjacked. On highway with a strip mall.*

He hit the blue arrow on his phone to send it and hoped John Henry would hear the text tone while sleeping, building up his buns, or whatever he was doing. Cooper knew better than to text Lilibet; even if she heard the text notification through her snoring, she would think he was trying to take sympathy away from her with some made-up crisis—God forbid.

The carjacker pulled on the side of the highway and slammed on the brakes. He aimed his pistol at Cooper and yelled more gibberish that sounded like he was saying, "Salty." He seemed to be motioning for Cooper to get out of the limo.

Before Cooper could do as commanded, the gunman jumped out and opened the door for him while waving his pistol between him and the darkness outside. Cooper put up his hands and stepped out of the limo, accidentally dropping his cellphone near his pavement-scuffed shoes or what was left of them. As soon as the gunman reached down to grab the phone, Cooper knocked him on the back of the head with both hands locked together for extra force. The man collapsed near the rear tire, and Cooper saw his stolen wallet fall out of the man's shirt pocket. He grabbed it with fingers that felt broken, and he took off running. The carjacker fired a shot, but Cooper jumped over the guardrail and slid down a high slope beside the raised highway, where he then lunged toward the closed strip mall. If only he could've gotten his phone back as well, but there was little time. Then he remembered his phone had a tracking app.

"Ha-ha! Go right ahead and keep my goddamned phone, you botch-haired bandit," Cooper shouted back at the now distant highway. He kicked an empty beer bottle out of his way and stomped through the parking lot toward the only store in the mall that still had its lights on. "I could be out on the peaceful ocean on my yacht right now, but oh no, my wife had to teach the Mayfields a lesson. Well, the only lesson they're gonna learn is how miserably married middle-aged couples kill each other after losing everything they own."

If Cooper had a hundred dollars for every crook who had tried to steal from him, forge his identity, or vandalize his properties over the years, he could use that money to take a lavish European cruise. Didn't these thugs realize that for every crime, they are creating and fostering a world that even they won't be safe living in? They were in essence, training and encouraging more of the same. Thugs robbing and killing other thugs. Rapists raping rapists. If they spent as much time doing something useful for society instead of damaging it, then everyone would be better off for it. It wouldn't do for Cooper to become president. He would say things that everyone else was afraid to say and get some shit done. He paused in the parking lot and realized that what he had done, his darkest secret, was just as bad. At least others would see it that way if they ever found out. But it was far in the past. Cooper didn't pursue a life of crime, and he felt bad about the former him. Was he a hypocrite for trying to justify his actions? Surely living with Lilibet had punished him enough.

Cooper had thought this all out in his years of agony. He considered himself a Christian, not the "Sell all your possessions, take up deadly serpents, and raise the dead," working definition of a Christian—more of a modern believer—that magic formula to attain eternity. Oh, okay, a *supposer* was more like it because his parents were at times. And one was always taught that no matter what you've done, repentance and forgiveness from God were all you needed. Burn a school or house down? Give it to Him. Molest someone's children until they grow up warped and slit their wrists? It's covered by His blood. Kill a pregnant mother who used her last frozen egg to save her marriage? Recite the sinner's prayer. Rape some man's philanthropist wife and give her AIDS so that she dies and goes to Hell for being an unbeliever? Problem solved—for *you* anyway. No need for the new you to fear confessing to the people you've wronged and risk going to prison. No one ever does that, or there wouldn't be many folks left to tithe. A dog must not return to its vomit once its slate is wiped clean, and that way, the cops won't ever be on to you. The Good Lord only asks that you never turn the other cheek; instead, learn karate for Christ, judo for Jesus, join Shot Guns for El Shaddai, and if all else fails, then write scriptures on a nuclear missile and send a whole country or two into oblivion, baby!

The ancient Bible got it backward, Cooper had grown to understand; the scripture is now interpreted: The righteous must never "give sinners your coat as well" when they sue you for your shirt. Instead, countersue those pesky woke sinners with every ounce of religious freedom the government has recently given you. Cooper far preferred the new beliefs but wondered if he should learn karate in case his ass got sent to prison despite his prayers and any hush-money lawsuits he might have to resort to if any godless nosy bodies dragged his past out from under the blood that had washed it.

When he reached the front of Happily Ever After Antiques in the strip mall, he collapsed on the iron bench bolted to the concrete to keep people from stealing it, but not from covering it in graffiti. If the Mayfields knew what was best for themselves, they would call for someone to come get them and take them back home. They would never come near Lilibet or him again. If Lilibet ever found out he had even suggested such a thing to the Mayfields, she would ruin his life.

A skinny, hunched-over man in his sixties opened the door to the antique store and turned around and locked it. He looked over at Cooper before pausing in his steps.

"Ah, you must have the magic formula, too," Cooper said to the man, still thinking about the power of belief.

"Huh?" The man held his hand up to his ear and wrinkled his face.

"The name of your store. I just figured—oh, never mind."

"Everything all right? You've got a bit of blood running down your neck there," the man said, pointing behind his ear for emphasis.

"I just got attacked and had my limo and phone stolen, and I don't have a clue where I am, but other than that, I'm just peachy. I'm sure it was something I deserved for being the wrong demographic for this new generation—which generation is it now that they have run out of alphabets?" Cooper hissed. It had finally happened. He had turned into his father.

"Attacked, you say? Man, I'll tell you: It's getting so bad you can't even go to your own funeral. My name is Cecil Thornton. Come on inside and use my phone. My help is out on maternity leave, and I had to stay late and do inventory—got audited . . . damn IRS."

"Thank you. My name is Cooper Pearmain, and I have an old home in the Garden District of New Orleans unless they took that, too. That's the thing about antiques; how many times can one chair be ethically taxed before you end up paying more in taxes than you ya paid for the damned chair ya can't even sit on? It's white-collar thievery, actually—especially if you're buying it for a business. That's where the government really gets ya," said Cooper. He followed behind the kind man, who locked the door to his store as soon as they both entered. The potpourri in the air still couldn't drown out the dusty embrace of an enormous collection of period furniture and bric-a-brac. The blend of wood and metal polish, mothballs, cedarwood, kerosene, and woodsmoke, along with centuries of bacteria and fungi breaking down, gave off more gas than a recovery room for colonoscopy patients.

Cooper paused to inspect a mantelpiece clock and matching candelabras that looked fit for the Palace of Versailles—mere stress balls for Lilibet to fling when one curl on her hair wouldn't cooperate. He had certainly been in finer antique stores in the French Quarter, especially on Royal Street, but Cecil had more pieces that would work better for eclectic if not contemporary homes. He took the cordless phone from Cecil and dialed Lilibet since he hadn't memorized John Henry's number. The phone rang over a dozen times.

"My wife is still mad at me. She'll never answer. Do you have a phonebook so I can look up my hotel?"

The man reached behind the counter and plopped a phonebook down in front of Cooper. "Primitive, but it should work if your hotel is local."

Cooper buried his nose between millions of tiny numbers and nearly became cross-eyed before he found the hotel and dialed the number. "Yes, this is Cooper

Pearmain. I reserved two suites there with you and, well, you're not going to believe this, but I just had my limo and cellphone stolen, and they dropped me out on the highway."

"Yes, a Mr. John Henry informed us of the incident," replied the hotel clerk. "The police are searching for the man now. Give us your location, and we'll send a shuttle to bring you back to the hotel."

Cooper gave the hotel desk clerk the antique store's address, and Cecil agreed to wait until the shuttle arrived before closing his store.

"Sounds like you are having trouble with the little lady," Cecil said.

"Believe you me, when it comes to Lilibet, there is nothing little."

"Now trust me on this," said Cecil, pushing his wire-rimmed glasses up his long nose. "What you need to do is buy her at least one gift that says you have been listening to her. Two gifts and she's smooth as silk for a few weeks."

"Perhaps you're right," said Cooper looking around the store. "She does keep bringing up how I got her the wrong gifts for Christmas . . . oh, and her birthday, anniversary, and Groundhog Day. I think she just says that so she can get a free weekend with my credit card."

"What does she talk about more often than not? For most women, it's jewelry, which I cannot help you much there."

"She loves Tiffany lamps, and the Art Nouveau works of Alphonse Mucha. In fact, she once said she wished she had lived in the day to have modeled for one of Mucha's seasonal goddess posters."

"You don't say?" Cecil's brows rose high over his glasses. He came from behind the counter, patted Cooper on the back, and motioned for him to follow as if he were leading him to a hidden brothel of naked beauties waiting with steak dinners and lit joints. Cecil pulled two sets of white-cloth gloves from a carved box on the shelf and told Cooper to put on one pair while he did the same with the other.

The naked beauties must be germaphobes like Lilibet, Cooper imagined. If Cecil pulled out a bedsheet with a two-inch hole in the center or a pair of long ugly underwear some religious people wear to ward off evil and soul-damning impurities during sex, Cooper was heading fast for the exit. He'd then jump in the nearest garbage dumpster and cry out "Impure, impure," like menstruating women had to do for seven days in the Bible. What bliss it must've been to be forced into seclusion outside the desert camp for a whole week every month. And Cooper wouldn't even consider killing two turtles or pigeons in order to get back inside the damned camp. Let his monthly curse turn wine bitter, make crops wither, make mirrors dim and swords dull. Let it drive dogs mad until their bites become poisonous or whatever it is the superstitious still believe.

His heartbeat began to return to normal after Cecil floated to a section of antique books in the back of the store and motioned for Cooper to help him pull a four-foot-tall book from behind the musty bookshelf. They each latched their fingers on the spine, slid the heavy thing in short intervals until it was free, and stood before them like a curious door for short people. A stocking stuffer for the Jolly Green Giant.

"My goodness, I've never seen a book this large in my entire life."

"This book is unimaginably rare, Mr. Pearmain— one of the biggest treasures for any real Alphonse Mucha collector. Only four of these limited-edition books were ever created in fact—poster-sized prints of every one of Mucha's works, including his interior designs."

They gently hoisted the heavy book on a reading table and opened the front cover as though it was an Egyptian tomb being entered for the first time in five thousand years. The color prints had faded but were still magnificent and inviting in their design. Much of the prints included fair-skinned lovelies with flowers in their hair, standing in mannerly poses, wearing flowing gowns in earth tones and pastels while surrounded by arched borders featuring rich repeated patterns.

"Yes, but how *much-a* is this Mucha gonna cost a retired old man who just had his car stolen and has a ton of lawsuits awaiting him because his wife conveniently lost her rare diamond ring?"

Cecil shifted in his leather wing-tipped shoes and tapped his index finger against his jaw. "For you, I will make a deal at thirty percent off. I will sell it to you for seventy-five thousand—plus tax, of course."

"Seventy-five thousand! My wife had better be as smooth as silk until she dies for that amount of money."

"She will love you forever; I promise you," said Cecil.

Before Cooper had fully realized what he had done, he had bought the rare book and, just in case, a four-hundred-thousand-dollar Tiffany floor lamp with a glorious peacock design—"Very rare," said Cecil. But nothing says "I love you" like a lamp so expensive you dare not risk blowing a moth off the glass shade—a shade that blocks out so much light that you can't see just how much your lucky wife has aged. But this didn't matter; together, they were going to put an end to Lilibet's nagging and bitterness for many years, hopefully. Cooper had truly listened and had yielded—his wallet, which the carjacker had narrowly stolen—or did he just have it stolen after all?

The hotel shuttle bus had arrived to salvage what bit of money Cooper had left, and the store owner helped load Cooper's purchases in the back of the bus. Cooper didn't know whether he should thank Cecil or if Cecil should thank him. But he took his receipt and certificates of authenticity well aware of the pit in his stomach that feared he, a successful copyright attorney, was the world's biggest sucker.

Back at the hotel, Cooper carefully hid the lamp and book in John and Ami's suite until he could surprise Lilibet with the gifts in the morning.

"Does my wife know about the carjacking and all?" Cooper asked the Mayfields. He knew it would be too much to ask that she would care about his safety either way.

"I tried knocking on her door while John Henry was

on his phone with the police, but she didn't answer," said Ami, with an apologetic frown. She was still in her nightrobe when she offered Cooper a washcloth to clean up the blood on the back of his head. Then she searched the internet on her cell phone about head injuries.

John Henry patted Cooper on the shoulder. "Oh, gee, my man. She should come around once she sees the gifts. If not, well heck, I'll marry you." John Henry's broad grin withered when Ami's eyes squinted on him deeply, knowingly. A look only mental-health professionals master from years of psychoanalyzing patients.

The police arrived, and Cooper filed a report on the incident. Minutes later, after Cooper kept repeating the same story of what had happened to him, the officer received a call from another officer named Costas.

"Good work. Hold on a minute." The officer muted his wireless radio and turned to Cooper. "Mr. Pearmain, you'll be glad to know we've captured the carjacker. He had stopped at a gas station to buy a pair of furry dice to hang on the rearview mirror. The suspect put up little resistance, they say—couldn't hurt a butterfly."

"Little resistance! That god—that *thug*—busted my head open with a loaded gun, nearly wrecked on the interstate, and then tried to shoot me." Cooper thought he was going to burst a tonsil; he was so livid.

The officer returned to his radio communication and then muted the device again. "Office Costas said he recovered your cellphone, Mr. Pearmain. You can pick it up at the police station in the morning. Oh, and by the way, he said great pics of your ass you sent to a man named Frank. We kept a copy for our records."

Ami and John Henry jarred themselves to attention and locked their eyes on Cooper.

"It's not what you're thinking," Cooper said to the young couple, before focusing his growing anger on the cop. "What was he doing looking at my private photos?" Cooper lowered his voice when he realized that he was yelling and shaking.

"Look, Mr. Pearmain, whenever there is a crime reported, we collect evidence from all parties involved. And from the looks of that photo, according to Officer Costas, it looks like you threw a damn parade."

"Frank is my proctologist; I'll have you know. I had a cyst pop up overnight and get infected. He wanted me to send him a photo since it was on a Sunday and the clinic was closed. I had to have ten stitches. Hardly anything to look at—turned nearly black—lots of puss. Do you need proof, huh?" Cooper tugged at his waistband; certain he could spit flames.

"That's your business who ya want to send nudes to. Now, a few years ago, I would've had to cuff ya and take you in," the officer said, waving his arms for Cooper to stop tugging at his pants.

"The good old days, huh?"

After the officer left, the Mayfields insisted Cooper sleep on the couch in their rooms since Lilibet still wouldn't open the door to their suite. *Oh, how charitable of every damn one of you since I'm paying for the rooms and the whole trip*, Cooper wanted to say. Never mind him and his crumbling spine; it would be his honor to spend the night on a sofa so narrow he would fall off if he twitched his finger—the finger he used to fish his credit cards out of his wallet—the wallet he nearly lost his life to rescue from a dangerous thug. The rock-hard plank he had been graciously allocated for the night would be splendid. *Thanks, and don't let me disturb you two snugly little lovebirds over there.*

Perhaps Cooper was too wired from his near-death experience and the nosy cops who must've had belly-busting laughs at his expense. All he could do was stare at the Tiffany Lamp and Mucha Book leaning safely against the wall. It wasn't wise to travel with such expensive rarities, so as soon as he could, he was going to take them and have them shipped to his home address. In the meantime, he couldn't just present the gifts to Lilibet as they were; he needed to wrap them in gift paper. He remembered seeing a twenty-four-hour pharmacy a half-mile up the highway, so he got the extra room key and his wallet and walked all the way to the store and back in the hot night air. He fumbled down the hotel hall and through the door with a stack of gift-paper rolls and bows and a gift card that said, "For my kind and loving wife," since he couldn't find any that said, "For my nagging, sociopathic, money-pit of a wife, in hopes that you'll never again say that nothing I ever do is good enough."

As quietly as he could, without waking the Mayfields, he spent over an hour wrapping the lamp and enormous book with the gift paper before attaching the silver bows

and card using transparent tape. Like Cooper and Lilibet's relationship, the gifts looked mismatched, wrinkled, and rough around the edges with a bit of silver on top. But hopefully, Lilibet would finally be pleased with something he did.

10

NOT MUCHA
ANYMORE

Cooper awoke that morning with the worst headache and backache of his life. Sleeping on the sofa surely hadn't helped. He should've had a doctor look at his injured head, but he hated hospitals and didn't want any more expenses than he had already accrued. Ami and John Henry had already dressed and had gone down to the hotel restaurant for breakfast. Cooper needed to get inside his own suite to clean up and get to his clothes. He tried his key card on the door, but Lilibet still had the deadbolt fastened.

"Honey dumplings, please let me in. I'm sorry that I offended you. I have something really special for you, but you need to let me inside," he said through the door.

Cooper could barely hear the television paused on some talk show. After waiting another minute or two, he tried to fight the anger building inside him. He went down to the hotel lobby and told the desk clerk about Lilibet locking him out, and they tried phoning her room, but she still wouldn't answer.

"Perhaps she doesn't want to be disturbed," said the clerk.

"Trust me, she's always disturbed. Anyway, my name is on the credit card. I am the one who reserved the rooms, not Lilibet, not Sleeping Beauty, not the president of the United States. Surely someone in this hotel can get the door open for me," said Cooper.

The clerk phoned someone from maintenance who arrived with a device similar to a crowbar, and together they went to Cooper's suite. The maintenance man knocked on the door and used the card key, but the bolt was still secured, so he inserted the metal bar through the crack in the door, which Lilibet suddenly decided to unlatch. She jerked the door open and was dressed in her designer red dress, heels, textured black stockings, and a piling of jewelry that clanked like a treasure chest being rummaged by a band of pirates.

"Oh, good heavens! What are you two doing, blocking the door? Are you morons? Move!" she said, pushing between them, marking them for life with her designer scent. A fog of steam poured from the bathroom where she had showered, and no doubt shaved and oiled everything below her powdered chin. Her eyelashes lowered derisively at the bar in the man's hands, but she avoided looking at Cooper before lifting her chin high and strutting toward the restaurant as if the hall walls were made of steel and she had magnets in her hips.

Gritting his teeth from his back pain, Cooper hobbled after her and grabbed her arm. Her heels dug into the carpet, and her head snapped toward him. "Get your hand off of me."

"Sweetheart, I just want you to come and see what I got for you last night. You're not going to believe your eyes. I promise," Cooper panted with excitement.

"I don't trust my eyes anymore; they should've seen the real you before my brain figured you out," said Lilibet, pulling away from him.

"Please, honey dumplings. I picked it out special just for you."

"Oh, all right," huffed Lilibet.

He put his hand behind her waist and eased her back toward John Henry and Ami's suite while she sighed through her pinched nostrils and puckered lips. She walked like she was squashing snakeheads all the way to the room.

Once inside the suite, Cooper lifted his hands toward the tall, wrapped gifts against the wall by the sofa. "Ta-da!"

"You don't expect me to unwrap that shit? I just painted my fingernails."

"Okay, I'll do it. I'll unwrap them for you, but first—" Cooper paused and grabbed the greeting card off the lamp. He hadn't sealed the card, so all she had to do was slip the card out of the envelope.

Lilibet didn't take the card. She rolled her eyes and made a shooing motion with her fanned nails, indicating for Cooper to take out the card for her, which he did. He

opened it and held it in front of her face. He didn't hear any response, so he lowered the card. Her painted eyebrows rounded, and her face elongated as though she was getting sleepy.

"I'll just put the card on the coffee table over there in case you might want it later." He then carefully unwrapped the lamp, slowly, tempting her with previews of what was behind the wrapping, as though the lamp was a leg in a striptease. Of course, if it were his leg, she would have made him bathe it and shave it so she could enslave it. When he finished removing the paper, he tossed the wrapping to the side like a pair of panties.

"An exceedingly rare and very genuine Tiffany floor lamp. I remembered you love peacocks, too." He plugged the cord in the socket on the wall so she could see it lit up in glorious stained-glass color.

"*Humm*," Lilibet said, with something between surprise and a constipated grunt. Her face remained unchanged, and she seemed more interested in an imaginary scratch on her fingernail, which she inspected under the light of the hotel lamp and not the Tiffany lamp, which was much closer.

"Okay, great. And wait till you see what else, Lilibet. Wait until you see." Cooper held his back and hobbled over to the last gift. He was so excited for her to see it; he ripped the paper off the oversized antique book in one swipe this time. "Ta-da! Don't say I don't ever listen to you, honey dumplings. Even though this was extremely rare and expensive, I thought well, not too much for my sweet thing."

He waited but had received a better reaction from a dying slug once, so with sweat beading on his throbbing face, he opened the heavy front leather cover and began leafing through pages the size of posters.

"*Mah*," she grunted, inverting her chin. "I'm not into Mucha anymore."

"WHAT? What are you saying? Mucha has always been your favorite artist. Your biggest wish was that you would've been alive back in the twenties, so he could've painted you like a seasonal goddess, remember? You even tried looking for an interior designer to do the whole house in the style of Mucha."

Lilibet fumbled with one of the curls over her forehead. "I can no longer support people who don't know who the hell they are or what they want. Mucha dabbled in freemasonry, and he dabbled in the Catholic Church, and then he dabbled with mysticism."

Cooper's head and heart were pounding at full throttle now. "What? But you don't prefer any of those groups. Hell, for the past four years, you wanted to plan a vacation in Prague just to tour the Mucha Museum, or are you going to deny that now, as well?"

With her red fingernails, Lilibet picked at the leading between the stained-glass panels on the Tiffany lamp as if it had dried glue from a dollar-store sticker on it. "Look, Cooper. When I say someone's my favorite artist, it might be Austin Osman Spare one minute or the guy who painted that, you know, that little country girl on those cheap snack cakes the next."

Cooper suddenly realized why he had learned to tune

out Lilibet—not pay attention to her likes and desires. She was always quick to offer a fight-to-the-death opinion, which she contradicted within the same day or sometimes within the same conversation. And waiting for her to place an order in a restaurant was like watching a pine tree shed all its needles: She was so afraid she would order something that wouldn't absolutely titillate her so she wouldn't even begin with a less risky appetizer. Now, as far as her drink order, it couldn't get to the table fast enough, and she thoroughly expected the server to read her mind on what she needed to wet her whistle.

"You just live to punish me, don't you?" hissed Cooper. "You have no idea of what kind of hell I went through last night. Now, if you don't mind, I have to go to the police station to get my phone and the limo."

"Why the hurry?" asked Lilibet, fluffing her hair in the wall mirror behind her. "You haven't had breakfast yet. That's why you're so cranky."

"I'll grab one of those 'cheap country cakes' on my way back. Unless I change my mind and fly to Paris for some French pastries." Cooper was sure his bitter grin appeared monstrous by now. "But I'll be sure to let you know when I change *my* mind."

Cooper stormed toward the exit door, and his foot got caught on the electric cord of the Tiffany lamp, and by the time he realized it, old Tiffany fell like a hewn timber and shattered into hundreds of pieces on the marble floor.

11

GLORY HONOLULU

Cooper was still in a foul mood by the time he got the limo and his phone back from the police. He had offered to autograph the copy of his ass that they needed to keep for their records, but the officers didn't seem amused for once. They had all obviously had a late-night party over it and were now hungover and ready to make some easy money parked under shade trees to ticket grannies for jaywalking to the fabric store. Cooper then tried to return the expensive Mucha book to the antique store for a refund, but the owner refused.

". . . After all I did to help you, Mr. Pearmain, I deserve some compensation," said Cecil Thornton. His nostrils pinched, and he kept tapping the same stack of receipts against the front desk as if they still weren't aligned perfectly.

Cooper leaned over the desk. "Do you even have a wife, Mr. Thornton?"

"Well, I—" Cecil's mouth tightened into a guilty

frown. And his shaky fingers fumbled to push his glasses back up his pasty nose, releasing the stack of receipts to a scattered mess again.

"I didn't think so," snapped Cooper. He grabbed the massive book off the counter and carried it back to the limo, feeling like he was a skinny lad back in college and moving his mini-fridge full of canned beer into the narrow dorms. He could always hollow out the Mucha book and store a grenade launcher in it, he determined.

His back was aching, so the hot sun on the leather seats helped ease his pain. Lilibet turned all the air vents on her while she propped her feet on the dashboard as if she were blessing the limo with a much-needed hood ornament—a dis-figurehead on the Titanic. Cooper stayed in the slow lane so the passing cars couldn't see Lilibet's old stubby toes glowing white.

"The sun is good for my gout," said Lilibet, spreading her toes wide.

If only the sun would help with the pain of Lilibet's voice in Cooper's ears. For much of the drive through New Mexico, Lilibet insisted everyone listen to the recordings of Yma Sumac on the car stereo, a double-voiced singer of exotica music from the 1950s who sounded inhuman at times. Ami and John Henry sat in the back seat with their heads buried in their brochures of tourist attractions. Poor kids: Cooper almost felt sorry for them. They actually believed they were going to get to do something fun on this trip.

After chanting along, with her hands dancing like charmed cobras in the air, Lilibet said, "You have to meditate, children. Cleanse your chakras—listen with your third eye, and the universe will whisper mysteries only the worthy can hear."

"Only someone in a straitjacket, you mean," said Cooper, struggling to keep his eyes open from little sleep. But with the vocals on the radio occasionally shrieking like birds, he kept jolting awake.

A bus full of men in soccer uniforms pulled up beside the limo while Lilibet was seductively waving her arms, seemingly at them, and she moaned with her eyes rolled back in her head. Cooper tried to speed forward, but it was too late; the men started hanging their heads and other parts of their anatomy out the windows while yelling catcalls.

Ami gasped with her hand over her face and slid down in her seat. John Henry strained his neck to see what all the fuss was about.

"I think I went to middle school with that guy," he said to Cooper and the others.

"What do you mean?" asked Cooper. "You can't even see his face."

"My old best friend, Erick Rand," continued John Henry. "Erick stayed at my house for sleepovers occasionally. Don't think anything of it, ladies; he looks for any excuse to get naked."

Cooper steadied the steering wheel and kept his focus straight ahead on the road. "Oh, for God's sake, Lilibet, do you always have to create a scene? I don't know about the universe, but you've certainly conjured up a few ass-teroids and a big dipper or two."

Lilibet's eyes sprang open, and her left dancing arm accidentally stabbed the panic button above the dashboard. An alarm began whirring, all the car lights began flashing, and a woman's voice came through a speaker: "Warning. You have enacted the emergency defense system. Please remain calm while we track your location and send authorities as soon as possible."

"Oh, shit!" said John Henry, getting a little whiplash from straining to see the bus still. "What are they going to do—send the entire Coast Guard after us?"

The car slowed to a rolling stop in the middle of the fast lane while speeding cars screeched past, blasting their horns.

"What's happening?" asked Ami, peeking through her fingers in case the buff bus was still beside them.

"I don't know. Someone must've turned off the engine remotely," said Cooper, looking for any emergency lights on the dash to indicate system trouble.

Within five more minutes, an angry disco of red and blue lights came rolling and roaring up behind them. Ami decided to search the internet on her phone to see why a car would just shut down while driving.

"Oh shit, they've got their guns drawn," said John Henry, when a swarm of uniformed officers began prowling toward the car with body shields, blocking the entire highway. Everyone in the car put their hands in the air, except Lilibet, for once.

"I'll take care of this," she said, opening her blouse and then the door when a bullet zinged a hole through the handle, inches from her hand, which she inspected with a frown. "They nearly chipped my fingernails."

Cooper could just see it now: he was going to have to pay for the rental company to buy a brand-new limo when they returned to New Orleans—if they made it home.

"What are you doing? Are you crazy?" Cooper yelled out the window at the officers. Had they decided to arrest him and his proctologist over his ass photos after all?

"All of you, keep your hands in the air and step outside of the vehicle," said a female officer through a loudspeaker.

Everyone did as they were told and eased out of the vehicle. Cooper's back was so stiff and achy; it was more like hands in his ears and not the air.

"Facedown on the ground!" the officer yelled, as if Armageddon were about to start.

"I'm not about to ruin my new dress on this filthy highway," said Lilibet. She lowered her arms and began strutting toward the officers. "Now, look here. You—"

"Down!" the officers yelled in unison before one of them fired another shot that left a hole in the bottom right of Lilibet's dress. She eased down on the hot pavement, cringing at the shed skin of a rattlesnake two feet beside her.

"Oh, Cooper. They are going to have their way with me," said Lilibet, while the officers began frisking them.

"I'm suing!" yelled Cooper. "I'm suing all of you. John Henry and I are attorneys. And you have made a huge mistake."

"Are you Cooper Pearmain?" asked the male officer, checking Cooper's ID from his wallet.

"Ah see, you've heard of me. Well, buster, you had better—"

"We got a report that this vehicle was stolen and that you were attacked," continued the officer.

"That was yesterday, you freakin' idiots!" Cooper growled, getting a mouthful of sand that was drifting on the pavement. "I settled all the paperwork with the police this morning and got my car back. They arrested my attacker. My wife was doing her spiritual chakra shit and accidentally hit the panic button."

The officer scribbled something on a small tablet and handed Cooper a sheet of paper.

"Oh, what? You can't apologize to my face. You have to write it down?" asked Cooper.

"That's not an apology; it's a bill for the emergency response crew and for shutting down the highway." The officer motioned for the crew to return to their vehicles. The fire trucks began rolling up their firehoses, the ambulances workers began returning their gurneys and equipment, and the police returned to their cars.

"What? Six-thousand dollars for, for nothing?" Cooper yelled, after looking at the amount due on the receipt. He dusted himself off violently, smacking his groin, which caused him to double over. When he tried to straighten up, his back went out, and he fell.

One of the men started to return with a gurney after Cooper hollered out in pain and rolled on the pavement.

"No!" Cooper held up a hand for him to stop. "I'll

just die right here among the tumbleweed before you do a damned thing for me. Oh, you would just love to send me another huge bill, wouldn't you? Oh, no, no, no, I'll be seeing all of you in court is what I'll do."

After Lilibet, Ami, and John Henry were able to carry Cooper back to the car, they finally resumed their drive to Sin City. Lilibet interrogated the Mayfields, asking them every intimate detail of their lives, while another wind, a softer wind, whistled through the bullet hole in the front passenger door, but this one Lilibet stuffed with the receipt from the limo rental center.

"Oh, come on!" she squawked. "Surely one of you was just a little teeny-tiny bit tempted to cheat on the other at some point in your marriage." She leaned over the seat and held her fingers an inch apart. "Just a teeny-weeny bit, huh?" When she got no response, her smile warped, and she slid back into her reclined position. She then took another swig of alcohol from a silver flask before returning it to her bag and steadied her pen and notepad in her lap.

"John Henry and I are secure in our commitment to one another, aren't we?" Ami's straight, flat bob grazed her shoulders as she nodded. "We would never cheat. Why? Are you writing down our answers or something?" Her bare face wrinkled, and she wrenched her fingers over her short gray skirt.

"Me and Cooper argue all the time about which one of us has the worst memory, so I'm just getting a little proof for when I talk about you two behind your backs." Lilibet squinted smugly over her raised shoulder, which hid her double chin as if she were so innocent and shy.

Cooper knew she was still trying to read the young couple, trying to get them to confess that they were the ones who had sold the Pearmain party story and photos to the New Orleans' press. Lilibet was a specialist at gossip herself, and the whole trip felt so wrong, so hypocritical. She never considered that the hearsay and speculations she whispered to friends and strangers about others could possibly be gossip. Gossip was for the lower class. She believed her revelations to be more like sharing concerns and admonitions that needed to be shared because she was the guardian of all that was still decent in the world. Only a select few knew how to toe the thin line between being a prude and being a slut, being a skanky slanderer and being a heavenly herald, and Lilibet was an honorary member of that club. Those who couldn't tolerate her sharing loving concerns at every opportunity were enemies destined to be excommunicated from her inner circle, anyway.

"I know you're just kidding. But like I said, there's nothing disparaging to say about our relationship. I knew the minute John Henry put this wedding ring on my finger that he trusted me to consult with him before making any major decisions. He does the same with me." With a bashful smile, Ami pivoted her knees and head as close as she could get to her husband and still keep her seatbelt fastened. Her eyes settled on her ring. "I'd be devastated if I lost this token of our love and dedication." Ami stroked her diamond ring while Lilibet's cold eyes settled on her.

"Bless yo little heart. Come on, just admit it, Ami Cable; you and John Henry never fight because you're trying to fit in with all the Southern women—perfect, submissive, and ladylike—a goddamn Stepford wife. You probably iron your husband's undershorts and cook him gourmet dinners in the missionary position, and never, I repeat, 'never' squash your sun hat you wore to the country club," Lilibet said in her overkill Southern accent, while wiggling her toes on the dashboard. "My husband likes an independent woman, don't you, Coopie?" She dug her claws near his crotch while they reached the border of Las Vegas. "He never questions my decisions."

Cooper got chills when the faint snort of stifled laughter broke the silence in the back seat. *Please don't let Lilibet have heard it*, Cooper pleaded with the universe. But it was too late. He could tell by Lilibet's drawn lips and rising eyebrows that she perceived one of the Mayfields had scoffed at her claim.

"There's a box of tissues in the container between the seats if you guys need one. I know this arid desert air always gets me all sinusy," Cooper said, while sniffling as convincingly as he could. He placed his fist over his mouth to fake a cough when Lilibet's hand came down hard on the steering wheel, forcing the limo to cut off a small SUV at the exit ramp toward I-215 East. The other vehicle managed to brake two inches from the concrete guardrail high over an overpass. Cooper caught a glance of the passengers being flung forward before jarring back in their seats with stunned expressions. Other cars on the interstate twisted in a maze of squealing tires and blaring horns. Lilibet maintained a stiff-armed grip of the wheel that matched her stiff jaws. Cooper was sure he had just had his ninety-ninth mini stroke because of his wife. One more, and he would surely be put out of his misery.

"What the hell are you doing? You almost ca-caused that car to crash over the bridge," sputtered Cooper. He regained control of the swerving limo and kept making the loop, wondering how he was going to get back on the highway to Las Vegas from here.

"I changed my mind. I want to see the Grand Canyon before we do Vegas. You will propose to me again on the Sky Cross. I want you to get me a new diamond ring and get on one knee and do it properly, and the way I'll know is if you are able to bring a tear to my eye."

Lilibet was incapable of a genuine tear even if she chopped a dozen onions while watching *Schindler's List* on the eve of Princess Diana's funeral. She was becoming increasingly volatile, and Cooper needed to have a talk with her and give his heart a rest, so he pulled over on the side of the road as soon as he merged onto the interstate.

"Are you nuts? We're all exhausted and almost on empty, and the Grand Canyon is at least another two-and-a-half-hour drive from here. I'm not doing it. The hotel is holding our rooms, remember? And it's too late to cancel, remember? I'm not paying for two suites that I won't be using."

"Yes, you are. Now put the damn car back in drive." Lilibet reached for the automatic transmission shifter, but Cooper grabbed her wrist, stopping her.

"I said, 'no.'"

"Have it your way," said Lilibet, as her pupils turned to blackened slits. "I'll find a new man to take me to the Sky Cross, and he'll grovel on his hands and knees to have me as his wife."

"You got the grovel part right," hissed Cooper.

Lilibet unlocked the door and stepped out onto the interstate. She swished several yards ahead of the limo, hiked up her red dress above her knee, and dangled her pasty leg over the solid white line of the road as countless vehicles whipped past. Cooper was sure he was blushing worse than he was sweating as he leaned his head out the window.

"What are you doing? Get back inside the car."

Lilibet snarled her lip at Cooper and hiked up her dress even higher. He knew this was another desperate cry for attention, and that he should get out in the middle of traffic and carry her ass back to the limo while she kicked and screamed like a damsel in distress, and he would wind up in a back brace afterward. But he was tired of the games and threats. He needed to put an end to her theatrics.

"Perhaps you should go get her, Cooper," said John Henry grimly.

"What I should do is floor the gas pedal with my eyes closed." Cooper found his arms rattling over the steering wheel. "I have had to put up with these stunts of hers for years, and I'm done, I tell ya—done! She thinks some romance-novel Fabio is just going to fall out of the sky and sweep her off her feet, so, let's see, huh? It's time she faces the truth no matter how harsh, no matter how brutally humiliating."

Lilibet stuck out her sagging boobs and rotated her exposed leg to make it sparkle like Ami had shown off her diamond ring minutes earlier. It just occurred to Cooper that she must've been jealous of Ami, who actually cherished her wedding ring. When the dark demon of jealousy overtook Lilibet, she would stop at nothing to one-up the person as she had done once at a Christmas party in Palm Springs. The hostess had printed "Casual attire" on the invitations, but when drunken Lilibet arrived and saw the sexy hostess in her sheer black minidress with strategically placed beadwork, she made such a fuss. She insisted Cooper drive her back home so that she could change into something dressy and sexy as well—a nearly two-hour trip one way. Cooper, of course, refused, and everyone at the party became uncomfortable. Soon Lilibet ripped the car keys out of Cooper's pocket and staggered out to the driveway, determined to drive herself. Cooper ended up grabbing Lilibet, heaving her over his shoulder, and locking her in the trunk of his car, where she remained as he drove her back home to stay.

And here Lilibet was again, with her insecurities on full display, determined to endanger herself and others on the road. Only now, with his bad back and her extra poundage, Cooper couldn't lift her to put her in the trunk. She was like a monster feeding and growing larger by the year. He was convinced they were planning a remake of *Mothra*, and Lilibet wanted the title role.

"She's really pitiful, isn't she?" said Cooper, cackling inside at every vehicle that flew past her, one cruel rejection after the other, not even braking one split second to consider the goods she seemed to be selling—*the bads*, he meant to think. Lilibet began to wobble from drunkenness and balancing on one foot. Did she think the interstate was a stage?

A large truck had paused beside Lilibet but drove away. Cooper's butt had become sore from sitting when a grinding and whistling brought everyone's attention to an eighteen-wheeler that pulled over on the side of the interstate just ahead of Lilibet. She turned and wobbled up the gravel shoulder toward the passenger's door. For once, she was able to pull herself into the cab without a forklift or Cooper's one good shoulder—amazing how self-sufficient a woman could be to get back at a man. Cooper just wished he had realized that before he had messed up his shoulder, his back—hell, his entire body, to assist the man mangler.

"We have to stop her," said Ami. "The driver of that truck could be dangerous. Every year thousands of people are abducted—"

"Yeah, but not old biddies. You should be more worried about the driver. That's who you should be worried about. The poor fellow has no idea of what he's in for. No idea!" Cooper half-believed what he said. He couldn't tell if the angst he was feeling was hurt that Lilibet would go, who knows how far, to make Cooper jealous or if he was worried that something bad might happen to her for once. And it was ridiculous that she always dragged him into these moral dilemmas.

The driver of the eighteen-wheeler turned on a signal to pull back onto the interstate. Cooper couldn't believe this was happening. He jumped out of the driver's seat and hobbled toward the truck while waving his arms. Before he could get close enough to the cab of the truck, it had merged back on the interstate at a steady speed. He caught his breath and gazed at the truck that now seemed the size of a refrigerator as it faded in the traffic. He hadn't even had the presence of mind to look for any identifying marking on the truck. Perhaps the Mayfields had memorized the tag number, at least.

He hobbled back to the limo to see Ami's and John Henry's faces now longer and paler than he remembered. Definitely, they were trying to give him a guilt trip. From the way Lilibet had treated them, he had imagined they would be dancing the back-seat Macarena while popping corks on champagne bottles.

"Oh, come off of it," groaned Cooper, fastening his seatbelt again. "You are studying psychology, Ami. You should know; there's some kind of disorder where victims of monsters like Hitler might miss him if they're around him for a long time. Well, did you get the tag number? I didn't get anything—no name on the truck."

"No, the tag was too dirty to make out the numbers," said John Henry.

"As always. Just like the damn gravel trucks—probably another kickback for the police. If I did something to conceal my car tag, the police would ticket me faster than an Irish tap dancer on amphetamines."

"We need to do something. I'm afraid Lilibet might be experiencing some sort of trauma-induced psychotic disorder," said Ami. Her lips clamped, and forehead scrunched into a pained look of apology.

"Are you serious? She causes trauma; she doesn't experience anything but euphoria from making me miserable. Anyway, my hands are tied." Cooper lifted his hands above the steering wheel. "I can't report a truck with no markings and a wife who willingly hitchhiked. Maybe it's a fetish she's finally come to terms with. You psychologists are always encouraging free expression these days."

Cooper began thinking of what he would do now: Wait for Lily-Butt to get tired of her little game and contact them or the police? Wait to get a notice that Lily-Butt is now the proud owner of two brother-husbands, the antithetical version of sister-wives? Cooper was not going to order a custom-built bed for three. Besides, things could get messy in the dark, and you had to be careful where you aimed certain things.

After he thought of all the possibilities, Cooper nearly swallowed his Adam's apple. If he didn't go searching every highway, byway, and back-alley after Lily-Butt, she would become even more volatile and might reveal his shameful secret. That would surely be the end of him. He started the engine and began looking for the first available gas station. He had an idea he would end up driving all the way to the Grand Canyon if he could even find Lilibet before midnight, especially on a highway with more commercial trucks than cars these days.

"I don't want to sound like an alarmist, Cooper, but Lilibet could be in terrible danger," Ami said, with her hand over her throbbing neck. "Don't think for one second that the trucking industry is void of disturbed men. There have been many serial killers who were truck drivers. It is easy for them to pick up strangers and escape across state borders. One trucker wore fake fangs and called his truck the 'torture room.' Another trucker carried around a woman's breast like a trophy. One preferred to take and kill mothers and daughters in front of bound fathers. One had a deadly obsession for red-headed hitchhikers. One trucker, we learned about in psychology, ran for mayor and preferred to slaughter his victims at truck stops. Some liked to photograph tortured hitchhikers. One preferred to leave happy faces near the bodies of his victims. Another even kept a disturbing DVD on how to hunt down and kill women in their homes. One trucker was massively obese and mixed the flesh of prostitutes in his hamburgers. And these are among some of the most famous cases."

"Okay," said Cooper, "But we're never going to get far until I get gas first."

A half-hour later, Cooper had filled up the limo's tank with enough unleaded to sustain a luxury jet and had returned to I-215 East. Ami and Cooper had bought a bag of popcorn at the gas station and were now sitting in the back seat, munching away like they were watching a kidnapping movie plot unfolding. Cooper became sick of the smell of stale butter and salt and annoyed with the sounds of them slurping soft drinks from paper cups. He had grabbed his own fast food, which was getting cold as he strained his eyes and neck, looking at every eighteen-wheeler that crossed his path.

"I don't know why you two didn't want a good old hamburger," said Cooper, finally taking a huge bite, burying his face inside the foil wrapper. "For some reason, I was craving one with extra ketchup."

After a long silence, Cooper slowed the limo near another suspicious eighteen-wheeler. "Is this our serial killer?"

"That can't be the truck that picked up Lilibet," said John Henry. "See the little green light behind the cab? It means the driver is gay and cruising for sex."

"Where did you hear that?" asked Ami, coughing up a bit of popcorn while Cooper began driving faster, more worried about Lilibet with each passing mile. He definitely was the poster boy for victims who miss their abusers. Why, oh, why had his parents taught him to be so damn agreeable growing up? Cooper didn't realize until it was too late that he couldn't establish a boundary even if he owned a fencing company.

"It's all, um, color-coded, like the hankies they used to wear around their necks or in their back pockets. Navy blue means they're looking for a little rumpy-pumpy," mumbled John Henry with a mouthful of popcorn. "I thought everyone knew that."

Ami leaned her head forward at him.

"What? I don't use truck-stop restrooms if that's

what you're thinking." John Henry's voice rose to a squeak. "I just heard it from one of the fellows at college; that's all. Look, all I'm saying is whoever picked up Lilibet must be into, you know, women—older women."

After a few minutes of silence, John Henry cleared his throat and said, "Maybe we should call the police. Maybe they can file it as a Silver Alert."

"Despite how we might look and act to you Generation Z-ers, Lilibet and I are not that ancient. If Lilibet hears that the police have a Silver Alert looking for her, she'll bed any teenage boy who looks twice at her and then set off every nuclear missile in this country and claim the damned things got excited to see her, too. Trust me; I. Know. Her."

* * *

Lilibet tried not to fall over in front of Cooper and the Mayfields. She didn't know how much longer she could hold out with her bare leg, *a sexy leg, damn it!* dangling over the white line of the interstate. *Aaah, you don't know what you're missing,* she said mentally to the occasional driver of a passing vehicle that she thought surely would stop for her. She would yell her thoughts, but she didn't want her limo audience to see her angry or worried.

She got chills. Delightful revenge was about to unfold. A maroon eight-passenger truck crammed full of men slowed near her. They leaned out of the windows whistling and making every variety of catcall in the books.

"Can you boys give a girl a ride to the Grand Canyon?" asked Lilibet, swishing her hips, ultrafeminine moves she had memorized from playing a streetwalker in a few films she had hated. She was far too good of an actress to play such lowly roles.

A handsome young man with a chiseled face opened the back door from the inside. One of three men crammed in the back seat, muscular legs spread wide in tight pants—ready laps for Lilibet to crawl over. He threw her a sexy wink under a sheet of curly bangs. Lilibet lowered the hem of her dress and sauntered into the highway to climb inside the truck. Oh, the groping she was about to get. Oh, the heated mixture of cologne, manly scents, that would overpower her sweetness. Oh, the danger she could be thrusting herself into—*thrusting and thrusting*. But even if it were her last, this moment gave her chills of satisfaction just imagining Cooper's stunned face at what he was about to lose. Her husband just thought he had experienced loss. He would have to find something or someone else to blame for his misery. Sure, Lilibet could leave Cooper's sorry ass any time she wanted, but this was the perfect moment. He was with a captive audience of backstabbers who would definitely have a story to sell to the press now. This would be better than any movie scene Lilibet had ever filmed—riding off into the sunset with a team of lusty lads.

Her first step over the white line was liberating. Her second step was blind and numbing. She was within a foot of reaching the man cave on wheels when the driver sped off, squealing every tire, leaving a chorus of stupid laughter trailing out the open windows into the lonely wind, which still carried a fog of burned rubber. Lilibet jumped back, knowing exactly what it would feel like to have someone fire a cannon two seconds after she had looked down the barrel at a bird's nest. Her ears were still ringing, and her heart was trapped in her throat.

"Curse you! I hope you cra—I hope you crash into a fuel tanker," Lilibet yelled to the delighted faces, now oval dots, gawking back at her in the rear window of the truck.

She couldn't even look back at the limo lurking there like a black buzzard in readiness for a sick cow to tip over. To keep them from seeing her heated, twisted face, she turned her back to the bulging-eyed buzzards and began walking farther up the interstate. What had Lilibet gotten herself into this time? She would rather get hit by a speeding church bus than admit failure and crawl back to the limo, crawl back and endure Cooper's self-righteous grin. Why the hell won't they just drive away and stop waiting for her to make a bigger fool of herself?

She was seriously contemplating removing her high heels and chance stepping on shattered beer bottles and discarded AIDS-tainted syringes when the gut-vibrating roar of a diesel engine came from behind her and slowed several yards ahead of her aching feet. She could have sworn she saw a lei of tropical flowers hanging from the CB radio in the center of the front window. The grass-skirted hula girls on the mud flaps seemed to be shaking their hips in a welcoming gesture. *Climb aboard ye wayside lady of loveliness.*

"Oh, Glory Honolulu! An eighteen-wheeler for an aching heeler," Lilibet said with a breath of relief as she hurried her pace to the passenger's door. She was going to get inside that truck cab if she had to break her neck to do so.

The door opened with the calm sound of chanting blended with steel guitars, ukuleles, and gourd drums. Lilibet managed to crawl inside the cab of the eighteen-wheeler and gave herself a minute to catch her breath before looking around. A lingering smell of incense invaded her nostrils, and her high heels became embedded in a straw mat on the floor. If the driver of the truck wanted her to change into a grass skirt, she would have to respectfully decline. She wore one once to a Hollywood luau and nearly caught fire when someone dropped cigarette ashes on her leg. The percussion section banged their drums faster because they thought Lilibet was doing some sort of hip-slapping hula dance, but she was only trying to put out the flames. She loved smoking grass, but not that kind.

"Thanks for stopping for me. I'm Lilibet Bathroy. I'll bet you never dreamed you would be picking up a famous actress, didja, big fellah?" said Lilibet in a flirty accent.

The burly hunk she had imagined behind the wheel was a bit distorted. Saggy in the chest area and sunken in the crotch under a faded denim fold where the zipper was clearly a decapitation danger waiting to happen at every rest stop. An overgrown boy—surely—with his smooth

face and brown hair greased back in a pompadour so high Elvis would have little-man syndrome by comparison. But the boy was old enough to drive, so that was all that mattered. And old enough to smoke as well. Under his rolled-up flannel shirt was the rectangular bulge of a cigarette pack. He punched the left signal to pull back onto the interstate when, in the right mirror, Lilibet saw Cooper hobbling toward the truck just as she had hoped, waving his arms like a shipwrecked fool now stranded on an island while the only ship vanished on the horizon.

"Please hurry. Go! Go! My husband's a monster. He's trying to kill me," said Lilibet, placing her hand over her lips to keep from laughing but knowing it would make her appear truly frightened.

The boy coughed against his left shoulder, jerked the gearshift, and sped forward. "Yeah, I know. Men are awful; they can't accept a woman like you for who she is. But don't ya worry now, Lilibet; that bigot bastard won't hurt ya as long as I got one inch of oxygen remaining in these lungs. Name's Darlene, Dar for short 'cause lemme tell ya, my gaydar was strong when I saw ya on the side of the road back there."

Lilibet's mouth became so dry she couldn't swallow. Her hunk in a shining truck wasn't a man in the sense that she had come to consider, but neither was Cooper as far as she was concerned. Dar ripped down the CB radio mouthpiece and held it to her bare lips. A few flower petals shed from the lei and landed on the floor near some organic snack wrappers she had discarded.

"Breaker one-nine; got your ears on? This here's Dar

from afar, shiftin' to the boogie and hammering down here on I-215 East outside Sin City. You gotta copy on me, you chopper warriors, chicken haulers, and Billy big rigs, c'mon?"

A fuzzy transmission of men and women responded with a gargle of lingo and numbers Lilibet could only guess was a long word salad for answering "Yup." The vibrating hum of the engine alone made it hard to hear, and the passing cars seemed so small from this height. Lilibet wondered how many women had flashed their breasts to Dar in passing. Too many cars slow down when they get beside an eighteen-wheeler. *Is that your gear shift sticking up there, fellah, or are you desperate to make a pass?*

"That's a big *no* on the city-kitties," continued Dar. "I need a convoy deployed—some eighteen-wheeled justice. We got an uptownie wife-beater in a prom wagon here on the boulevard, and he's bumper-stickering me hard. Got his old lady with me, and she's 'bout ready for a band-aid buggy. Copy?"

"Ah, yeah, ten four, Dar from afar. Moving in," replied one of the other truckers that Lilibet could understand anyway. Dar returned the CB mouthpiece to the box above her head and checked all the mirrors. Cooper probably turned right on the next exit to get gas, Lilibet imagined. She knew he would try to catch up to her at the only place she had mentioned going—the Grand Canyon Sky Cross. But would Dar actually take her there? Or was there some resurrected Lilith Fair happening nearby?

"You little shit! How dare you call me an old lady?" hissed Lilibet, noticing a bronze statue of a woman in a grass skirt on the truck's dashboard. Under it was a seashell to catch the ashes from little colorful cones of incense. In a cup holder sat a wooden mug carved to look like a tiki totem head, and in this mug, Dar kept spitting her chewing tobacco on occasion.

Dar turned up the Hawaiian music again and slammed her shaking fist on the steering wheel. "Please don't use foul language like that. It contaminates our auras, and we're all supposed to be vessels for the goddess of all goddesses. In the ancient texts, you would've been put to death over that—put to death—thrown in a volcano! But I can tell you're an unbeliever. It's not your fault—not your fault, so I'll overlook it this time."

Dar's under-plucked eyebrows sank jaggedly as she squeezed her eyes shut and chanted a bunch of two-letter words, each ending with a vowel from A to O and sometimes Y—*Why?* That's what Lilibet wanted to know. Dar looked like she was about to sneeze out a bunch of baby goddesses and restart the universe. What sort of nut job had Lilibet allowed to offer her a ride?

She mustn't show fear.

"How do you keep *your* vessel clean by smoking those cigarettes up your sleeve there?" Lilibet patted the box protruding under the woman's plaid shirt. "And that spittoon you have there's about to overflow. I've seen sludge pits at commercial waste facilities look less toxic than that." Lilibet knew she would end up down a rabbit hole by asking those questions just as she had by asking questions in her own faith growing up. But she delighted in seeing people squirm.

"Oh, that? That's my celestial cigarettes and transcendental tobacco made with special blessed herbs. The goddess allows 'em, especially for smoke offerings. It helps my witness," said Dar, as eighteen-wheelers and motorcyclists started forming a convoy behind Dar's truck. Still no sign of Cooper. Had he given up on Lilibet so soon?

"Your . . . *witness?*"

"Yeah," grunted Dar. "At the truck stops, ya know? All the truckers gather there to smoke and shoot the breeze. It's a great way to fit in and share my testimony. When I get a burden for souls, Mahinalani causes my hands to turn red and hot. Lets me know they need my help. It's part of my gaydar the goddess gifted me with."

Lilibet kept quiet and tried to think of a response that wouldn't be offensive or cause Dar's hands to burn any further.

"Where ya headed to?" asked Dar, rubbing her chin against her arm stiffened on the upper part of the steering wheel. "Look, I know you're scared 'bout your husband and all. I can get ya to the Church of the Goddess Mahinalani, and they'll offer ya shelter. Their home base is in Hawaii, where she will one day re-emerge from the Pacific Ocean near the end of the Age of Aquarius. But we have smaller sanctuaries scattered about. Great things are happening. The Mahinalanians put me back on the right path; praise Mahinalani. The great goddess can do the same for you, but you need to get lei'd first."

"Listen, honey, I appreciate the ride and all, but I'm not into that sort of thing," said Lilibet, scooting closer to the passenger door. She had just as soon lick a casino ashtray.

"Of course, not . . . because the dark alien forces have you bound. They've been binding souls ever since the Great Flood ended and Mahinalani appeared as a rainbow at certain coordinates across the globe at the gridlines between the Earth's pyramids—and pyramids are triangle-shaped, you know." Dar gave Lilibet a chunky wink. "The sneaky little aliens used to walk among men and dominate them like they did on the islands where they first appeared. Since the flood, they are forced to transcend the astral realms and dimensions, seeking out all that their spirits might walk into and control—especially unworthy men who near the open portals. That's why I always keep a fresh lei of flowers nearby. It's part of my mission, my calling—" (Dar began muttering gibberish in a trance as though she was speaking to a multitude from atop a mountain.) "Thus sayeth the Great Mahinalani: 'Search the streets for fellow children of the rainbow who are lost and hurting, Dar, my child, and bring them unto me.'"

"Mahinalani?" mumbled Lilibet. Somehow, she had missed this one in her studies of the multitude of gods and goddesses over the millennia. Gods always happen to have regional names, but at least this one was a woman for a change.

"How dare you say her name incorrectly—so

carelessly? It's blasphemy! The goddess of goddesses' name is pronounced Mah-HE-nuh-LAH-née." Dar kept repeating the name until tears rolled down her cheeks, and she was swerving on the now dark interstate. "My trust in her is so strong I could let go of this steering wheel, and she would drive this shipment of organic vegetables to its destination, and I wouldn't have a scratch."

"Now, just hold on there, Elijah. I don't want no one taking the wheel but you," said Lilibet, raising her left hand toward the steering wheel. "*Your*, uh, faith might go unscratched, but *mine* would look like I fell in a meatgrinder. My aura's contaminated, honey; it's damned near as toxic as your spittoon."

Part of Lilibet wished all this fantasy grabbing were true. How often she had hoped and prayed for miracles to scrub away that dark day in her past—the day that had changed her and Cooper beyond repair. Ultimately it was all a plastic token dangling at the bottom of an endlessly long string attached. Lilibet could no longer pretend except in movies; she was not a virginal princess in a crystal palace of pleasantries; she was as toxic as life had made her. But she could survive, exist bearably within the luxury their money could afford. And in her world, the real world, she was allowed to release her anger occasionally. To endure fantasy grabbers, you had to use a lot of imagination, or it would be like opposing magnets trapped together in a discarded pillbox.

"Mahinalani can fix you if you let her. All you need to do is renounce the dark aliens and get lei'd in a special ceremony under the sky, in the breath of nature, and recite the ancient chant. And lemme tell ya, even that husband of yours will have no more power over you." Dar slapped her calloused hand over Lilibet's left hand. "You'll be free to live and love without contamination."

Lilibet thought of a way to play along and get what she wanted. She hoped. First, she sniffled remorsefully and then dabbed her dry eyes with a hanky from her purse.

"Oh, I do want to be free, Dar—to live and love and get laid. And I know a perfect spot for you to do whatever it is (she waved her hanky at her) you need to do to me: the Sky Cross at the Grand Canyon."

Dar retracted her hand and lifted it near the light of the CB radio. "I don't think my hand has ever been this hot and red." She leaned back in the driver's seat and stiffened as if waiting for a cramp to pass in her leg. "Oh, man. Look!" She pointed at the moon through the front windshield. "I can't believe it. Mahinalani has sent me a moon dog as a sign."

Lilibet angled her head every way possible but couldn't see anything unusual except for Dar, whom she needed to keep humoring, or no telling what might come of her after she was ravished under the stars. At least she wasn't a virgin; being sacrificed in a volcano was fun in films but not in real life. The earth would surely spit Lilibet back out like an unripe persimmon.

"Oh? What kind of dog?" she asked, wondering why Mahinalani would need a cosmic dog. Of course, the ancient Egyptians had Anubis, the dog-god of the afterlife, and Hinduism has dogs who guard the doors to heaven and hell. But what Lilibet found most peculiar was that the Catholic Church holds dear Saint Roch, the patron saint of dogs, especially considering that the Jews and even Jesus in the Bible called everyone without Jewish blood "a dog," which was defamatory slang for a male prostitute at that time, much like the replacement three-letter word homophobes used today. Or was there some esoteric implication, beyond dyslexia or basement conspirators, that dog spelled backward is god? Since Saint Roch Feast Day is observed to celebrate the birthday of all dogs, who get to attend mass and roll around in the aisles like old-time Pentecostals still do, then perhaps godly dogs were significant.

Lilibet's parents had joined a Pentecostal church for a few years when they thought their Baptist pastor had become too worldly. Which meant Lilibet and her mother had to stop cutting their hair and start wearing long dresses even to go swimming. Girls in one pool and boys in another, of course. Lilibet remembered the church members rolling around on the floor in the sanctuary, crying and making all sorts of animal noises. She remembered the enraptured congregation yelling out praise and messages in unknown tongues, also called glossolalia. The few friends Lilibet had made hated being forced to be there. And so, to play along with the whole "saved thing," as they called it, they taught her a devilish way to use the foulest of curse words during the long church services. Completely unbeknownst to their pastor, the visitors, and their parents, the kids learned shocking curse words in Malaitian, Russian, Hungarian, and more obscure languages. And they managed to scream them out without having their raised hands shot down by bolts of lightning or detected by those members who supposedly claimed they possessed the Gift of Knowledge and Discerning of Spirits. Lilibet can't remember the exact language she had used at the time, but she had yelled out in the choir loft, "Suck my big juicy tits, you bunch of Bible fuckers!" Hearing the men in the church cry out "Amen," or "Can I get a witness?" in return was absolutely hysterical to the kids, who laughed about it later as they recapped the whole event in the parking lot or at someone's house.

"I still don't see anything," Lilibet said to Dar, who was grinning up at the moon. "But I hope it's not a beagle or basset hound. Surely the great goddess would never waste a pedigree on some common hound. They really are the dumbest creatures on the planet."

Dar shook her arms in frustration. "Not a real dog, *duh*. A moon dog is a lunar halo, like a sun dog, that Mahinalani gives her children as an answer to prayer. It's a sign, just like my hot hand. You see, the dark aliens don't want you to be attuned to nature, but we're going to free you. To the Grand Canyon, we must go."

Lilibet was certain Dar's "hot" palm would look like a starched white glove stuck on the Devil's plump red ass, but what the bloody ever. The girl's holy hand couldn't melt a chocolate chip. Now, if two nail holes suddenly appeared in her hands, they might be talking. God, Lilibet missed the parties in Hollywood. The conversations there were near orgasms by comparison. She might as well have moved to Mars with the dark aliens.

Another hour later, while Dar still kept checking her hand for redness and heat, Lilibet spotted Cooper's limo trying to pass the remnants of the convoy that had surrounded Dar's truck. Dar radioed her fellow truckers and asked them to tighten the line. Cooper pressed down on the limo's horn when another eighteen-wheeler cut him off from pulling up beside Dar's truck. Lilibet got goose bumps of pleasure. Cooper would never again doubt that Lilibet could find another man or a "Dar" who would take her in at the first flash of her leg. She could feel the truck speeding up as though they were plummeting to Earth in a metal trashcan.

"Hurry, Cooper's still back there. And we need to get to the Sky Cross before they close at eight," said Lilibet, who rolled down the truck window and gave the middle finger to Cooper.

Dar frowned when she spotted her arm sticking out the window. The truck swerved. "You aren't doing anything impure, are you?"

"Who me? No, I'm just—I'm offering a bit of worship to the great goddess. Offering a bit of praise for the major change that's about to happen."

Within twenty minutes, they reached the tourist center for the Sky Cross. It looked like a tiny, bricked box dangling on the edge of a flat earth. To the left of the building, a glass walkway arched way out, seemingly to infinity and back.

Dar grabbed the lei of flowers and put it over her head. She jumped out of the truck while three other eighteen-wheelers pulled into the parking lot and formed a line to block the limo from entering. A few rough-looking men and women on motorcycles drove between the trucks and asked if Dar needed any help.

She spat out her chewing tobacco near her boots. "The driver of that prom wagon is named Cooper. Don't let him anywhere near the Sky Cross," said Dar.

After the bikers nodded and manned the gaps between the trucks, she waked heavy-footed over to the passenger's side of the eighteen-wheeler and helped Lilibet out of the cab. Lilibet danced up to the ticket window, occasionally looking over her shoulder to see if she could spot Cooper trying to break through the line, see him seething with jealousy.

"Okay, here you go; two tickets," said the clerk at the ticket window. "You're just in time. Ten more minutes, and the admittance gate is closing."

"Lilibet! What the hell are you doing?" Cooper yelled from afar.

"I'm getting laid under the sky, Coopie. And then I'll be free of you," she yelled back and grabbed Dar's hand. Cooper would never know Dar wasn't a man, not from this distance anyway.

They walked hand in hand out on the glass bridge over the Grand Canyon as the sun began to set and tourists had about cleared out. The view four thousand feet above the bottom of the canyon was breathtaking. The distant roar of engines sounded like the

motorcyclists were perhaps leaving or doing stunts. Cooper must be crapping his pants, Lilibet imagined as they walked farther across the glass bridge. It's a good thing Lilibet wasn't afraid of heights like Cooper; otherwise, she would be traumatized already. She would probably become a puddle on the glass floor, unable to move. The flowers on Dar's lei were peeling off one by one from the wind circling the canyon. Lilibet gripped the glass railing, and it was a good thing she had; Dar had released her hand and had knelt on one knee in front of her.

"Lilibet, before you get lei'd and become a new person, you must first deflower me, right here in front of Mahinalani."

"What?" Lilibet nearly choked from such brazenness. "Shouldn't we wait? I mean there are a couple of children still on the bridge. Besides, you can't be a virgin . . . why, a big strapping Dar like you, I mean—"

"I meant the necklace of flowers around my neck. You must take them off me first."

"Oh!" breathed Lilibet before unhooking the lei from Dar's thick neck. With shaking hands, Dar then took back the flower necklace and looked up at her while her pompadour hairdo wiggled from the wind like a tall gelatin mold being slapped by a naughty child.

"Before you get lei'd, Lilibet, you must get a little moist. Ask Mahinalani to dip her hand into the clouds and wash you of all impurities, especially those imposed on you by mankind."

Lilibet lifted her arms toward the heavens. "Hear my petition, O Great Goddess, Mahinalani: Dip your heavenly manicure into those milky-white clouds and slosh your eager hands all over my voluptuous body and remove the impurities, especially those caused by nasty boys like Cooper Pearmain."

Speaking of impurities, Lilibet had already been doused in them the minute Dar's flannel shirt came untucked and exposed her butt crack above her leather belt and tight blue jeans. Dar started to continue with the ceremony, but the revving of a motorcycle grew intolerably loud. Lilibet looked over her shoulder, and it was Cooper; he had somehow taken possession of one of the motorcycles and was riding it across the glass bridge. The remaining tourists scrambled to get off the Sky Cross, taking no time to look back over their shoulders. Behind Cooper, the remaining motorbikes were giving chase, followed by two security guards yelling and wielding pistols.

"Shoot 'em," the older guard shouted.

"I can't. If I miss, the glass might break," the younger guard yelled.

Cooper hopped off the motorcycle, squared his jaw, grabbed Dar by her shirt collar, and snatched her off her knee. "Listen here, fellow: this woman is already married . . . to me."

Lilibet felt like a ten-foot-tall Oscar Award. This couldn't have turned out any better, even if it were a movie script starring her and Daniel Craig. She had never seen Cooper so dominant and sexy, but she

couldn't let him off so easily.

"Don't you lay one finger on my new—on Dar. I've had enough of you and your—"

Before Lilibet could tell Cooper exactly what she thought of him, Dar's lumpy face tightened into shades of red. Her thin, dry lips and eyes squeezed into slits. She grabbed Cooper's right arm near the elbow and flung him over her shoulder like a sack of laundry. She carried him to the glass railing and dangled him over the edge, holding him by his right arm while his left hand swatted against the glass wall, searching for something to grasp for support.

Lilibet's blood slowed and became chilled. She couldn't believe what she was seeing. Had she gone too far again? Was someone else in her life about to die? Cooper didn't cry out for help like Lilibet would expect, especially for a man afraid of heights. Why wasn't he yelling his head off?

Old torments flooded Lilibet's brain again: *Cooper was expecting to die at your hands. You got what you wanted, and it all failed. He's ready to leave this world because he's tired of dealing with you, you evil, manipulative woman. Ha-ha-ha! Your parents and church were right about you. You should've listened instead of pursuing mammon, instead of becoming the harlot and polluting yourself with the Beast and all its shallow offerings. You, Lilibet, you have sold your soul and are the daughter of Satan.*

Lilibet found herself tugging at her hair while the other bikers dismounted their motorcycles and waddled over toward Dar in their leather chaps, their expressions a mix between anger and confusion.

"Stop! Don't hurt him," Lilibet said. "I . . . I lied. Cooper doesn't abuse me. He . . . he never—"

"You are in denial. The alien contamination has gotten to your brain; your submission to them has tainted your ability to have faith," said Dar, shaking so hard her eyes were bulging, and her jowls vibrated. "You cannot serve both Mahinalani and man. You must choose your master. My hands don't burn for no reason."

"Don't let go of that man. You don't want to do this," said the younger security guard. His voice and hand trembled as he tried to steady the pistol, which he aimed at Dar. While he kept her within a clear and clean shot, the older security guard leaned over the railing as far as he could to grab Cooper's flailing free hand.

"Grab hold," the guard said, grunting as they reached for one another. His uniform hat flew off and fluttered down into the depths below.

Lilibet's heart and lungs compressed when Dar released Cooper's arm and dove like a sumo wrestler at the young guard's legs, flipping him over the railing. It all seemed like a film edited in slow-motion. The young guard's eyes expanded into bulging globes of horror, blurring behind the curved glass wall. His screams became quieter the farther he plummeted to the bottom of the four-thousand-foot canyon. With the arrival of the police across the canyon, it sounded like a shrewdness of Chinese gibbons had invaded America with a shrill chorus of sirens building in short bursts and others with their rapidly firing whistles.

A female biker, wearing a shirt with the word "Rebel" in red letters, arrived on the back of a motorcycle driven by a stocky man with a strawberry-blond beard to his bottom rib. The two had narrowly evaded the police and security at the ticket office. The woman took off her helmet, which had a brown ponytail attached to the backside, and she placed it over her heart after seeing the guard fall to his death. Lilibet knew the talk around Tinseltown was true: short-haired women did sometimes wear ponytail-helmets so it wouldn't appear like two men embracing on their badass bikes.

Oh, come on. You wanna look like a real rebel? Take off the damn ponytail, then. Or at least make the man sit in the back and hold onto you, Lilibet laughed mentally.

She wanted to run to the edge of the wall and help the older guard lift Cooper back over the railing, but this was all too much, too painful. She sank to the glass floor in a blinded daze as visions of the past shot into her brain and heart like railroad spikes. Drunken visions of the stars over an unfinished second-story frame of what was supposed to be her future home. Cooper deceiving her, denying her simple things that could advance her acting career. The lack of walls, boundaries that Cooper wanted, but Lilibet had been raised to never have or expect. Her parents appeared in her head with their constant scolding.

"Listen here, Lilibet: you cannot be an actress. It's ungodly and will lead you into a sinful lifestyle."

"*. . . You will most certainly not be leaving the house wearing that skirt and makeup, little lady—looking like a teenage Jezebel, enticing boys. You'll end up pregnant. And just you stop with all that pouting and go and give your daddy a kiss and tell him you're sorry and you love him.*"

"*. . . No more buts and whataboutisms, little lady. You will most certainly not stop confessing your sins to God and the church; the Bible commands us to. I don't care if Brother Steve uses you as an example of the dangers of sin. If it's for the edification of the church, we must die so that Christ will live through us.*"

"*. . . There are no secrets in this house, Lilibet. I demand to know everything you and the girls from your school did at that sleepover! You talked about birth control, didn't you? You will not be having sex before marriage. You've always been so selfish. You will marry a Christian man and tend to his needs and have his children the way God intended.*"

Again, Lilibet found herself looking over the edge of her unfinished dreams, her unestablished boundaries, into a silent darkness that concealed the devastation that she had made of her life. This was all her fault. If she had ever convinced herself she wasn't a monster, then that illusion had ended.

The other half of her, the survivor side that had broken free of her suffocating past, knew that the guards should have been better trained to oversee such emergency situations. Nobody asked Cooper to break the rules and ride a damn motorcycle onto the Sky Cross like a fool. Surely, that had kicked this disaster in motion more than the few little lies Lilibet had told Dar, a delusional and gullible ignoramus, who was, yet again, just another person trying to control Lilibet.

12

POOR WITTLE
COOPIE DROOPY

Cooper was sure that his arms were now three inches longer and that he would never be able to bend them like he used to. He had been so terrified, hanging over the edge of the glass Sky Cross, that he had pissed his pants again. Of course, part of that was from getting older and having a weak bladder. He didn't like to think of himself as a weakling or fearful. All through his school years, he tried lifting weights on pulleys, but more times than he cared to remember, the weights had lifted him in the air instead.

He tried to catch his breath while three sets of police interviewed everyone involved. A female officer finally managed to lift Lilibet off the glass floor of the bridge. The night sky was flashing red and blue from all the emergency responders in the distant parking area near the edge of the canyon. The police arrested the

---

motorcyclists for holding Ami and John Henry hostage. The Mayfields sat on the bumper of an ambulance while paramedics examined them. Cooper lied and insisted that he didn't need any medical help. He was already dreading the money this was costing him.

Lilibet got her balance, stuck her bottom lip out, and came charging toward Cooper with her hands outstretched. He drew his arms up to his head as he sat against the glass wall railing.

"Oh, Coopie, I'm so glad you're all right. I was so worried about you that I actually nearly fainted. It's a miracle I didn't crack my head open or something," said Lilibet in a high-pitched tone reserved for babies, a tone Cooper had learned never to trust to have an ounce of sincerity. She had deceived him too many times, and he was immune to it.

"Please, arrest me," Cooper begged the officer. "I'm . . . unstable. I, uh, tried to kill myself, and then I murdered the security guard. I also bombed the federal building in Oklahoma City, and I killed Amelia Earhart."

"They caught the bomber already, and unless you're a hundred years old, you couldn't've possibly killed Earhart," said the officer, shaking his head with a sigh.

"Did I say, Earhart? I, uh, meant Jimmy . . . Hoffa. I'm the one who shot him at the Ambassador Hotel in Los Angeles." Cooper squeezed his eyes closed and tried to lift his aching arms in a pleading gesture. He was too stressed mentally to grab any more random moments of history and place himself there. He was now tempted to tell the officer the truth of what he had really done.

"Right," the officer said with a sarcastic whine. "And I'll bet when old Hoffa parachuted off the Hindenburg after you blew it up, he never even saw you hiding in the grassy knoll behind the fence."

"Lock me up for life. I beg you." Cooper said to the male officer beside him. Maybe he could get solitary confinement in a nice, padded cell where they would never allow Lilibet to visit him. Or maybe they would put him in an institution, dope him up, and he could sit in front of a window, rocking an imaginary puppy in his arms all day.

"Hoo boy. Just when you think you've seen 'em all," the officer mumbled, wrinkling his forehead. He pulled out a pair of handcuffs and ordered Cooper to scoot forward and place his hands behind his back.

"Whuh—why? Whatever for?" Lilibet began breathing hard, and she forced herself between them.

"He's under arrest for trespassing and endangering others, for starters. Also, the boys in prison are in serious need of some comedy."

Lilibet clamped her claws on Cooper's receding hairline and shoved his head around slightly. "But he's obviously out of his wittle ol' mind from the trauma of it all. My wittle Coopie droopy was only trying to save me from being a victim of a sex cult, weren't you, sugar booger? That woman over there is crazy." Lilibet pointed to Dar, who was now in handcuffs and snarling at everyone. "She wanted to perform some sort of alien purification ritual on me—said it needed to be done in the outdoor air. It was like something out of *Skyclad Biker Babes of Beltane*, which I'm sure you remember me starring in. Of course, you might not recognize me with all of these hot and heavy clothes I'm wearing."

"No way! You were in *Biker Babes of Beltane*?" asked the female biker who had the fake ponytail on her helmet. She stiffened when the officer fastened handcuffs to her wrists behind her back. "My older brother watched that when he was recovering from his hernia surgery. He said for the first time in his life he was glad someone invented bras—sagger baggers he called 'em. I actually kinda liked the movie myself."

"Oh," Lilibet's curled-down lips lifted with a smile as she sprang forward and adjusted her windblown hair and wrinkled dress. "Which scene with me did you like best?"

"The ones with that Rex Heat character. He was smokin' hot. Of course, he was dancing around a bonfire." The woman added the last part when her boyfriend or husband frowned at her.

"Get outta here. You were an actress?" said the officer with a smirk. "Boy, you and your husband can come up with some whoppers."

Lilibet stopped shaking her breasts and seemed to give up on any recognition from the officer. Her red lips opened askew. "Yes, I am an actress. And little did I know I was being dragged up here to my death. Her real name is Darlene, and she almost crashed the eighteen-wheeler just because I said a curse word. She told all those truckers and bikers to go after Cooper and our dear friends, the, um, Mayfields."

"That will be determined by the court of law," said the officer, angling the cuffs over Cooper's wrists, ready to clamp them.

"Dar . . . she hates men. She threw Cooper and that security guard over the railing like they were garbage. I saw it with my own eyes. No respect for law enforcement. But Cooper and I do. And you want to arrest my fine law-abiding husband for trying to save the woman he worships—the woman he finds to be the sexiest, most talented, most charitable woman on the planet? All my fans will be very unhappy about this. They'll probably boycott the whole state." Lilibet turned to the female biker. "You saw that woman kill the guard. You were right there beside your motorcycle. From one biker babe to another, tell the officer the truth."

"Yeah, I saw it, okay? And I was shocked. Your husband was barely hanging on for his life on the other side of the wall. There was no way he could even have touched the guard who died. 'Dar from afar' flipped 'em both over the rail. Look, I'm sorry we got involved. We thought your husband was the danger when we got the broadcast, but now we know Dar is nothing but a rachet jaw. Your husband obviously ain't no wife-beater," the woman admitted with her head down low.

"Nope. He don't look like he could squash a beer can with two hands. No offense," said the male biker, also being handcuffed.

"Trust me; when you've been married to my wife for as long as I have, there are few things left that offend me," said Cooper, feeling like a puny old wimp ready for the nursing home now. Much to his regret, the officer returned the handcuffs to the back of his belt and helped him get on his feet.

"I'm going to let you go this time, Mr. Pearmain. I talked to the management of the Sky Cross, and they said they do not want any of you to set foot on this property ever again."

"Aw, come on. You are just going to let me go? Don't you have some arrest quota to make—Disney trip planned for the kids?" Cooper held his wrists out as the officer continued walking away toward the parking area. Lilibet swayed over to Cooper and stood in front of him with her hands on his shoulders. Cooper strained to lift his arms but managed to knock her hands off him.

"You were such a chivalrous dear, sugar booger, showing the world that I'm your wife. LILIBET ME WIFE. ME OWN HER," Lilibet roared in a ridiculous caveman accent, grunting, and spinning around all hunched over like a Neanderthal. She stopped and ran her claws tenderly down his cheeks. "Coopie does have a backbone somewhere under all that—"

Cooper squinted darkly at Lily-Butt. "Don't even try to act like you care about me. You nearly got me killed like the security guard who tried to help save me. He is dead because of the stunt you pulled. Hell, you could've killed the Mayfields, too. Those truckers nearly crushed us on the interstate. Are you happy finally? Have you finally gotten the attention you've been craving?"

"It's obviously who I am and what I do. Tell me what you really think of me for once. Just say it, and then we can stop pretending." Taking a tissue from her purse, Lilibet swabbed a few tears that slipped down her cheeks, leaving burrows in her pancake makeup. Cooper knew she wanted him to assume otherwise for once, but he wasn't falling for those tears being anything but tears of suppressed laughter from a woman with a twisted sense of humor.

"Since when do you care what I think?" said Cooper.

The tissue in Lilibet's clenched fists ripped in half, and her bottom teeth appeared between her freshly applied lipstick. "Why can't you just admit you hate me and want to be rid of me? Why can't you?" She stomped ahead of him as they proceeded to join the Mayfields, who stood like lost children in the parking area after the ambulance turned off its lights and drove away.

Lilibet swung her purse and hooked it back over her shoulder like a cowgirl roping a steer. "Always wanting to discuss the past. 'It's time to have that talk,' you always say. Well, I say you're a big ol' chicken shit. And you had better be thankful I kept you from going to prison." She stopped and turned around to face him. "I could have you sent there, and you know it. But if and when I do, it won't be for some ridiculous story; it'll be for the truth."

"You don't know the meaning of the word," hissed Cooper, before they exited the Sky Cross.

13

TOILET THERAPY

After resting for the night and half the next day in a hotel near the Sky Cross, Cooper regained enough strength in his arms and back to continue driving the dusty trek back to Las Vegas, located at the southern border of Nevada. Perhaps it was the extra pain killers he had taken, but Lilibet had never been nicer, except when the Mayfields suggested they should cut the vacation short and return home.

"John Henry and I have prayed about this. It's not that we don't appreciate the offer of you considering us to come with you on vacation or anything," said Ami, with a blushing smile. "It's just, well, there has been a lot of drama and close calls ever since we left New Orleans. And John Henry, he's a big tough man and all, but he gets stressed easily. I'm sorry, babe, but you do." She patted his hand halfway on the leather seat between them. "And, well, we do have a lot of exams and stuff awaiting us after spring break is over. I'm sure you

understa—"

"BULLSHIT," blurted Lilibet, applying lotion to her hands and inspecting her manicure in the front passenger's seat of the limo.

Ami's eyes nearly crossed, and her mouth clamped shut. John Henry's neck snapped toward the side window where he watched the white lines on the highway blur into the distance. Ami sneaked a pinkie finger toward him over the seat as if signaling for emotional backup, but his forehead appeared to be glued to the glass now.

"Oh, how heathenistic of me. You kids are offended by cursing. Let me use more appropriate language from your Bible: 'Eat shit and drink your own piss!' as Rabshakeh would say." She looked over the seat and, with a coquettish grin, batted her long lashes. "Look, I know I can be a bit much for some people. But I promise I won't spread shit on your faces like God said he would do. Name that scripture."

Ami and John Henry slowly turned their head toward each other with confused expressions.

"*BEEP!* Times up. It's in Malachi. Oh, honestly, don't you do-gooders ever read your damned Bibles? Actually, I used to love Sunday school when we had to name our favorite scriptures. That didn't last long with me in the room, lemme tell ya." Lilibet gave a throaty giggle and noticed the Mayfields' long faces. "Oh, now look what I've done. But I want to make it up to you—I want to make it up." Lilibet's painted lips curled high in the corners with devious delight. "I have the best connections in Hollywood, need I remind you? And you know what I'm going to do to make it up to you? I'm going to try and get you both walk-on roles in a film. You never know where it could lead."

"Um, thanks, that's really swell and all," added John Henry, as if by a silent prod from Ami. "We, um, wouldn't want you to go out of your way or anything. You can just drop us off at a safe location, and our family can come and get us. They don't have anything better to do."

"Ugh, you kids today are such fuddy-duddies. And I won't take 'no' for an answer. Keep driving, Cooper," said Lilibet. "This is way more fun than sitting at home on your cellphones tweaking, twitting, twerking, or whatever it is you do, and you know it. No life outside your damn phones. I'll bet you two sit in your living room, and all you know how to do is have phone sex. Now my Cooper here, when he has to have it, he has to have it." Lilibet licked her lips with a grin. "One time he missed his kidney transplant, he had waited years to receive, and the kidney had to be destroyed."

Cooper knew Lilibet was just trying to redeem his reputation with gross exaggerations as if it would make up for all the crap he had to take from her. The truth was, Lilibet was supposed to have driven Cooper to the hospital for his kidney transplant, but she was drunk that day and nearly burned the house down. She realized she had no clean panties in her dresser drawers because she didn't trust the maid to touch her "delicates," as she called them. So, she had hand-washed an old pair of panties with dish soap, and after a few squirts of perfume, she tried to speed dry them in the microwave. Cooper smelled something awful and saw smoke blackening the white ceiling. He came running butt naked out of the shower too fast, slipped on the slick tile, and got a concussion. It was a memory that remained permanently embedded in his lungs. He had nearly died from the billowing stench of Lilibet's panties.

Ami snapped her head toward the window on her side and watched the roadside arts and crafts stores as the limo sped past them. Her jaws clenched. "Our sex life is perfectly normal, thank you. John Henry and I maintain an open and honest partnership; don't we, baby?"

John Henry nodded adamantly. With his right fist, he made a playful jab at Ami's upper arm until her forehead bumped the window. "Ya got 'er right there, partner," he said in a cheesy cowboy dialect that seemed to say, "A'ight there, Ami, looks like we're a-gonna be going to Vegas after all."

The sun had set by the time they arrived, so the lights of the Strip with its casinos, clubs, restaurants, and grand hotels, were aglow in neon colors. They checked into their luxury hotel and began freshening up before dinner. Both their suite and the Mayfields' adjoining suite were similar. Massive fresh floral arrangements on the entry-hall tables, sprawling butter-toned walls adorned with oil paintings and ornate mirrors. The furniture was mostly traditional carved wood with brown-leather cushions that an elephant would feel comfortable mating on. Cooper knew Lilibet would be pleased deep down in her icy core. The most prominent feature in both suites was the wall-to-wall window views of the Vegas Strip that commanded the eye far more than the widescreen televisions built into the walls.

The door to the bathroom finally opened, and Lilibet danced leg-first into the room. Cooper got his comb stuck in his hair and thought he was hallucinating. He was already woozy from the pain medicine he had taken for his back. Lilibet had either ripped or cut up to her fanny the entire length of the red dress she had worn two days ago. Her greased-up, goose-pimpled legs looked like those of a fresh-plucked chicken.

"What, in all that's holy, happened to your dress?" Cooper managed to free his comb along with a plug of his already scarce hair.

"Because of that late-night carousing you did back at the border of New Mexico, the cops shot a hole in the bottom of my dress. I thought, what the hell, I'm in Vegas; I'll just turn it into a miniskirt."

"A miniskirt? More like a crop top. And I was not carousing; some thug carjacked me because I had to sleep in the limo when I couldn't get into the hotel room, which was paid for with my money, need I remind you? Anyway, don't even pretend you're going to wear that, that crop top to dinner."

Lilibet spun around, brandishing her red lipstick like a knife. "Why shouldn't I?"

"Well . . . what if you fall? I won't have my wife showing her who-ha to all of Vegas." This was only a partial concern for Cooper. Still, it was better than him saying he didn't want her putting her stretch-marked blubber on display like she was a pyramid of long-expired and uncooked dinner rolls on a party platter, the kind some creepy hermit might serve the FBI when they discovered his underground bunker in Central Park.

"I've seen you looking at Ami's legs," Lilibet snapped. Her lips puckered tight before she blotted the excess red with a tissue. She prissed up to Cooper. The fat on her ghostly white legs jiggled with every step. "I intend to have fun while I'm here, so I'll go to dinner in the nude if I decide to."

She ran her right claw down Cooper's fragile spine and dug her knuckle squarely on the one herniated disc that threatened to rupture.

"I need you to do something for me tonight," she said seductively, which was only the cool icing on a molten lava cake underneath.

What? Cooper wondered. Sacrifice a virgin so Lily-Butt could bathe in her blood? Kill some snow leopards at the Vegas Zoo so she could have a coat made for a one-night-only occasion? He wouldn't dare say this, of course, not unless he wanted to end up on a hospital stretcher.

"I'm going to distract Ami and John Henry long enough for you to search their luggage for anything suspicious. I know they've been recording us on their phones. Ami's phone rang in the car when she was pretending to be talking to her friend from college. I saw her blushing worse than Aunt Margaret did when her vibrator fell out of her purse at baby Joey's baptism. The damned thing turned on and wiggled past the preacher's feet and under the front pew. Poor Aunt Margaret looked like she was trying to catch a pink snake. She moved to Spain after that."

Cooper turned around to protect his spine. "Come now, dear. I don't think anyone would go to that extreme."

"Oh, you don't, do you? You have no idea how bad our church used to mess with people's minds and control their lives. As a matter of fact, Aunt Margaret started wearing a hijab in public as soon as she got to Spain."

"You've got to be joking. She converted to Islam because of a vibrator?"

"No, she converted to a life of shame and secrecy. I could have ended up like Aunt Margaret, but I'll be damned if I am going to hide this candle under a basket. I'm going to put it on display for all men to see. And that, baby, is biblical." Lilibet shoved Cooper away from the mirror. She twisted around to see how her butt looked in the mirror and began singing "Pull up to the Bumper" by Grace Jones.

"If the Mayfields *are* recording you, it's only because Ami is an obsessed fan of yours; you said so yourself. Isn't that the price of fame, as celebrities bemoan?"

"Fans will sell stories on stars like me in a heartbeat, Coopie—just because I didn't take time to sign autographs while on the operating table for a nose job— just because they want to be me," sighed Lilibet, lowering her shaking head while spreading her bejeweled fingers over her silicone-shielded heart. "I only started writing Ami's and John Henry's answers on that notepad of mine to let them know I was on to them because I know that's what Ami has been doing at every damn rest stop. She doesn't have a weak bladder, as she claims. She has been using restroom breaks to write down stuff about us."

Before Cooper would say what needed to be said, he looked around the hotel suite for the nearest sturdy object in case he needed to defend himself: a lamp with a clay base sculpted to look like a maiden emerging from a clamshell that resembled a hoop skirt.

"For someone who acts like they don't like to be the subject of juicy news stories, that stunt you pulled—hitchhiking with an escort of trucker terrorists to the Grand Canyon—should be quite the cover story, lemme tell ya! I'm beginning to think you secretly want to be in the news. Have you for one minute considered, or even had a flutter of guilt, that a security guard got killed because of your little attention stunt, huh?"

Lilibet's breasts and head rose with a jolt as if she had recovered a much-needed breath. She lowered her eyelids and diverted her gaze.

"I saw the notepad in Ami's purse, Cooper—oh, but I know you and your little love affair with them. They can do no wrong." Lilibet traced a heart in the air with two fingers. "You're gonna claim she's using premium, acid-free, stitch-bound paper to wipe her little fanny."

"All right, Lilibet. But I don't think you need to go to any extremes to distract the Mayfields. Once they see you in your tube *top* (Cooper emphasized the P in "top"

with a popping of his lips), they probably won't remember where the bloody hell they are."

Cooper could feel a numbing tingle, a firing in various places on his body, and was sure it was nerve or neurological damage from the stress that his wife had caused him over the years. He should be used to the unknown demons lurking behind the next door by now. He had no idea of what devious plan she was cooking up next—what life-altering humiliation he was about to face.

Lilibet flashed Cooper an insidious glance. "Well, at least somebody will be looking at me. As for you, look for anything suspicious that you can. Mainly, I want you to find that notebook of hers. Now, she'll probably be carrying a sexy little evening bag for dinner and not that huge ugly luggage she usually does."

"So?"

"Sooo," Lilibet said, jerking Cooper by his coat lapel, "she won't have room for that damned notebook. She'll have to leave it in her room, which is where you're going to use those blind eyes of yours."

Lilibet thrust her breasts out and posed with one leg crossed in front of the other at the door between the suites. She knocked, and John Henry opened it. His chin dropped to his chest and whipped upright.

You thought she was in her slip too, didn't you, Buns Henry, baby? Cooper thought. He tried not to laugh, in concern that his back would snap in half.

"What happened? Um, I mean, are you ready for dinner already?" John Henry asked.

With a vixen of a smirk, Lilibet leaned against the doorframe like a spider catching John Henry in her web. "Yes, but before we go down, you and Ami have to come see the sunset from the third-floor lobby. If you catch it exactly right, the sun shining over the casino roof across the street looks like an angel with its beautiful little wings spread."

"Lilibet thought the same thing the first time she saw her hemorrhoid scan," said Cooper, dodging behind the protective door of the closet.

"All right, I guess. Ami was just flossing her teeth," said John Henry. Cooper could hear Ami suddenly dry heaving in the sink.

Five minutes later, Ami joined the others in the hall outside their suites. They kept a distance from Lilibet this time. Her eyes fixed on the huge purse strapped around Ami's shoulder, and her chin receded in a frown.

"Ami Cable, now I love that black cocktail dress you're wearing, but you cannot—must not—carry that atrocious knapsack. It looks like you're going hiking in the Himalayans."

Ami's lips flattened into an apologetic smile, and her shoulders shuffled in a shrug. "I didn't bring another purse."

"Then leave it in your room. It's an eyesore," said Lilibet, grabbing at her purse straps.

"I might need it," said Ami, clutching it to her thin waist.

"For what? You look like you crawled out of a teepee with a papoose strapped over your shoulders. Cooper is

paying for everything. And with as little makeup as you wear, you can refresh the color on your lips with a damned cocktail cherry."

"Well, all right then," said Ami, waddling like a duck back to her suite.

"Hurry up; you don't want to miss the sunset," said Lilibet. "I know how much you kids like angels."

When Ami returned, Cooper paused as he and Lilibet had planned. "Oh, gee, I sure hate to miss it—God and all the saints, forgive me. I'll have to take a raincheck on that solar angel, apparition, or whatever it is." He rubbed his perfectly fine stomach. "The pain medicine has my colon protesting my esophagus. You all go ahead, and I will catch up in a bit."

Cooper returned to the hotel room, entered the Mayfields' suite, and searched everywhere for Ami's beige purse. He felt like a home invader, but why should he? He was paying for their room, after all. He gave up and tried to open their luggage, but they had locked it. What would they have to hide except for some Bibles, perhaps? Wouldn't the people who steal need those the most?

He looked over at their bed and noticed the pillows looked lumpy in the middle. He pulled the top cover back, and there was the purse. He unbuttoned it and found the questionable notepad. The first few pages had what appeared to be notes Ami had taken in her psychology classes in college. Another page flip, and Cooper found exactly what Lilibet had suspected. Pages of notes describing Lilibet's behavior changes, which he

began reading.

The main aspect of the Pearmains' personalities is atypical for couples in middle age and seems to be a result of stagnation that has caused them to unleash indignations on anyone and anything. Lilibet, in particular, displays a heightened tendency to engage in agitative expositions. She could be using sadism as a defensive strategy, whereas Cooper's defense mechanisms have either become ineffective, or he perhaps was unconsciously drawn to Lilibet to fulfill moral masochistic needs instead of sexual since he appears to have little libido.

Sadomasochism is one of the most complex issues of the human condition. If truly sadomasochistic, Lilibet's domineering tendencies to engage in all forms of domestic violence can possibly substitute as a normal sexual relationship to release endorphins and other hormones. For such an individual to have successful intercourse or other fulfilling exchanges,

he or she must exhibit some measure of cruelty. Or it could be another way to leave her mark on society, stemming from a strong need to be remembered, worshipped perhaps.

I suspect some sort of deep repression in her childhood has left her instinctual needs unsatisfied. Some sort of authoritarian attempt to break Lilibet's will has caused her to test boundaries or test trust. By taking pleasure in her dominating behavior, she has found a pathway to displacement, in which unpleasant emotions such as anger and guilt are fixed onto a scapegoat that she believes to be sub- or non-human, thereby avoiding any emotional baggage from an unlovable object that cannot betray or hurt her.

It is my diagnosis that Cooper has developed masochistically to behave submissively and endure humiliation, with the illusion of inducing guilt from his

abuser or perhaps as a self-effacing remedy to his own guilt.

Judging from Lilibet's latest display of psychosis, perhaps her disconnect from reality and her acts of hostility are nothing more than aesthetic aspirations to produce art or prove herself an overlooked exemplification of one who possesses the true talent of deception, which is the foundation of the dramatic art of acting.

Voices outside the door startled Cooper, and he shoved the notepad back inside the purse and returned it between the pillows. He barely squeezed through the door to his own suite before the Mayfields returned, looking underwhelmed. No angelic epiphanies, although Cooper sure had a few; he couldn't believe what he had just read. According to Ami, he and Lilibet were poster children for sexual deviancy. Although many of the things she wrote seemed to resonate with Cooper on some level. If he hadn't had to rush, he was sure he would've found notes where Ami recommended an exorcism to cure their troubles.

"Did you get what you needed?" asked John Henry, popping his head inside the door to Cooper's suite.

A cold sweat dampened Cooper's forehead. Did the

kid suspect him of snooping through their things? Or was he going to lay holy hands-on Cooper and cast that spirit of sexual deviancy out of him and Lilibet?

"Relief, I meant," added John Henry, patting his belly. "I know what it's like when you have to go really bad."

"You know what? I think it has hit me again. Sorry." Cooper rubbed his stomach and pushed the door shut, nearly pinching John Henry's fingers in the doorframe. He pulled Lilibet far enough away from the wall so the Mayfields couldn't hear their conversation.

"Ahhh, I can tell by the look on your face. You found something, you naughty boy," said Lilibet. Her eyes enlivened, and she licked her lips. One of those brief moments reminded Cooper of the woman he had married, the happy woman that had seduced him gently and seemed to respect him.

"You're damn right I did. They are the informants. Ami is so obsessed she's making psychological evaluations on us." Cooper used the word "us" because Lilibet would be extra enraged if she knew it was mostly unflattering information about her, especially sexual evaluations. And, too, Lilibet was now snuggling against Cooper, rubbing her claws up and down either side of his spine.

"Mama's poor baby; you did all of this for me even with your achy breaky back. You know what we're going to do, Coopie? You know what?" she said seductively.

Hopefully not try out the industrial leather sofa right now, Cooper prayed.

"Go ahead and pucker those lips of yours," whispered Lilibet, eye to eye, breathing hot alcohol fumes across his face. She could literally take his breath away. It was as Cooper had feared. The sofa was in Lilibet's sight, and it was probably trying to crawl out the window right now. He leaned his head forward to kiss her.

"Not that!" Lilibet jerked her head back with a snarl. "You'll ruin my lipstick. I meant to put those lips together and blow those pipes. It's time; the Mayfields are going to pay the piper. We are going to punish them no matter what it takes."

14

HURRICANE LILIBET

Sitting between Cooper and the Mayfields at a table for four that evening, Lilibet kept her head behind her menu, waiting for the cosmos to tell her what she should order, lest she make a mistake and order the A5 Kobe steak imported from Japan and it just not satisfy her cravings. Everyone knew not to order even a glass of water until Lilibet had made up her mind for her entire course, and the waitress had already come and gone three times, surely wondering how many tips she was losing for the evening. Cooper felt quite a connection with the restaurant. Across the entire place, lighted sculptures trickled with water much like Cooper's bladder every morning. The glass ceiling was recessed and offered a broad view of the stars for the patrons to gaze at, as they did at Cooper's old broad, who thought she was still a star.

"You should've brought your crystal ball, honey dumplings," said Cooper, patting her exposed thigh under the table, or at least the exposed skin he thought was her thigh.

"Decisions, decisions," she mumbled, glancing around the menu at Ami and John Henry with fierce eyes. "I like to carefully plan what I'm going to chew to pieces and then spit out. Isn't that the celebrity diet secret the press is creaming themselves to share with the world? Why don't you go ahead and order us all drinks, Cooper dear?"

"Great idea. What are you two in the mood for tonight? Virgin Marys?" Cooper asked the young couple.

"I think I'll have a hurricane," whispered Ami with a blush, as though ordering an illegal substance, and then eyeing her husband for approval.

"Sounds good, actually," said John Henry, grinning back at Ami. His dimples framed his perfect white teeth with giddiness at their decision to face the boogeyman under the mattress.

Boy, a real hurricane you both are about to get. Hurricane Lilibet. Cooper bit the insides of his cheeks to keep from snickering, and then he flagged the waitress and ordered four Hurricanes. "Double, tall, and straight please."

"Almost like you, Coopie," hissed Lilibet, returning her face behind the menu with a look of nausea at the Mayfields.

After the waitress brought out four towering Hurricanes and placed them on the table, Lilibet jumped up from her seat.

"I suddenly remember; it wasn't the sunset that looked like an angel—it was the lights of the Vegas Strip . . . the way they glow behind the casino across from the hotel. We must go and have a look. It'll only take a second," Lilibet said to John Henry and Ami, who kept eyeing their Hurricanes in front of them as if the drinks were naked and aroused men they weren't supposed to see. John Henry quickly jerked his head back and closed his moistened lips that were first to inch toward the protruding straw.

"Excellent idea, Lilibet. Maybe the angel will give you an epiphany on what you should eat tonight," said Cooper, knowing this was his cue to stay at the table and get the real hurricane blowing. While they were away, he took from Lilibet's purse her flask of high-proof grain alcohol and poured as much as he could into John Henry's and Ami's drinks. He returned the flask to her purse just before Lilibet returned with the young couple. Ami's eyes seemed permanently frozen in a bored roll while her husband was scratching the corner of his nose, partially concealing his shifted grin and sighs.

Lilibet, who had been walking way ahead of the sheepish couple, paused to adjust the gold bracelets on her arm. "I don't understand why the damned angel didn't appear. I've seen it several times," she said. "Maybe it only likes certain people. Spiritual beings are particularly good judges of character, you know?"

Another waitress approached their table. "What happened to that Analise gal?" asked Lilibet, seemingly affronted that anyone could possibly grow tired of waiting on her no matter if he or she had to leave a six-inch heel-scuffed trench in the floor tiles from returning to take her order. Lilibet's servers should never mind missing out on sleep, much less marriage, having children, or even grandchildren in the future.

"She's having feet cramps, so I'm taking over her section. Are you ready to order?" asked the new waitress in a huffy tone.

"Oh, I can't decide. I think I'll just order a bunch of appetizers instead." Lilibet read off an extensive list of starters that she wanted. "Make them half-orders if you can. My stomach cannot hold a lot of food. Oh, and separate plates please; I don't like anything I eat to touch—well unless it's a tag team at a hunk fest. There's one for your psychology book, Ami Cable." Lilibet shoved her drink straw in her mouth, and her long lashes stretched like exclamation marks.

While Ami's whole body stiffened, Cooper wanted to make a personal analogy with that last comment but decided the looming hurricane would be enough drama. After everyone had placed his and her orders, Lilibet scooted closer to the table.

"It's time for a game—a drinking game. I'll ask the questions," she said, and the Mayfields agreed. "Take four big gulps of your drink if you lose. First question: Who all here has had over five operations no matter how minor."

Cooper and Lilibet raised their hands. Lilibet knew she would win that question since she had more cosmetic surgery than someone with body dysmorphia. In fact, Cooper once remembered her drunkenly joking at a funeral that she was born a Filipino male, much to Cooper's horror.

The young couple's eyes enlarged after their four gulps of alcohol. Ami made a noise between a gasp and a giggle, and she fanned her face with her white-cloth napkin.

"Next question: Who all here has ever used a rotary-dial telephone?"

Cooper and Lilibet raised their hands.

"Wait—a what?" asked John Henry, wrinkling his forehead and loosening his top button and tie as his face slowly turned red.

"If you have to ask, then you obviously lost the question. Drink up, buttercups," Lilibet ordered. She made a toast with her glass and took a long sip herself.

Ami's head swirled, and her eyes enlarged until she resembled a western tarsier on its wedding night.

"I t'ink we better *ass* the *nest* questions," slurred Ami before giggling.

The waitress wheeled out a cart of Lilibet's appetizers and filled half the table with enough small plates to feed a classroom of children.

"Oh, my goodness; that's way too much food," said Lilibet, holding on to her drink. Cooper was so embarrassed he wanted to snatch the tablecloth over himself. Ami laughed so hard she snorted.

"Do we need to move to a larger table?" asked John Henry, who apparently noticed all the customers' heads

turning in their direction as the waitress seemed to be bricklaying; there was so much plate transferring.

"Nonsense," said Lilibet, as the waitress balanced the last plate on the table's edge near John Henry.

Everyone began eating, and Lilibet didn't need to ask any more questions. The Mayfields were sipping their drinks between every other bite. Their eyes were glassy, and they were so relaxed they were slumping in their chairs, gazing at everything like newborn babies.

"We should all go to the casinos. I'm feeling luck flowing through my veins," said Cooper, after finishing off his redfish.

"That's probably the hurricane. He-he-he. I don't *fink* I can stand up," said Ami, nearly spilling the last bit of her drink.

"You two go ahead. I'll help Ami back to her suite," said Lilibet, while Cooper paid the bill and left with John Henry, who tottered behind in choppy little steps.

* * *

Ami clung to Lilibet's shoulder and began slipping in the hall outside the restaurant. Lilibet released her hand and let her fall to the black marble floor.

"Poor thing. Happens all the time. Get a luggage cart," she ordered one of the door attendants in his red shirt, black vest, and pants they all wore.

The attendant returned five minutes later, and together with another attendant's help, they lifted Ami off the floor, sat her on the gold cart, and wheeled her down the hall. Ami giggled and kicked out her bare legs while the cart rose up the elevator. At the suite door, the attendants lifted Ami and carried her to the Mayfields' bed. While one man held Ami's arms and the other man gripped her legs, which were sprawled, Lilibet sneaked her cellphone from her purse and snapped a photo of Ami with her white panties showing.

Now, this will be a photo to sell to the press, Lilibet thought, just imagining the scandalous headline: "Fusty College Shrink Is Acknowledged Lusty Minx!" With vindictive glee, she imagined having to tell everyone, "No, the camel toes aren't albino at the Vegas Zoo; it's just Ami glad to see the men in uniform—any uniform."

The attendants left, insisting they didn't need a tip, as they craned their necks back at the bed for one last peep at Ami.

"Let us know if you need any more assistance," the attendant with the nicest ass said.

"That should be all unless she starts doing those damned scissors with her legs again. I don't know why I have that effect on young girls," said Lilibet, before shutting the door on the tip of the other attendant's nose. The boys' hesitant departure reminded her of when she once ordered her Great Dane, Beatty, to its room after she spilled a tray of hamburgers she had cooked for a party—a party too painful to remember. If only she could throw it again.

"Here, let's get you comfortable," said Lilibet. She began removing the pillows from under the bedcover to prop under Ami's head when she spotted Ami's purse in the center. Her cellphone was sticking out the top, so Lilibet took the phone and put it on mute and record, and then she propped it upright on the nearby dressing table and made sure it was aimed directly at Ami.

"You liked that drinking game; I could tell," said Lilibet. Her fingers were still shaking; she was so stunned that everything was going as she had planned. For once, she was going to reward Cooper for standing by her side in this plan. Mama was going to do something special for wittle Coopie-poo.

"Yeah," giggled Ami, writhing on the bed with her eyes fixed on the ceiling.

Lilibet slinked toward the end of the bed and wiggled Ami's big toe through her shoe. "I have another game you'll like even better."

Ami shook her head vehemently. "Can't—I can't drink nooo more. I'm emaciated."

Lilibet agreed but knew she meant "inebriated." She removed Ami's flat heels she kept fumbling to kick off. Just as she imagined, Ami's toes were unpainted, just like her fingernails.

"You don't have to drink for this game. It's called Confess or Strip. If you don't confess, you have to take off one article of clothing."

Ami giggled and rolled on her side for a few seconds. Her hair was now stringing all over her face.

"First question: how old were you when you lost your virginity?"

"Nooo," Ami laughed. "That's a naughty question. Naughty, naughty."

"You have to take off your dress then."

Ami tried to sit up but collapsed back on the bed, where she squirmed and tugged at her dress until she finally pulled it over her head. Her breasts were so small she wasn't wearing a bra.

Only big pale breasts were sinful; it's what Lilibet learned as a teen, unconsciously, from her parents, her community, and the geography magazines and documentaries that freely depicted bare-breasted women from various tribes outdoors. Lilibet's tits were downright lecherous.

But why can muscle men and really fat boys go without a bra or shirt? I don't see any difference; she remembered asking her mother before getting smacked on the bottom with a frying pan. Apparently, boys wearing bras was sinful, too, according to her parents, especially her dad. Lilibet didn't mean to come out of the womb an inquisitive renegade. But she learned quickly that some rules just were and didn't have to make a speck of sense. And they didn't require an explanation, especially those of a religious nature.

"Okay, next question," said Lilibet. "Have you ever fantasized about another man while having sex with your husband?"

"Ohhh, I can't hear you." Ami covered her ears and shook her head with a drunken grin brightening her face.

Lilibet would never be able to answer this question honestly in front of Cooper. Like the big breasts things being more sinful, she was well aware of the limitations Hollywood had for years regarding frontally naked male actors. They had better be fat, hairy, at least fifty, and filmed in lighting no brighter than a single candle, or the American prudes would absolutely lose their shit. And if the actors' cocks were any longer than one inch ice-cold flaccid, they had better be filmed from a foggy distance or running for their lives past the camera. If, God forbid, there was more than one naked male actor in any given scene, they had better be in a locker room before or after a kick-ass game or with all eyes on the ceiling in a military inspection before going off to war. If not, the actors had better be filmed at careful angles while they beat each other to a bone-crushing pulp. This all came about thanks to the Bible-thumpers' greatest overruling commandment: "Love thy neighbor as thyself."

"*Beep!* You lost. You have nothing left to take off except your panties," Lilibet said to Ami, hoping her camera was recording everything.

After Ami was butt naked, she began rambling incoherently with a grin so big her pink gums were showing. Lilibet got a devious idea. With Ami's phone on mute, no one would hear what they were really saying.

"Huh? Oh, I understand. You have syrup on your breasts. You had better wipe it off before it dries and gets sticky."

In clear range of the camera, Ami began rubbing her breasts and giggling, "Bresticky tick . . . ."

"What is it now?" asked Lilibet. "Stomach medicine, you say. I have your medicine right here under my necklace. But you have to get it yourself. It's hard to find."

Ami reached up and began feeling all over Lilibet's breasts, searching for the medicine she had convinced her she wanted. Lilibet knocked Ami's hands off her breasts and lightly slapped her across the face, acting as horrified as a cheap camera could record.

"You molested me, Ami Cable! How dare you? I knew you had a thing for me, but I'm not that way." Lilibet sheltered her breasts with her hands and turned in circles. "What will all your little college friends and family think, huh? Oh, and your poor husband; he will be devastated."

"Molested," Ami giggled, seemingly unaware of what Lilibet was doing as she grabbed Ami's phone and began sending the video clip to everyone on her contact list, including John Henry. But the person Lilibet took the most delight in sending the clip to was in the list under the name Pastor Chastain.

"To hell with the great commandment. I, like the rest of the world, still prefer 'An eye for an eye,'" said Lilibet, hitting the send button. "And boy are they going to get an eyeful."

* * *

Cooper felt like he had entered a lighted Christmas village, except it was hot and the streets were lined with palm trees. He crossed the busy intersection to the gambling casino with John Henry staggering behind him. He couldn't help but worry about what Lilibet was planning to do to punish Ami. It couldn't be pretty. Cooper had to keep reminding himself that the Mayfields were bad people who deserved to be paid back for trying to ruin Lilibet and him—the dirty little snitches. After what the Mayfields did, he couldn't believe they would have the gall to accept a vacation all expenses paid by Cooper. But hadn't Lilibet punished them enough already?

"John Henry, young fellow, to make it in the business world, you have to be willing to risk everything. Now I've paid for everything else, but we are each going to gamble with our own money tonight."

John Henry paused in the street and swayed. "Oh, I dunno, Cooper. I, *hic*, promised Ami we would keep saving to pay off our college debt. She wants to have a baby as soon as, *hic*, as soon as we get more settled. Okay, twins, but who's counting?"

Cooper pulled the boy, who was still holding up four fingers, safely out of the street when a passing car nearly hit him; the driver sounded his horn for another block.

"Look, John Henry, if I'm going to be able to recommend you to the bigwigs in the business world, I need you to show me what you're made of . . . be a man."

"But I've never, *hic*, gambled before. I don't even know how to play poker."

"There are slot machines. You can pull a lever, can't you?" Cooper steadied John Henry's shoulders to keep him from wobbling so much.

"Yeah, but I didn't bring any cash, only credit *cars*."

He knew John Henry had brought his wallet on the

trip just in case. Men were always prepared. Besides, the boy's buns were like soccer balls, as Lilibet described them, but the right one wasn't an inch fuller naturally. He wouldn't need a wallet or a bank if Cooper's plan worked, but first, he roughed up the boy's face with a few slaps and pinches to get him to sober up a little.

"Ow, ow, ow," John Henry whined and batted his Bambi eyelashes.

"The casino we're going to takes credit cards, my man. All you have to do is give them a valid form of ID. They verify your account, and you're good to go."

"*Goo* to go," slurred John Henry, with a boyish grin, as if he had suddenly been freed from the restraints of a suffocating bureaucracy. He didn't seem to realize he was gripping a parking meter to keep from falling over.

Another block down and Cooper recognized O Fortuna Grand Casino with its giant roulette wheel entry lit up in neon tubes of red, green, and white. A golden orb of light spun around the wheel, inviting you to come inside and lose your ass. Cooper lifted his arms like a painting he had seen of Moses standing before the Sea of Reeds.

"Here we are, my boy; the place where your whole life is about to change."

John Henry lifted his arms as well, and together they entered the casino and at once began looking for the front counter through a crowd of people.

"Get out your wallet and be ready," whispered Cooper.

John Henry reached around to his right back pocket

and tried to unbutton the flap. He strained so much it looked like a bug was crawling on his butt, and he couldn't find it. "I can't do it, Cooper. I guess we had better leave."

"What? Quitters never get anywhere in the business world, my man. To be a great attorney, you are going to be meeting one crucial deadline after the other. You are going to have to be unflappable in the face of a viciously shrewd audience. You are gonna have to learn to solve any and every problem using your critical thinking skills. Now here, look at you. One attempt to unbutton your pocket, and you're ready to crawl back to the hotel like a scolded puppy," Cooper huffed and smacked his fist in his hand with every point he made.

"Like a scolded puffy," aped John Henry, smacking his fist limply into his hand. He stuck his butt out and began feeling his right pocket, looking for the button, until he gave up and began tugging on the wallet through the fabric of his buttoned pants.

"Stop, stop!" said Cooper. "You look like you are trying to eject a watermelon through a pinprick."

When Cooper thought no one was looking, he bent over as much as his back would let him and began fiddling with John's pocket button. He finally unbuttoned it and reached his hand inside. But the fabric was so tight against the boy's butt, Cooper couldn't pull out the wallet. He froze when he heard a little girl's voice in a panic.

"Ooo, Mommy and Daddy, why does that man have his hands in that other man's pants?"

The mother covered the girl's eyes and pulled her toward the door while the father grimaced back at Cooper over his shoulder. "There're kids here, for God's sake. What's the matter? They outta hotel rooms in West Hollywood?"

"I told ya we should've stayed in Mississippi, Harold," said the mother, on the verge of tears. "We just got here and look what happened." She fumbled for the exit door handle with her free hand.

"You ain't kiddin', hun. We got 'em like that in good ol' Alabamer—but not like THAT. It's jes' sinful," said a heavyset woman waiting near the door, munching on a bag of caramel popcorn shoved in the front pocket of her gray jogging pants. A vein bulged on her receded forehead, clearly visible with her hair tightly bunned on top in a red polka-dotted scrunchy.

"I'm so sorry. Which sin were you all expecting to get an eyeful of here in Sin City—the sin of 'reviling?'" yelled Cooper, before managing to wrench out the amber leather wallet.

"I ain't gonna argue. You, sir, are rude," the woman muttered, spitting out flecks of popcorn.

Cooper ignored the gawkers and opened the wallet, finding two major credit cards in the interior sleeve. He slid them out and handed them, along with a driver's license, to John Henry.

"You gave me both cards. How much am I betting? I only have 'bout a thirty-thousand-dollar limit between 'em." John Henry's eyes tried to focus on his cards.

Cooper braced his hands against John's shoulders

and pushed him toward the front counter. "As much as they'll approve you for, my good man. To win big, you must risk big. That's how I became successful."

"Risk big," repeated John Henry, before he eased up to the counter. About ten minutes later, he returned, holding a handful of colorful ceramic chips.

"They gave me all of it, Cooper—thirty thousand dollars. And it's all right here in these chip thingies. What, *hic*, game am I going to win at?"

Cooper grabbed his arm and pulled him through the slot machine section where people sat glassy eyed on stools while pulling levers, pushing buttons, and pouring coins into the machines. John Henry stopped walking and pinched his nose.

"Dude, what's that awful stink? Is that the craps table you were telling me about or did the toilets back up in here?"

Cooper put his arm around the boy to keep from talking too loudly. "A lot of the gamblers become so addicted they wear disposable adult diapers, so they don't have to leave their machines for restroom breaks."

"Oh, no," the boy said, dizzily, "I'm too young. I don't wanna end up stuck in here wearing nursing home shorts." He bent his head as if checking to see if Cooper might be wearing a diaper.

"Never you mind that. You need to focus on winning. Moolah, moolah, baby. Now, let's get going." Cooper pulled away from the boy and led the way past the blackjack and roulette tables until he found the lottery game he remembered—the Sweepstakes Spinner.

Throughout the casino, sporadic cheers, dinging bells, childish game tunes, and cries of "I won!" charged the atmosphere. Hell, even a terrorist alarm in a casino would make people think someone had hit the jackpot, but John Henry didn't need to know that secret. Cooper could just see a terrorist now, a female for a change, dressed in a unisex vest, tie, and white-collared shirt, coming up to John Henry, holding a serving tray in one hand and a machete in the other. "Congratulations! Would you like to be dismembered in a lump sum disbursement or an annuity today?"

"Now listen, my friend," Cooper continued with an urgent whisper. "You have a greater chance of winning if you bet on smaller numbers, but you don't want to do that. That's not what we came for."

"We come for the big bucks," said John Henry, kissing his handful of chips. He wobbled, and his eyes grew teary. "Gee, Cooper. Nobody ever believed in me like you. My parents never ever have. I wanted to be in a boy band, you know, but they said I would, *hic*, starve to death. They said the same thing about everything else I wanted to be. 'You have to be an attorney like your father, John Henry,' they said. 'You have to go hunting and kill them deer like your old man, John Henry,' they said. You have to marry a nice girl and learn to belch and scratch your—'"

"Right, right," Cooper interrupted. He needed to do something fast before the boy became a slobbering spectacle. "So, my good man, you aren't here for piddle squat. You're—"

"No, not wearing a diaper," mumbled John Henry, rattling his head.

"No." Cooper humored the boy. "You're gonna put all your chips on that one gold slot on the wheel. And, my good man, those chips will make that slot worth nearly. Ten. Million. Dollars. Just think how that'll change your life, huh? You can do naked ballet on Castro Street if you want to. Are you feeling lucky?" asked Cooper, playfully jostling the boy to get him charged.

When the dealer called for the next person in line, John Henry picked up the chips he had dropped and marched between the velvet ropes up to the Sweepstakes Spinner. He placed his chips on the table on the one golden wedge. The dealer raised his eyebrows but accepted the bid and let John Henry give the wheel a spin.

"That-a boy. Big money," Cooper shouted.

John Henry reached up and pulled down on one of the golden handles, and the enormous wheel dragged him underneath until he had no choice but to release the handle. Cooper offered his hand to help him from the floor while the wheel began to slow to a stop.

"And the wheel has landed on wipeout. Sorry, spinner, all of your money was just wiped out," the dealer called out and raked in thirty thousand dollars' worth of chips for the casino, as everyone nearby moaned John Henry's loss. "Next. Who wants to win big money?" the dealer called out.

"What? You mean I lost? That's it?" asked John Henry, looking sickly pale now. He staggered sideways, watching his chips disappear.

"That's the way it sometimes goes, friend. Next time put a little more zing in your spin." Cooper lifted his hand in a wheel-spinning gesture.

John Henry stared blankly with his mouth ajar, his hands shaking. "Are you sure? I heard a buzzing sound and thought I won."

"I think it's your cellphone in your front pocket," said Cooper, pointing to the boy's pants.

"Do you mind moving aside?" gargled an old man, shaking his chips in a white gym sock while an unlit cigar flicked between his crusty lips.

Fishing out his phone, John Henry looked at his texts. "I got a text from Ami. Aw, she's gonna kill me when she finds out I maxed out our credit cards. We were planning to have twins with that money." He looked closer at his phone. "Oh, she sent a video." John Henry hit the play button and watched while the bridge between his eyes tightened into a fold of stunned wrinkles, and his bottom teeth protruded. He stumbled backward against a marble support pillar and slid limply to the floor right on the spot where someone had spilled a drink.

Cooper grabbed the phone, which had fallen beside the boy's leg, and finally saw the texted video of Ami naked and groping Lilibet's breasts.

"Oh, gee, buddy, I know this must be awfully hard. I didn't want to upset you, but Ami made a pass at Lilibet on the dance floor back in Arizona, and she begged her for more naked photos of her. But I never imagined it would come to this." Cooper wasn't lying with that last comment. He wished he could have been there to help with the orgy video instead of watching a boy sobbing on the floor of a casino. He guessed it would be inappropriate to have another look at the video.

John Henry's chin dropped to his chest. "Aw, man! My wife is, *hic*, into ugly old women in granny panties? How can I compete with that?"

Cooper gritted his teeth at that comment but needed to stay focused on his plan. That would be the best punishment. He set his phone on video record mode and eased down to the floor beside the boy, certain his back wouldn't let him stand up again.

"You're too much of a pushover." He put his arm around the boy and shoved him so that his head nearly hit the floor. "You know what we need to do? You need to show that two-timing wife of yours that real men can play at their game."

"Oh, gee, Cooper, I'm flattered but the, *hic*, only time I experimented with another guy was in middle school. I realized that a fellah needed to get on one side of the fence or the other after that. I had enough of straddling."

"I didn't mean with *me*," whispered Cooper, shocked at the boy's drunken confession. He decided now was the best time to turn off his phone. Oh, the juicy news story this would make. "I was talking about the nice little strip club up the road a ways. I'm gonna pay for you to have the most smoking-hot girl in the club. Oooh, she'll just make your mouth water, Johnny boy."

"Like you do." The boy blinked at Cooper with red eyes.

"Um, I, uh, had no clue you found me, you know, good looking," said Cooper, realizing he had turned off the recorder a bit too soon.

"No." John Henry grimaced. "I meant you drooled in your sleep when you were sharing our suite the other night. I thought Ami had left the bathroom faucet dripping."

Cooper was double glad he had turned off his phone. "You have to stop all of this crying. I promise you, for the right price, you'll forget about Ami."

After several wipes of his wet face on his shirt sleeve, John Henry nodded his head and stood up. The big puddle of spilled blue drink was now gone. Had Cooper drunk too much as well?

The boy flagged a casino assistant to help him lift Cooper. Once on his feet, he shuffled to the casino bar and ordered another double for John Henry just in case he sobered up enough to change his mind. While Cooper waited for the drinks to go, he couldn't help but wonder how far Lilibet went with Ami than the video had captured. Had she done it to get revenge, or did she perhaps enjoy herself too much?

15

THE HOT
STOCKING

Music poured out of some of the lounges, clubs, and passing cars as Cooper led John Henry two blocks south to The Hot Stocking strip club. John Henry paused near a lighted palm tree and seemed mesmerized by the huge stockinged leg wearing a neon red high heel as big as a compact car. The mechanical leg kicked out over the entry from the top of the club.

"Isn't she a beauty?" Cooper slapped John Henry on the shoulder and followed his gaze upward. "Wait until you see the girls inside, my good man. Lilibet wouldn't call me a drooper if she saw me with these chickadees."

Cooper approached the ticket window and paid for two Gold Card VIP tickets. "Now, as soon as we get inside, you can go to the club review and watch the show, but that's not why we're here. We're here for a private show. We need to look for the owner in the lounge, and you tell him if you see any girl that really gets your motor purring. And I'll take over things from there."

"Okay," said John Henry, but the sparkle in his eyes began to fade again, and his head lowered as if guilt were overcoming him.

The club was dark except for pockets of pink and amber lights near the sitting areas. The music from the club review was jazzy and pounding, accompanied by the rhythmic hoots, howls, and whistles from the crowd of men gathered in leather chairs around the stage. Women in various stages of dress slithered and spun on mirrored stripper poles across every room's perimeter. From the end of the open corridor, a buxom woman with blonde hair down to her rhinestone G-string slinked toward Cooper and John Henry, doing a prowl-like dance.

"Hey, fellahs. I'm Lisa. Would either of you be interested in a lap dance?" she asked with a voice like a baby doll. She ran her hand across John Henry's smooth cheek. He didn't seem to realize he was gawking at her plump oiled jugs with nipples so long eagles could perch on them.

"I want 'er, Cooper. I want 'er," said John Henry. His chest pumped under the grazing of the woman's fingertips around every button on his shirt.

"Who? Lisa? But you just walked in the door. You haven't even seen the other girls."

Lisa's plump pink lips formed a playful smirk. And her exposed hips swayed like a red cape attracting a bull as she slithered around him. She buried her upper teeth into her protruding tongue and batted her long lashes over her doe-like eyes.

"Ooo, mmm," she cooed, as she squatted with her face inches from the boy's zipper. John Henry froze and tried to look down without lowering his head.

Cooper plucked three hundred dollars out of his pocket and slipped the bills to John Henry as inconspicuously as he could. "Put it in her G-string, my good boy. You have to show the girls here you're worth their time," he whispered.

"But she doesn't have a guitar," whispered John Henry, before his mouth gaped and eyes enlarged. "Oh, I get it. G-string is a nickname you old-timey fellahs call a girl's—"

"The string with all the rhinestones that ties between her legs." Cooper shook the boy. He was beginning to think he was wasting his money. Bankrupting John Henry wasn't enough. How could he get any more evidence against such an idiot? The boy would probably end up making paper airplanes with that wad of cash Cooper gave him. He could just see the boy throwing the planes at the girl's loins and squealing, "Weeee! This is flight 47 coming in for a landing."

With trembling hands, John Henry held the money by the folded edges and tried to squeeze it under the jeweled chain of her G-string. He dropped the cash instead, and Lisa took off her right high heel, pinched the wad of cash between her toes, and lifted her leg straight in the air where she took it between her long fingernails, allowing the boy a gratuitous look at her crotch, which had a lot more rhinestones than on some girls Cooper was seeing in the club.

"You get more with me, baby. Do you want to go to the red room? It's the most private," she cooed.

John Henry nodded stiffly. The boy's awkwardness reminded Cooper of an old *Frankenstein* movie he had seen as a kid. A reanimated corpse with needs greater than his mouth and brain could express.

They passed several curtained-off VIP rooms and one where Cooper caught a glimpse of a dancer doing a trick with the mouthpiece of a hookah that put smoking in a whole new light. The men seated around the girl pumped their fists and cheered as if the girl had just qualified for the Olympics. John Henry craned his neck to see more of the hookah girl as they kept moving to the back of the club.

"You were right, Cooper; the girls here are smoking hot. But, *hic*, how do ya think they keep from getting tartar buildup down there?"

Cooper tried his best not to laugh, and soon they arrived at a VIP room that had sexy red lighting and a large round sofa made of soft red leather, and it dominated the center of the room.

"You might want to give me your cell phone," Cooper whispered to John Henry. "I have a feeling things are about to get steamy in there. And you don't want to leave your pants lying around with pickpockets everywhere."

"What about my wallet?" asked John Henry, handing Cooper his cell phone with shaking hands.

"You can keep that; you don't have any money left,

remember?"

John Henry's lips shifted in a hopeless frown, which Cooper had to quickly fix. "Don't worry about that. Just remember what Ami did to you and let your inhibitions go."

While Cooper waited outside the VIP room, he held the extra cellphone inside the curtain, recording what he could. Not long into his spy mission, a woman in a police uniform appeared out of the smoke and pointed her black pistol at Cooper.

"Ah-ha! I caught you filming one of our girls in there. I'm going to have to arrest you, you naughty, naughty boy."

"No, no, no. It's not what you think," stammered Cooper. "You see, my friend is in there, and I was holding his—"

A stream of sweet alcohol sprayed his mouth through the pistol—a fake. The officer began unbuttoning her blue top. Cooper released a deep sigh. He realized she was one of the strippers acting out some men's fetish. Still, she might tell on him, so he fished the last of his big bills out of his pocket and handed the cash to the woman.

"It's all I have left. But keep your clothes on; I'm not interested in a lap dance or anything," said Cooper, trying to keep his voice down to avoid disturbing the action he hoped was going on inside the VIP room.

"How dare you? You don't know what you're missing, buddy." The woman squirted Cooper in the face again and then shoved the pistol in his mouth before

stomping off through the club. Cooper jerked the pistol from his mouth and hid it in his jacket before anyone saw him with the thing and mistook him as dangerous. He peeped through the curtain again as he held the phone just inside the velvet flap, hoping some action was happening by now.

John Henry peeled off his white underwear, revealing two thick foam pads in the seat. This was far beyond the enhancement underwear Cooper had seen on television ads; this was ass prosthetics. And it was now obvious where the spilled blue drink at the casino had vanished to; the underwear padding had soaked it all up. Buns Henry was more like Sponge Henry in more ways than one.

Cooper tried to keep the recording steady while John Henry tossed Lisa's G-string to the ground, paused as if stunned, and then fell on top of her.

"Oh, yeah! I'm totally okay with it," the boy said, as the two collapsed on the round sofa between groans of ecstasy. Cooper blinked his eyes to see if he was drunkenly hallucinating. John Henry's naked hindquarters appeared to be straddling a mirror. Underneath his loins was another set of pendulous balls, although smaller. Cooper jerked his head back in shock and then looked through the curtain again, and now the only thing which he could liken the sex scene to was a gentle sword fight between their loins becoming more aggressive with every hump and groan.

"Buckle up, buttercup. You're gonna feel a little love stick," the woman's voice deepened.

"Oh, Lisa, that's the spot. You found my hidden cookie. Oh, yeah! Uh-huh."

Cooper's scalp tingled, and his stomach became fluttery. Lisa wasn't a liar; she *did* offer the boys something extra! And it apparently took extra rhinestones to conceal the fact.

John Henry couldn't be blind and that numb—unless Cooper had given the boy too much alcohol. Cooper wasn't sure he'd ever be the same after all he just witnessed and videoed, but there was no time to delay. He pulled the cellphone to his face and texted the recordings to everyone on John Henry's contact list, starting with his wife, Ami. But he couldn't bring himself to text it to the boy's pastor he later found on the list of contacts. No telling what his church might do to him. Conversion concentration camps were so inhumane they were outlawed in many states but not in the Dirty South.

Immediately John Henry's phone began receiving texts and calls. Cooper put the phone on mute so it wouldn't alarm the lovebirds behind the curtain.

> *It's the middle of the night. Everyone's been calling us. Fred nearly had a heart attack, I'm afraid. What has happened to you and Ami? Please call me ASAP*
>
> Read a text from John Henry's mother-in-law between texts containing scriptures and I'm praying for you threats.

Wow, J.H., you're all-over social media already. I'm so disappointed, though; I didn't know you wore falsies

> A text from the yard guy read, along with several flame emoji.

This is disgusting. I cannot believe you or somebody sent this to me? I'm blocking you. You'd better hope children aren't seeing these nasty videos

> Read another text.

Dude, I don't care if this is you coming out of the closet, but, dude, couldn't you have found another way to let everyone know? PS Could Ami send me more of her sex tape? It got cut short

> Read a text from a guy named Brandon Garret.

Hooo-leee fudgesicle, John Henry! My eyes are melting here!!!" Is this a joke??? SICK

> Read a text from a guy named Benjy.

What's the matter with you and Ami? Are you two doing drugs now? Your parents have been trying to reach you both

> Another texter named Aunt Rita sent.

I hope that is Ami you're screwing. Wait, no, I don't. I'm so confused. What's going on? Where are you?

A girl named Kelli Lewis texted along with a string of emoji Cooper couldn't figure out.

This is so unlike u both. I'm afraid u and Ami have been abducted by a sex cult. If u need help just text the code word bluebird, and I'll send the police

Someone named Mandy G. texted.

Cooper's flesh became icy. What if someone does send the police to Las Vegas, and they find out that he sexted the pornographic video? This surely would be considered revenge porn at best. Either way, Cooper could face jail time. He needed to get rid of the phone as soon as possible, but he couldn't help replying to one text, the one from the yard guy.

I was wearing the falsies for you. You can still cut my yard if you want, but I've found someone else to trim my bush. Oh, and they really know how to plow and fertilize my garden, too.

John Henry

Laughing inside, Cooper hit the send button and rushed toward the exit. John Henry was a grown man; he could find his own way back to the suite. Once

Cooper reached the busy Strip and got lost in the shuffle of the pedestrians, he started to ditch the cellphone in the first trashcan he came upon. He paused and got a better idea. He wiped his fingerprints off the phone and dropped it on the sidewalk. Thieves were everywhere these days; surely, someone would pick up the phone and keep it. And, hopefully, they would be blamed for sending the video of John Henry's drunken infidelity.

Six large steps forward toward the first intersection, a woman's voice called out, "Hey, mister, you dropped your cellphone."

Well, wouldn't you know? The only honest tourist in all of Vegas, and they just happened to be the first to find the phone. If it had been Cooper's wallet or cell, well then sayonara, goodbye bank account. Cooper didn't even look behind him and instead walked as fast as his back would let him up the bustling Strip.

"Hey, mister—excuse me, sir—you dropped your cellphone," the same woman panted, as she ran after him.

Cooper increased his pace to a near jog now, shoving past pedestrians and narrowly missing a collision with a twin-baby stroller, a four-hundred-pound scowling woman on a walker, and a gang of men with face tattoos.

"It's not my phone. Leave me alone," Cooper yelled over his shoulder, and in a split-second decision, jaywalked across the Strip. He knew he was in trouble as soon as the white beams of a car's headlight engulfed him and the unmistakable screech of tires on pavement rang in his ears. He looked to his left just as the black hood of the car smashed into his side, sending him face-first into the car's windshield. With his chin on the windshield wiper, he saw a man and woman in the front seat and a boy and girl in the back seat. Through the bloody glass, their faces were contorted with shock, especially the children, who now had the top layers of their ice-cream cones smeared all over their faces.

While Cooper remained face down on the hood, and traffic honked at the congestion blocking the road, the owner climbed out of the car and inspected his vehicle for damage.

"It's not my fault. You crossed the street illegally. I didn't see you," the driver spat with a quiver in his voice.

"Cooper? Are you all right?" a familiar man's voice called out from somewhere nearby.

Cooper wasn't all right. His head was killing him, and he could feel a chipped tooth directly behind his busted upper lip. If by some miracle, he wasn't paralyzed, he was sure he wouldn't be able to stand upright ever again without help. And with his nose pressing against his left cheek, he was sure he would always be able to breathe the dusty West wind before it reached his mouth.

John Henry leaned over the car and placed his hand on Cooper's back. "Are you okay? I'd call an ambulance, but I can't find my phone."

The boy's words sounded concerned, urgent even, but he had a fixed smile and glassy eyes that seemed to have never seen any heartache tonight—a look, a glow of having found nirvana.

"No—no ambulance. I'm okay, I think. Help me down and let me try to walk," Cooper said.

The driver and John Henry gently pulled Cooper off the car hood and carried him back to the sidewalk where he tried to stand on his feet. Nothing seemed to be broken except for his nose and front tooth. But when he tried to walk, a piercing pain shot through his spine, and he would've collapsed had they not been on either side of him, offering support.

Flashing blue lights paused on the road beside them, and a female officer stepped out of the car. Cooper reassured the driver, who hit him, that he wouldn't sue and that his back was already giving him trouble.

"A gang attacked me and stole my phone, officer—I mean John Henry's phone—and I was running for my life. Can you just help me back to my hotel? I should be fine after a night's rest."

Cooper knew the police didn't even bother to write reports on stolen personal items anymore, and he didn't want them prying into what exactly had happened. Too, he kept looking over his aching shoulder, worried that Joan of Arc would spot him and come running with the discarded cellphone—the sexting evidence he had illegally sent to dozens of John Henry's close contacts. He could almost feel the shock and rage across the country, see it building in the night sky, or perhaps it was all the flashing neon lights. Still enraptured, John Henry rubbed his chest with an inward gaze.

"I dunno, Cooper. You look like H-E-double-hockey-sticks in mid-July."

"You might as well say 'hell,' my boy, because, trust me, you will after tonight."

"We should get you checked out at least," said John Henry.

"You mean this?" Cooper pointed to his bloody face. "This is nothing compared to years of being married to Lilibet. Now just leave me here if you can't get me to the hotel. I'll crawl back by noon tomorrow."

The police dropped Cooper and John Henry off at the hotel just a few blocks from where the accident happened. One of the doormen borrowed a luggage cart so that they could place Cooper on it to transport him to his suite. Three or four hotel guests shot condescending looks at Cooper while the doorman wheeled him into the elevator.

"You better stop frowning, or your face will end up like mine," yelled Cooper at the guests.

"Had a good time back at The Hot Stocking, didn't ya, little buddy?" asked Cooper, when his shoe got pinched between the elevator doors. He asked more out of awkward guilt for what they had done to the Mayfields, especially with John Henry coming to his aid when the car hit him. Why did the boy have to be so nice when he was secretly a snake?

"How did you know?" the boy asked.

"You've, um, sniffed your fingers at least five times for one thing."

John Henry blushed and then grabbed the front of his shirt and began pulling it in and out to cool his chest. "I changed my mind. I don't want Ami to know what happened. *Gah*, what am I gonna do, Cooper? What am I gonna do?" He began a drunken sob again and looked over at the doorman, who quickly locked his eyes straight ahead at the control panel.

"For starters, you're going to straighten up and be a man," groaned Cooper, looking up at him and the roof of the elevator as the little bell chimed, signaling they had arrived at their floor. He cried out in pain as the wheels of the luggage cart rolled over the elevator-door track on the floor, jarring his back. Soon the cart stopped outside of Cooper's suite.

"Can I stay in your suite tonight—just until I get up the nerve to face Ami?"

"If it's okay with Lilibet," said Cooper.

The attendant knocked, and Lilibet opened the door in her leopard-print robe and black-feathered slippers. Her head jerked back when she saw Cooper sprawled out on the gold cart, but she seemed more stunned to see John Henry teetering behind him.

The attendant and John Henry helped Cooper get into bed. And by the time Lilibet returned with Cooper's pain medicine, John Henry had passed out on the leather sofa.

"What is he doing here? I can't believe he's even speaking to you after you videoed him. He did a number on your face," she said, handing him a cup of water to swallow the pills.

"John Henry doesn't know I videoed him yet. I got rid of his phone and then got hit by a car; all for you, honey dumplings," he said snidely.

Lilibet held up Ami's cellphone with a snicker forming on her lips. "Ami doesn't know I sent her video out either. She conked out as soon as she raped me. But you, Cooper, you really impressed me for once. And to think I doubted you had the backbone to pull it off." She untied Cooper's shoes and jerked them off but seemed afraid to touch his black socks. She grabbed her bottle of hand sanitizer and greased up to her elbows.

"Happy for once, are we, now that we ruined a young couple's lives? Well, I don't have a backbone left thanks to you; I may never be able to walk again."

"*Waaa-waaa.* You're always such a titty baby. Get some sleep, wittle baby, because war is gonna break out tomorrow when those dirty rats find out what we did to them." Lilibet spun around with laughter and collapsed on the bed, deliberately shaking the mattress.

16

DRINKING GAME
BLAME

A pounding on their suite door awoke Cooper and Lilibet at 8:18 that morning. Lilibet sprang out of bed, threw on her robe, and walked past John Henry, who was still asleep, sprawled across the leather sofa with a pillow over his head. She unlocked the door connecting the two suites to find Ami wringing her hands and her hair stringing around her face.

"Sorry to wake you. I'm just worried about John Henry; he never came back last night." She peered around the doorframe, looking for him or Cooper.

"He's over there on the couch—still asleep. He's not happy about what you did to me last night, and neither am I—and the rest of the civilized world, for that matter. Now, I know it must be excruciating for you to control your lust for me, but I must insist you never get within three feet of *this* ever again." Lilibet swiped her hands from her breasts to her loins.

Ami tilted her head forward and slightly to the side while her eyebrows scrunched, and her chin receded—a repulsed look Lilibet had last seen on an animal documentary when a man had to stick his arm up an elephant's rectum for some medical reason.

"What are you talking about? Is this a joke?"

"I wish it were. My breasts will never be the same." Lilibet pulled her robe tighter over her. "You don't remember? You got awfully drunk last night and became a sex maniac, humped everything in sight. Don't worry, I sanitized the television remote." Lilibet picked up Ami's phone off the table near the door and showed her the video. "I had to take this from you to save what's left of your reputation. I managed to delete the worst parts before you sent it out to all of your contacts. Collecting naked photos of me is one thing, but secretly recording me is way over the line. I just hope my acting career isn't finished because of this scandal."

Ami's face turned purple, and she wobbled in the doorway when she saw the nude video of herself writhing on the bed. "Wait. This is—this is me? I did this?

"Well, it wasn't Mother Theresa, was it?" said Lilibet, with satisfaction so substantial a whole cheesecake would be a gulp of air by comparison.

"Are you saying I sent this—I sent this to all my friends?" Ami checked her texts and phone messages.

"There seemed to be a hundred from what I recalled," replied Lilibet. A shocking amount for someone so damn boring and mousy. Perhaps Ami had joined a homely mannequin convention. Or they were like those sock puppet friends and followers people pay for on social media, which Lilibet had heard about.

"Yep, your husband, your family, and your pastor. They seemed quite upset, to say the least." Without wrinkling her face too much and risking ruining her cosmetic surgery, Lilibet put on an expression of sympathy as best she could.

Ami stumbled backward and collapsed on the floor near the foot of her bed.

"Why did you have my phone?" sobbed Ami.

"Don't you blame me, missy. You passed out after I tried to get you to stop sending the photos of you victimizing me. I was able to delete a few before they downloaded, uploaded, or whatever you kids call it. I'm not good at all this modern technology. You had just better hope I don't sue you once I finish my therapy sessions. And my fan base; don't even get me started with them. They will be out for blood once they get wind that their queen, Queen Lilibet Bathroy, was raped by a—by a dirty little *hypocrite*."

Ami's eyes moved from their locked and swollen position on Lilibet back to her cellphone. "Wait! You didn't tell me about this text from John Henry. He sent a video. Ami's fingers fumbled to hit the play button, and she held her hand over her heart while she watched the video of her husband with the stripper. Cooper had told Lilibet all the juicy details about them before going to sleep last night.

"I guess John Henry was so devastated at what you

did to me; he wanted to get you back—it's a self-destructive behavior that happens all the time in unstable relationships. You should know that with all your psychology studies," said Lilibet, relishing every millimeter that Ami's sparse eyelashes rose in disbelief at what she was seeing. "But doing it with another man, well, that shows how miserable he must've been in his *marriage.* Isn't that what you two called it?"

While Lilibet drummed her long fingernails on the doorframe, Ami threw the phone across the room and curled into a ball on the carpet by the bed. She wailed so loud, Lilibet was positive the hotel security would be knocking on the door shortly. This reminded Lilibet of *Auberge Purge,* a French movie in which she played a maid in a hotel that was built with body parts of women in its mortar and framework, and even in the rugs and drapery. Men seeking supremacy designed the Auberge with an hourglass shape, like Lilibet's figure used to be. The check-in, cafeteria, gym, and event center were in the breasts and head section of the hotel. All of the sleeping quarters were in the skirt section. But the hotel rebelled against its male builders, and when guests retired into their rooms through the narrow waist of the feminine timepiece, the hotel sucked them into a time warp and devoured the men, husbands, and boys, and left only grieving widows and daughters who went mad from the experience. Lilibet's favorite scenes were when the men used the toilet bowls or bidets, which inevitably took a bite out of crime.

Ami's sobs were getting louder and needed to be

stopped.

"Don't be upset, Ami dear; you'll ruin the rest of my trip."

Lilibet spread her fingers over her heart and angled her head. "We can get you some counseling . . . for your addiction to me. Or maybe that college of yours has a professor who might be willing to take you on as a case study."

Ami rolled over on her hands and knees and hardened her eyes on Lilibet like a rabid dog. "I'm not obsessed with you! Something's going on here. I want to speak to my husband." She stood up and rushed toward Lilibet, who blocked the door with both arms lifted high on the frame like Jesus crucified; that's what she was.

Cooper must've heard the commotion and managed to crawl out of bed finally, Lilibet realized, when he scooted sideways behind her, all hunched over like Quasimodo with dried blood on his face. Of course, the little wimp stayed at least six feet behind her, bracing his hand on the hall table, still trying to garner sympathy for his spineless back.

"Not obsessed with me, huh?" In her warrior angel stance with her wings spread, Lilibet sucked in her cheeks with delicious anticipation. "You're a liar and a snake. Cooper found the notepad in your purse and told me about the book you are writing about me—about us. It's all shit. No wonder you wrote half of it in those roadside restrooms."

"Oh, that. It's not what you're thinking," said Ami, drying her eyes on her sleeve as the redness in her cheeks faded.

Lilibet's smirk widened. "Don't even try to deny it. You already told me you wrote an essay on me when you were studying underground films. But now you are obsessed by what I do sexually. You and John Henry were the ones who sold the story and photo about us to *The Big Easy Journal*—that I abuse animals and I'm some drunken nymphomaniac and Cooper is impotent and henpecked." Lilibet turned around and slammed her hands on her hips. "Tell her you're not henpecked, Cooper." Lilibet's nostrils flared.

"I'm . . . I'm not henpecked," said Cooper, lifting his head briefly.

Lilibet turned back toward Ami. "And Cooper and I have not lost all our money and standing in society. All along, you two were really describing yourselves."

Ami's phone rang a happy little melody so unfittingly, and texts continued popping up. She looked down at her cell as if blood were now oozing out, and she began shaking again.

"Oh gosh. My parents are calling. What am I supposed to even say to them?" Her bloodshot eyes pleaded for help as she paced in circles.

"The truth is always best—no matter how brutal— no matter how destructive," said Lilibet, knowing she should get the World's Biggest Hypocrite Award. The truth of her life and Cooper's was something that had gnawed at her very core for years. It wasn't fair that she had to live with the guilt and blame she tried her damnedest to forget. Not while tabloid-tickling, yuppy snakes like Ami, in her sheltered (receive-a-trophy-for-showing-up) world, got away with trying to destroy people's lives. Ami was hiding under the nobility, the superiority, of her therapist degree while having her mommy and daddy take care of the rest. Lilibet scrubbed houses to put herself through acting school. The only bill her parents ever footed for Lilibet was her boyfriend named Bill McDermott when they footed his ass out of their house because he showed up to take her on a date wearing long hair and skin-tight bell bottoms.

"But, Momma, if God truly intended men to have short hair, it would stop growing once it reached their eyebrows." Again, that was another bit of Lilibet logic that her parents couldn't respond to except with threats of discipline.

Lilibet's parents didn't even want her to get an education past high school. "You'll become one of those bra-burning free-thinkers, and I won't stand for it," her father had said, the first time the word *college* ever slipped out of her mouth. The only activities they intended Lilibet to take part in were church-related. Lilibet thought she would lose her ever-loving mind, sitting on rock-hard pews, hearing the congregants groaning for an hour the invitational hymn, "Just as I Am," throwing in extra Shakespearean English as if they were in anguish from crawling over Hellfire brimstones for two days, which they had. She knew they were hoping some hidden soul would finally pop up from under some overlooked pew and come sobbing to the altar to move his letter of membership there. Then the

church youth group would go to the local burger joint, one fun minute down the road, and make small talk while splitting orders of stale fries and watered-down sodas—every damn Wednesday and Sunday night of her youth.

"Isn't this fun, kiddos? See what being washed in the blood can do for you? His blood now flows through your veins," Pastor Booth would say, leaning over the youth table to inspect his property in his rose-tinted glasses and polyester suit that smelled as if he had washed it in musky cologne. Bobby Ray Booth, the pastor's son, whom Lilibet's parents wanted her to marry, found his father's "Washed in the blood" catchphrase particularly funny one night after he had squirted a whole package of ketchup on sixteen-year-old Lilibet.

One last-nerve-testing night after church, Lilibet had had enough of Bobby Ray Booth's antics. When he had shoved the last ketchup-covered toothpick in her hair, she grabbed his necktie that was so wide it could double as a table runner. She jerked the tie so hard, his face slammed into his chocolate pie he had yet to inhale. Bobby cut his face on the foil tray around the pie and was bleeding on his chin and forehead.

"Wasn't that fun? See what being washed in chocolate can do for that bad blood on your face?" Lilibet remembered saying, before her parents had jerked her up in the middle of the burger joint and spanked her buttocks, getting grease on her white cotton dress from their swatting hands, much to her deep humiliation. The youth group snickered behind their paper napkins while

Pastor Booth loomed over Lilibet, cradling his King James Bible.

"Be ye not deceived, Lilibet; the blood-washed will most certainly pay for their sins here on Earth. But as long as you remain faithful to God Almighty and this fine church, you won't spend all eternity suffering in the flesh-eating flames of Hell."

"Oh, she's covered in the blood all right, Pastor Booth," said Lynn Snodgrass. Pinching her nose to keep from snorting, Lynn pointed at Lilibet's buttocks. And everyone knew her parents had swatted her so hard they had knocked her menstrual pad loose.

She had become withdrawn after that and spent the rest of her teens avoiding church and school activities. She stayed mostly in her bedroom, watching as many movies as she could on her little black and white television until her parents took that away, too.

"Satan has got a hold of you, little lady," her father said, smashing her television with a sledgehammer. "No more movies, or magazines, or anything. You are going to take off all the makeup and bitch baubles and memorize your Bible from cover to cover and ask the Lord to make you an instrument for his will and stop all of this sulking."

"That's not who I am. I don't want to be a nun or a preacher's wife; I want to be an actress," said young Lilibet, resenting her parents more than ever each passing day.

"You will obey the Lord," growled her father.

"I don't know that I even believe in the Lord," hissed

Lilibet, before the backside of her father's hand smacked her in the face.

When she stopped crying, she begged her father to take her to a psychologist instead of her pastor. "Maybe a real doctor can help me be a better person."

"Absolutely not. Out of the question! Psychologists and all are of the Devil. They'll turn you against God. And only He can make you whole."

Yet here Lilibet was, well past the prime of her life, and the flames of Hell continued to eat at her. Eat, eat, eat. At least what was left of her life was in her hands, and she was going to draw blood for blood—take life where life had been taken.

"Let me through the door, Lilibet. You can't keep me from seeing John Henry," said Ami. She shoved past Lilibet and plowed through their suite until she found her husband face down on the leather sofa, moaning Lisa's name. Ami took the pillow from over his head and smacked it down hard over his upper back. He rolled over and held his hands over his face, squinting at the light until he seemed to realize it was Ami standing over him.

"How could you?" cried Ami.

John Henry bolted up from the sofa. "I guess Cooper told you about the lap dance at the strip club, huh?" he said. His chest rose and sank as if he had run from a bear.

Ami continued hitting her husband with the pillow. "Oh, so screwing is what you call a lap dance, is it? It looked to me like you were dancing butt naked in his lap. Cooper didn't tell me anything. You texted me, and apparently everyone in the world the video . . . which I'm just now seeing . . . but still." Ami clasped her fingers over her trembling lips. "I'll never be able to get that image out of my head. Did you enjoy it?"

John Henry began biting his lips as his blush deepened and the whites under his eyes lengthened as tears formed. His head snapped toward Cooper.

"You mean somebody videoed it? Cooper, you videoed it? You were holding my phone for me." John Henry looked across the room. "Where's my cellphone? I want my phone now." He felt in his pockets but only found his wallet. His expression sank even deeper.

Still bent over, Cooper limped forward and took another pain pill from the bottle on the bedside table. "I was, uh, waiting for you to finish your business outside the VIP room, and a gang of men surrounded me and took your phone. I guess they filmed you screwing the stripper. They had face tattoos, for heaven's sake. I barely got out of there with my wallet and my life; that's when I got hit by the car."

"Oh God, oh God. What all did the video show?" asked John Henry, sitting on the edge of the sofa, rubbing his knees raw with his hands, looking like he was about to throw up.

"If you're wondering whether anyone recognized you, don't ever doubt that they did." Ami scrolled through her texts and found the video of him, which she played for him to see.

John Henry gripped his forehead under his disheveled blond hair. His voice rose so high and distraught, it was hard to understand him. "That's it. I'm finished. I'll never be able to practice law. I'll never be able to show my face again."

"Oh, I wouldn't worry about your face if I were you; it's every other inch of you they'll recognize, sweet cheeks." Lilibet held up her phone. "I got the text, too."

John Henry jumped up and rushed over to the picture window overlooking the Vegas Strip, which appeared so much more innocent by daylight. Did he think he could jump through the glass? Should Lilibet have suggested they get a suite with a balcony instead? The boy pressed his forehead against the window and rolled his head side to side.

Lilibet shuffled sassily to a mirror and began brushing her hair, flipping it out in places. "Yeah, and you can lose that padded underwear also. Everyone knows you're flat as a pancake now."

Ami rolled her eyes as if she had been expecting this public discovery for years. "Still, how could you, John Henry?"

"You've got some nerve," said John Henry, pushing away from the window. "I saw the sex video you sent me of you and Lilibet. Cooper is right. What's good for the goose is good for the gander. I only did it to get you back."

Ami sniffled loudly. "Yes, the video showed me naked and touching Lilibet's chest area. I swear I don't remember doing anything."

"Chest area? Did you hear that, Cooper? Is that Christian for 'tits' . . . kinda like sassy instead of sexy?

Honey, until I had to slap you, you pounced on me like a dog in heat and groped my big juicy tits like they were life jackets, and you were drowning. I'm just glad I removed the worst parts of the video before you sent those out, too. Oh, Cooper, I still feel so violated. Come hold me," Lilibet cooed in her girliest voice. She re-enacted a silent movie damsel in distress and flung her arm over her weary head as her back arched and her breasts protruded.

"All right, Lilibet, all right. Just give me an hour or so to get there." Like a crab, Cooper shuffled his feet sideways until he finally reached her and buried his head against her breasts, which were eye-level to his bent posture.

"If I had been in my right mind—if I hadn't been drunk maybe—I wouldn't have done anything," said Ami. "But you, John Henry, you knowingly did it with a . . . with a man."

John Henry looked around sheepishly as if there might be a fifth person lurking in the room. "Look, I didn't know Lisa was a 'he' . . . at first."

"So that's the name you were moaning in your sleep a few minutes ago. You knew at some point who was screwing you, yet you just kept begging for more. I never saw you with that much passion. Not with me. There's no fixing this. We are calling for separate cabs, and we're leaving now. I want a divorce as soon as we get back to New Orleans, even if we have to pay for it with our credit cards."

John Henry's head lowered, and his shoulders

drooped. "I guess I won't be able to change your mind now."

Ami's head pushed forward, and she stopped blinking. "What did you do, John Henry?"

"I . . . lost all the money in the casino last night."

Ami backed up, and her mouth dropped. "What? All of it. Are you sure?"

"Every dime," mumbled John Henry.

"That's the only reason I agreed to this trip. We weren't supposed to spend any of our money. How could you? Oh, that's a stupid question. What are you not capable of doing? That's the real question."

"You should be asking yourself that question, missy," Lilibet said to Ami, while applying a final coat of hairspray to her platinum perfection. Seeing the young couple's downfall was better than any soap opera Lilibet had ever watched.

"Yes, Lilibet, I was making notes on you and your relationship with Cooper. I was doing it for my graduation thesis in psychology on toxic codependency. But I never planned to reveal whom I was writing it about. That would be unethical. It would go against the oath of confidentiality. I swear that neither John Henry nor I sold any story of you or anyone to the tabloids—to *any* tabloid. Tell them, John Henry."

"No," he said, shaking his head. "I don't have a clue what you all are talking about."

"They think we sold a story and photos to the newspapers, exploiting their behavior at Cooper's retirement party," continued Ami, with a sigh.

John Henry scratched a bulging vein in his neck. "You've got to be kidding me. Then why did you invite us on this trip with you?"

Ami folded her arms and frowned at Lilibet and Cooper. "To punish us. Isn't it obvious? I'm starting to think something is off with their stories. I'm starting to think they slipped something in our drinks before that drinking game, they made us participate in last night."

"Wait. I do remember someone taking a photo of you and Lilibet, sorta quick and to the side," John Henry said to Cooper. "It was that little girl who was with the older man at your retirement party. She snapped a photo when you two were arguing in front of the fireplace, and then she slipped the camera to the man like it was a microchip or something. I thought it was an odd time to take pictures. But her father didn't, I guess. He patted her on the back like she had done a good thing."

"The only girl at my party was my niece there with my brother, Stan." Cooper placed his finger over his upper lip and wrinkled his forehead. "Surely, he wouldn't betray me like this. Of course, I should've known. Stan has always been stinking jealous of my success. He thinks we stand to inherit a healthy retirement from our uncle. I wouldn't put it past him to make it look as though I can't manage money, so Uncle Bart would see that and cut me off."

Although Lilibet wouldn't put any scheming or unscrupulous behavior past Cooper's brother and niece, she couldn't believe Cooper would risk ruining their plan to take down the Mayfields with this speculation. Not when they seemed to have succeeded so marvelously. If she were wrong about the Mayfields, Cooper and everyone else would never forgive her.

"Don't fall for John Henry's story, Cooper. They are bullshitting us. They deserve everything they got and worse. What will the mental-health professionals think when they hear Ami Cable here is a nymphomaniac rapist and her husband is really a—"

"Shut up, Lilibet. Shut the hell up," growled Cooper, eyeing her disappointedly. He aimed a black pistol at her, a pistol he had removed from his jacket pocket.

"You wouldn't dare!" yelled Lilibet. "It's all that pain medicine; it affects you. I told you to be careful."

"Oh, tempt me and see if I have a backbone; I'm begging you. I'd be more than happy to put myself out of the shame and misery you have caused me." With his bottom teeth jutting, Cooper pointed the gun closer to Lilibet, who backed up with her hands in the air and her eyelashes up to her eyebrows.

Ami and John Henry tiptoed toward the exit door. "Please, just let us go. There is no use for any of us to keep pretending. Me and John Henry will leave you two and go our separate ways."

Cooper gripped the pistol like a madman. "What you're going to do is get in a nice orderly line and act like nothing is wrong. We are going to all go to the parking garage and get in the limo, and if any of you try anything, and I mean anything, I'll shoot you on the spot. Understand?"

John Henry mumbled in agreement.

"I can't hear you." Cooper aimed the gun at him.

"Yes!" everyone said in unison and headed through the door into the hall while Cooper kept the gun aimed at them in his coat pocket.

Had Lilibet finally caused Cooper to snap, to surrender to a darkness that had been building under his cordial surface, as she had feared for years? Or had his big lie caught up with him despite Lilibet not revealing it to a soul, which was a miracle for her? She had never been able to lock a secret behind her luscious lips for very long, but it might be time to let the truth vomit right on out in this case.

17

REACHING THE
BITTERN BEND

Cooper kept as fast a stride behind Lilibet and the
Mayfields as his aching back would let him. He was
painfully aware that he must've looked like a lumbering
gargoyle stalking its prey, especially with the suspicious
glances they received while filing six feet apart out of the
elevator with glum, hungover faces. Perhaps it was the
pain medicine making Cooper behave illogically. He had
no idea if what he was plotting would do anything except
get him in more trouble than he had already found
himself—not including all the lawsuits and fines
awaiting him. It was a terribly impetuous decision to
hold Lilibet and the Mayfields hostage. Like the time
Lilibet insisted Cooper make a midnight run to get ice
cream in his pajamas with only a tablespoon of gas left
in the tank. He also feared that someone related to the
Mayfields, or one of their friends, had notified the police,

which would lead them to Vegas. Cooper remembered the text replies sent to John Henry's phone; the police would no doubt think Cooper was a sex-cult leader, a human trafficker, or something diabolical.

It was time to leave.

"That's it. Now, everyone in the car," ordered Cooper, aiming the water pistol at them through his pocket when they arrived at the limo in the parking garage under the hotel. "You." He pointed the gun at Lilibet. "You're driving, and you're gonna go exactly where I tell you."

Lilibet snatched the keys from Cooper's left hand and stomped toward the driver's side door. For the first time in many years, she wasn't running her mouth. The water pistol Cooper had so elegantly received from the stripper was fooling them . . . so far, but he feared the power he felt brandishing it could become addictive. Lilibet started the engine, and Cooper looked back at Ami and John Henry. They were each hugging the car door nearest them, keeping as much distance between themselves as possible. Lilibet pulled out onto the Strip and soon began driving down I-15 South with dead silence in the car. Cooper told Lilibet to take West Flamingo Road toward Las Vegas Boulevard South. Soon the traffic slowed in front of a building with a billboard featuring half-naked men under shimmering gold letters announcing an all-male revue that night. Cooper felt like a hairy slug compared to the hunks posing up there in their smooth, oiled bodies.

"I'm sorry, John Henry, did you need to stop for

another lap dance?" Ami asked him icily.

John Henry didn't respond. He leaned his head against the glass as though he might take a nap.

Smooth sailing for another ten minutes, and much to Cooper's relief, the traffic became backed up in front of a far less controversial business—Final Oasis nursing home. John Henry turned his head toward Ami like young Regan did in *The Exorcist* when she had grown fed up with having holy water sloshed in her face.

"What about you, huh?" he hissed at Ami, with a reproachful lift of his left eyebrow. "There might be some excellent groping in there in Final Oasis? You can always feign dementia again."

Ami's eyes and nostrils narrowed to slits at John Henry.

"I am not anywhere near old enough to be in a damned nursing home if that's what you're suggesting," growled Lilibet. When the road congestion eased, she floored the gas pedal, giving everyone whiplash. Cooper removed the water pistol from his coat pocket and aimed it at Lilibet.

"Shut up and continue on to I-15 South."

"To LA?" squawked Lilibet.

"No, to Afghanistan. Of course, to LA," said Cooper, before turning the pistol on the Mayfields. "Now listen up, you two. Do you want to end up like me and Lily-Butt here?"

Ami rolled her eyes while John Henry kept his face pressed against the window as if in sorrowful contemplation. A sorrow that had gutted Cooper when the boy's eyes pleaded for help in the suite when he found out the recording of him had gone viral. A sorrow the boy had shown when he thought his wife had cheated on him first, right after losing all his money to pay for the babies they had planned to have. In a way, Cooper felt like he and Lilibet had killed their babies with this plan that she had dragged him into. It wasn't the first time Lilibet had blood on her hands.

"If you're trying to save our marriage, it's too late. We are done—finished," said Ami, closing her eyes and leaning her head back on the seat. "We'll sell the home after the divorce and, of course, we'll have to drop out of college since we're broke now. Not that anyone would ever hire us."

Tears rolled down John Henry's sunken cheeks. "There's no use in me pretending any longer. I realize now that I'm gay. I've been fooling myself for years, trying to be what my family expected me to be. I'm sorry I hurt you, Ami. I was hoping it would just go away if I kept the faith—kept pretending. But now the entire world knows. I guess we'll both be jobless."

Lilibet snorted through her nostrils and steered the limo as though she would ram any daycare bus or hearse that got in her way. "Oh, don't be so negative. No one wants to be around that. Besides, there's always work to be had in the porn industry. Until you hit thirty anyway. So, you better get to humpin', pumpin', and suckin' while you can. It's all about good work ethics."

Ami cried into her hands, and Cooper felt more awful than he had ever felt in his entire life. He knew, deep down, that he and Lilibet had utterly destroyed an innocent young couple with no chance for their redemption . . . unless they became ministers—well, Ami could, perhaps. He should have put his foot down the minute Lilibet wanted to take the Mayfields to Vegas for her sick, unfounded revenge party, when all along it was Cooper's brother, his own flesh and blood, who had sold the story to the tabloid. And not just "a story," the truth, the goddamned truth, it was! Except Cooper had more money than was reported—well, until Hurricane Lilibet wiped that out with this hellish trip, they were on.

This was the end as far as Cooper was concerned—his marriage, retirement, reputation, everything. And he was going to give the trip an ending none of them would ever forget. Cooper was going to be the first to tell. That was his intention anyway. Unless Lilibet told on him first, and at this point, he had no thunder left to steal. He deserved whatever punishment and humiliation he got. And if he had anything to do with it, Kingdom Lilibet was about to tumble to the ground brick by evil brick. They both had been leaning towers barely standing for way too long.

"This is going to be a long drive," Cooper warned the Mayfields, before again telling Lilibet every road to take for about three hours, which was fine with him; he needed time to think his plans through, time to prepare for a finale so big even Lilibet couldn't ask for a better role.

"Cooper, where the shit nuggets are you taking us?" asked Lilibet, with a few beads of sweat forming on her forehead. She was probably having alcohol withdrawal from having to keep both hands on the steering wheel, Cooper imagined.

"I'll tell you where I'm about to take you. Ami, you might want to record this on your cellphone."

Ami's head jerked. She had almost fallen asleep from the emotional stress. She fumbled through her purse and hit a few buttons on her phone with shaking fingers.

"You see, John Henry and Ami, you're about to witness something that needed to be settled a long time ago. You are going to see why it always pays to be honest. Lies they build and build and build, and you find yourself telling more lies to distract from the first ones you told. With that said, honey dumplings," Cooper addressed Lilibet, "why don't you be the first to tell. I know how much it will mean to you. Go ahead, tell the Mayfields the truth about me. You've been threatening to for decades now."

Lilibet's gripped the steering wheel so tight little blue veins popped out around her knuckles. Her jaw protruded, and her high heel pressed the accelerator. The engine growled the rage she was suppressing behind her pursed lips.

"What's to tell? I think they see it aaalllready," said Lilibet.

With eyes wide alert, the Mayfields slipped each other petrified glances. Their chests swelled and collapsed. Cooper wiped his dry forehead with his free hand and leaned near Lilibet's face.

"Look at my forehead, Lilibet; it isn't sweating

anymore. You've held my secret over my head our entire marriage. So go ahead; nothing would give me deeper satisfaction than you letting the world know. Shall we make a visit to the local news station? Shall we stop and buy a megaphone to announce it?"

Lilibet kept her head and eyes locked straight ahead. "Cooper Pearmain, you had better not be taking me where I think you are. This isn't where the birds are, is it?" she asked, when he ordered her to turn on Ventura Freeway.

"What's that?" Cooper held his hand to his ear as if hearing the distant voice of sweet vengeance. "Well, what do you know? A little gossip birdie told me it is. Now, take Sunset Boulevard to Nightingale Drive," said Cooper, lifting the pistol from his lap just in case she balked at returning to the curvy and narrow maze of roads of the Bird Streets section of Hollywood Hills. The section they were supposed to have left behind them forever.

Lilibet stopped at the gated entrance at the base of the Santa Monica Mountains. Her fingers twitched on the steering wheel, and her tensed jaw shifted left and right.

"Ha! Poor little Coopie. You forgot about getting past the gates. And you had me drive all the way here for nothing."

"And you forgot we still own the property at 47 Bittern Bend—what's left of it anyway. We couldn't sell it, remember? I'm sure the tour buses still stop there to tell the tales and horrify the tourists." Cooper steadied his pistol. "Now, roll the window down and enter the code. I know you remember it, and just remember I'm watching you."

Lilibet carefully entered the long passcode. She rolled up the window as the iron gates opened, and she drove between them. After turning up several rising streets, she floored the gas pedal.

"I'll not let you do this, Cooper. I'll not!" screamed Lilibet. She squeezed her eyelids shut, and the limo sped forward, cutting through the corner of someone's well-manicured lawn before crashing into a curved brick fence. The airbags in the limo exploded like a gunshot.

After the ringing in Cooper's ears abated, he could see Lilibet with her head pressed against the headrest. She was groaning while a jet of steam rose out of the hood of the limo that now resembled a giant crushed toaster from what Cooper could see through the windshield so cracked it had turned as white as a sheet of ice. Ami and John Henry were fumbling to find their seatbelts to unlock them. Cooper opened the front passenger's door, climbed out, and stretched his throbbing back as much as it would let him. He reached in his coat pocket, grabbed another pain pill, and swallowed it dry. It got hung in his throat, causing him to cough while a metallic sulfur taste filled his mouth. He tapped the gun against the back window.

"Out of the car, all of you. Don't forget your phone, Ami. I want you to record the end."

Ami and John Henry scooted out of the limo and stood near the back trunk before Lilibet finally emerged from the driver's seat with her hair looking like the snakes on Medusa's head. She kept her eyes on the road instead of the beautiful houses and landscapes. Surely, she felt like a soldier who had returned to a war zone. Cooper glanced casually around to see if anyone had come running out on the streets or were watching them through doors or windows, triggered by the noise of the crash. So far, the neighbors seemed oblivious—probably busy with their interior designers upgrading mirrors and chandeliers deep inside their walk-in closets, he imagined.

"Get moving, all of you. The property—the grave—awaits just around the bend here. Anyone try to yell for help, and the end will be sooner.

"I'm trying to *move*, but for some reason, I have a limp now," said Ami through clasped teeth, hobbling with her hands in the air.

"What do you expect after being in the car with a washed-up actress who just tried to re-enact the end scene of *Thelma and Louise*, huh?" asked Cooper. He wished he had John Henry's padded underwear about now to wear as a neck brace. He seriously considered making a grab for the padding, but it surely wouldn't help his case that he wasn't a sex-cult leader if the police came after him. *No, officer, I'm as unsexed-up as they come*; he imagined himself truthfully mumbling through the musky fabric that had just supported the man's dangly bits while Cooper had held a gun to his back.

"Limp a little quicker," he said to Ami. "And put your hands down; we don't want to draw more attention to ourselves."

When the road made a sharp turn on the undeveloped dead-end street, mostly obscured by trees, Cooper swallowed, and Lilibet staggered drunkenly. Still standing before him, like a wooden skeleton, a massive, ruined sepulcher, was the partially completed mansion that he had spent so long with an architect designing during the earlier part of his marriage to Lilibet. The home sat on a hill, and both stories had fifteen-foot-high ceilings. The pill dissolved in his throat, leaving in its place a lump of sorrow and dread. He could feel death calling to him from the very foundation of that skeletal home's frame.

"Keep walking," he said, forcing Lilibet and the Mayfields to walk up the concrete steps through the middle of what he had planned to be a formal garden with banana and palm trees spilling over a winding stone fence. A perfect gathering place for the Hollywood parties they had planned to throw under the stars and fairy lights while a bartender served guests their choice poisons behind a bar they were going to drape in sheer white fabric or whatever fabric that would match Lilibet's dress for the occasions. That way, everyone would know who always got to go to the head of the line for the alcohol.

"Here we are. Nothing has changed. It's all the same. Are you happy, Cooper?" asked Lilibet. She jerked her head back and stared down the property with a scowl as if daring it to reveal its secret.

Everything had changed. The grass had encroached

over much of the path, and small trees had burst through cracks in the concrete. And the rectangular pools of water on both sides had become overgrown with algae so syrupy it made Cooper nauseated from its vomit-green color alone. If it weren't for the spray-painted graffiti that skateboarders and punks had graced the interior walls of the pools with to add the dystopian touch, they so preferred, Cooper would believe he had stumbled upon an abandoned settlement in a jungle. The city would probably have torn down the unfinished construction at 47 Bittern Bend had the secluded road not been built just for Cooper and Lilibet's home, invisible to people passing through the Bird Streets. The city must've known what was good for the majestic and peaceful community by allowing it, and to think Lilibet had sworn they were fans of hers for allotting them the private road.

"Get that phone up, Ami, and make sure you are recording all of this. You see, Lilibet planned this whole trip. While you and John Henry went with her to look at that bullshit angel, she wanted you to see, that was only a distraction for me to spike your drinks."

"They did put something in our drinks. I told you, John Henry," said Ami. She walked in front of Lilibet, keeping one eye on the recording on her phone.

"Aw, Cooper, I trusted you. Why would you do that to us?" asked John Henry. He looked around the property as if looking for an escape.

"You see, John Henry, little buddy, that's what happens when your wife becomes paranoid and controlling, and you do nothing to stop her. Lilibet just knew you two had sold the story about us to the press, so she wanted to get you to confess. And when she thought she got her evidence, she convinced me to help her destroy your reputations."

"You mean *you* sent the video of me to my friends and family?" Ami asked Lilibet.

"Pass that question to Cooper. He has all of the answers now," said Lilibet, stumbling as they began to climb the front stairs to the house taken over by ivy.

"Yes, sweet Ami," Cooper sighed. "Lilibet took advantage of you while you were drunk, and she edited the footage to make it look like *you* had violated *her*. She has always been good at playing the victim. She sent the recording to everyone, as if it came from you. And I talked John Henry into going to the strip club to get revenge on you. The poor boy was in tears when he got the video text. I'm ashamed to say that I recorded him with the stripper and sent the video to everyone on his contact list. There was no gang who took the phone from me."

"But he had sex with a guy—the stripper was a guy, and now he thinks he's gay. Is that what you still believe, John Henry? Or is this all Cooper and Lilibet's fault, too?" asked Ami. She studied her husband's reaction with glassy eyes locked and desperate for a response. An unsettling mask of fading hope.

John Henry picked at the peeling paint on a white column supporting the front porch, removing layer after layer of the neglected facade.

"Before you answer, John Henry. Please think about everything you had with Ami and everything you stand to lose. Don't let what happened to Lilibet and me happen to you and your lovely wife."

John Henry kept scraping chunks of paint off with his fingers, watching them fall to the concrete porch. Cooper would've gotten on his knee if he could. Instead, he leaned against the column to face the boy, who now seemed like a stranger at a family reunion, a very dysfunctional family.

"Look, little buddy, if I could undo the destruction, we caused you and Ami, I would . . . in a heartbeat. I know it's hard to trust me here, but the key to reconciliation is still in your hands."

Lilibet lifted her arms and shook them. "Cue the fucking violins, somebody. Don't become like old Lilibet here, whatever you do. It's obvious John Henry doesn't want to talk about his intense passion for beans and sausage now, Cooper. Besides, the only one holding the key is you. So, open the goddamned door, and let's get this shit show over with."

Cooper's cheek twitched into a snarl at Lilibet. He shoved the key he kept on his keychain into the deadbolt, imagining it was a knife into her vile flesh. He unlocked the door, unsure of what condition the interior would be in. If it were as bad as his and Lilibet's interiors had become, then he imagined the worst. At best, some black bears had made it their yearly habitation, perhaps. At worst, some cult group had been using the place to perform ritual sacrifices, child-bride weddings, or even mass castrations in order to purify themselves in hopes that the sky chariots would whisk them off to Heaven during some comet flyby known only to the chosen members. About all Cooper remembered at this point was that the bottom half of the mansion had mostly been finished while the top floor had no solid roof and half of the walls there were missing except for the framing.

The door squeaked open, and a musty smell wafted through the opening. Inside the wide foyer, the ceiling drooped and had turned brown in places from rainwater. Thank goodness it didn't rain much in the region, or they probably wouldn't be able to get through the door. In the living and dining areas, typing-paper-sized sheets of plaster were barely hanging on the ceiling worse than the dandruff Cooper's father used to suffer with at times. The old drapes sagged on their brass rods from the added weight of dust. Cooper had not imagined everything looking this dismal, but some of it was the shattered dreams and old memories instead of the debris scattered on the floor. He and Lilibet must have been so distraught when they had abandoned the property, they had left the cabinet doors open. Records scattered on the floor in one corner where a stereo once sat near some built-in shelving. Garish upholstered chairs where rats had chewed the stuffing out in corners. Some corn pads Lilibet had peeled off her calloused feet and had tossed on the floor near a baby rattle and children's picture books. The old big box-style television with a shattered screen where Lilibet had thrown her cocktail glass the night she didn't hear her name called for best actress in an underground film. A room of unused, outdated exercise equipment just behind a door hanging by one hinge. Cooper and Lilibet had never really moved into this house. Lilibet had been too itchy to start decorating the bottom floor and have it homey and welcoming for those rare moments she stopped by to check on the construction.

John Henry paused near an old *Life* magazine on the floor with orange and blue crayon marks on the cover. "I'm sorry, Ami. I'm sorry you got dragged into this awful mess because of them. I still love you, but—"

Cooper pushed John Henry toward the base of the staircase. "Think about what you had together and be honest. Otherwise, you'll both end up drunken and bitter like Lilibet and me. Now before I take you upstairs to show you the secret Lilibet doesn't want the world to know, I'm going to let her tell you my secret." With his hands, Cooper made a drumroll on the carved newel post. "And now, ladies and gentlemen, heeere's Lilibet."

Folding her arms, Lilibet stood there defiantly until her eyes became glassy and distant. Cooper held the gun to her back and made everyone ascend the stairs—the stairs he had one day hoped to drape Christmas garland—hoped to see his children playing on as he had done when he was a kid. The stairs he wanted to carry Lilibet up after they officially moved in—a chance that never happened because of one drunken, fitful night, one of many nights that Lilibet forgot there wasn't a camera filming her in her hopes for a prestigious award.

With Cooper pointing the way with his pistol, they

climbed the steps ahead of him. Ami pushed against the railing on every step to take the weight off her injured leg.

"All right, since Lilibet here has decided to keep her nagging mouth shut for once, I'll tell you what I did. You see, I, William Cooper Pearmain, never—"

Lilibet burst into tears and leaned against the mildew-covered wall on the staircase. "Don't, Cooper. Don't do this."

Cooper motioned for her to keep climbing, which she did, holding onto the railing with both hands now.

"I never even graduated from college. Yes, yes, it's true. I worked my whole life as an attorney with a fake diploma. There, I said it."

"Why are you still toying with us? You just admitted that your brother, Stan, sold the story and not us?" said John Henry, placing his arm around Ami to comfort her.

"I want you to video my confession and send it to all of your friends and family. I, William Cooper Pearmain, am the phony! I should be ashamed, not you or your wife. I never would've even graduated from college. I made it to my senior year and realized one of my professors, Robert 'Bowlegged' Bowen, was intent on failing me because he hated my father for some reason. My father wouldn't say what had caused the bad blood between them. All I could figure was the two became rivals in middle school once. I would've reported my professor to the college president, but the two were good friends. Old Bowlegged was always trying to pick a fight with me. He even dragged me out of Sociology and claimed that I had copied another student's test paper. The idiot professor didn't know that the student at fault had taken the same test after my class had ended. He forgot he had made the student sit beside his desk as a punishment for talking, and the student copied off my test while the professor stepped out of the room. But did I get an apology for being humiliated and falsely accused? Hell no! It just made him want to take me down even worse.

"Just before the end of my senior year, I became desperate and told my brother, who said he would take care of it. I had no idea 'taking care of it' meant he would break in the college that night with a can of gasoline and some matches— 'justice for our father' Stan considered it. You see, with my mother selling half of our possessions to pay for my college, she would've been devastated if I didn't graduate, and it would've finished my ill father off to think Professor Bowen failed his son because of their old feud. While I was at home asleep that night, Stan burned down the entire university. All their records were destroyed, but Stan didn't know Professor Bowen was still inside the university, grading final exams. Old Bowen managed to crawl out a window, but he suffered from so much lack of oxygen, his mind was never the same—to the point he didn't remember any of his students. But he claimed all of his students had passed their finals. But my brother had found my test papers, and Old Bowlegged had given me an F, so he burned it in the fire separately."

Ami and John Henry cringed on the upper-staircase

landing. The afternoon sun filtered through the treetops and two-by-fours of the unfinished walls on the second story. Lilibet was breathing hard now, and she refused to look at the right side of the house, just as Cooper expected. But why was she being so quiet for the first time in her life?

John Henry let go of Ami, who kept her grip on her cellphone. "I don't understand, Cooper. How did you get such a prestigious job without a college degree?"

"I lost all self-confidence and doubted I could actually pass the finals exams when we were all told we would have to take the tests over since they had burned. The college board was split over whether we should be made to retake the tests, so I had a fake diploma made and then passed the bar exam in California, which was proof that I shouldn't have failed Bowen's class. My clever brother pretended to be a bigshot attorney and recommended me for a job in LA. He was setting me up to receive lifetime kickbacks for helping me achieve success. It should've been obvious from the beginning that Stan sold the story about me and Lilibet to the press to get me back. You see, I told him before my retirement party that I couldn't keep helping him out financially. He implied that I owed him and should help put his daughter, Farrah, through college since he was the one who helped me graduate and get a job. My niece is the one you saw taking the photo at my retirement party."

Cooper walked carefully over the plywood flooring on the upper level. With distant eyes, Lilibet clung to a wall stud as though it was the mast of a sinking ship. The sweet scent of the gardenias Lilibet had wanted planted around the house's foundation traveled up through the open framework.

"And that one mistake I made as a young man, my lovely wife here has used to manipulate and torture me with every damned day of our marriage. So, you see, I am spineless. But I did try to make amends for it all by helping those less fortunate attain college scholarships. It was the least I could do. Nevertheless, I brought you all here to put an end to the torture—put an end to what should have been ended a long time ago," Cooper continued, waving the pistol flippantly.

"Please, Cooper, for all that was good and decent about our time together, I beg you to stop," sobbed Lilibet; she slid down the wall stud into a squatting position on the subfloor.

"That's the problem, Lilibet; the only thing that was good and decent in our time together—even that you killed. Cooper looked straight into Ami's phone recording. "The good thing was our only child, Misty." Cooper's face began to quiver, so he turned his back from the recording to hide an anguishing release of tears. When he felt he was able to continue talking, he turned back around to face Ami. "My baby girl was barely two years old and the sweetest, most beautiful little girl you would ever lay your eyes on. Of course, Misty wanted her mother's attention, too, but Lilibet was determined to win an Oscar for once—always busy trying to star in one failed movie after the other and had no time for a snot-nosed rug rat, as she called children."

"Not our child, Cooper. Not ours," Lilibet muttered, gazing into the distance as her head swirled drunkenly.

"She had just come from one of her Hollywood parties, drunk as usual, so I had to pick her up and had Misty with me. On the way home in the dark, I decided to swing by our property here and see how the construction was coming along. Which was what you are seeing the remnants of now. We all came upstairs, and Lilibet discovered that I had changed the construction plans and had not added a rehearsal studio onto the house plans for her, but that I had added a smaller office for myself since I was making most of the money. Lilibet started foaming at the mouth; she was so pissed. She intended to grab Misty and leave, but Misty wouldn't come to her, so she charged at her—I suppose forgetting we were on the second floor. Naturally, Misty backed away from Lilibet and fell over the edge on the right side of the house and died."

Tears poured from Cooper's eyes, and he wiped them on his sleeve. He remembered the brief moments in time how Misty would crawl into his lap while he was sitting in his favorite chair after a hard day's work. She would just look up at him and dare to touch his razor-stubbled face with her tiny hands. And almost every time, it was the same questions from Misty: "Mommy not here? Mommy go to party? Me love Daddy." She would then lay her little head on his chest and sometimes squash Cooper's newspaper. But he never minded. He would gladly never read another newspaper, book, or anything again if he could have his baby girl, his little angel, back in his life. Many nights he would play rocky horsey with Misty on his knee, and she would hold on with every limb and squeal, "Again, Daddy, again!" until Cooper ended up nursing a leg cramp that jolted him awake from a deep sleep.

And when Misty *was killed*—died—a huge part, the best part, of Cooper died as well. He had to take off work for two whole months, where he mainly remained in dark isolation. He lost so much weight he developed a bleeding ulcer. It took a while, and at first, he wasn't sure he would ever be able to hold a normal conversation again, much less argue a case in court. During this time, Lilibet drowned herself in more movie roles, parties, and booze. And then she started taking prescription drugs on top of the recreational drugs she freely gleaned at the parties; she sometimes didn't stagger home until the next day.

"Everybody deals with depression differently," Lilibet had assured Cooper while rehearsing for the role of a serial killer.

When he had seen a hickey on her neck in those grieving days, Lilibet claimed one of the actors couldn't control himself while they were filming a sex scene. For some suspicious reason, over half of her sex scenes always got cut by the director, or that was Lilibet's excuse when she forced Cooper to watch the dreadful films that he tried his best to get behind.

"Lilibet and I agreed never to reveal the truth to anyone," Cooper said, in front of the recording cellphone, blinking his eyes to dry the tears. "We decided to claim it was an accident and never speak of it. As hard as I tried not to, I despised Lilibet for her reckless behavior and drinking. But, as you now see, I couldn't leave her because she had something on me as well—her spineless husband. I hope you can forgive us for trying to transfer our misery onto you. Lilibet, are you happy? You finally had one true fan, and even that you have destroyed."

"No. No, I'm not happy." Lilibet pulled herself up from the subfloor by gripping the wall stud.

"What? You finally dialed 1-800-I-REMEMBER?" hissed Cooper.

She dusted off her dress near her knees and then pushed her hair out of her face. "You don't think I have had to live with the pain, the regret for what happened to my baby girl?" Her face darkened, and her bottom teeth protruded from her grimace.

Cooper was used to this. Lilibet was putting on another act—the act of her life. If only she could see how grotesque she looked right now with her twisted face, dilated eyes, her dress about to rip at every seam. She swished toward him with a vile determination as if to destroy him. Stepping one high heel in front of the other like a panther stalking its prey. If Lilibet wanted an act, then Cooper was going to give her an act.

Cooper squared his shoulders and frowned at her. "No, I'm afraid you never had time, running your own fan club under a fake name."

"We all make mistakes, mister perfect, mister I'm-so-kumbaya," hissed Lilibet. "Oh, I knew, I knew you wanted to leave me after that night. I knew you wanted to make me suffer alone. Hell, you wanted to leave me before I even got pregnant; just admit it, you spineless coward. That, Cooper, that's why I started to drink more—to prepare myself for the pain. You have no idea how much rejection a film actress suffers every day of her career."

Like James Bond, Cooper's lips formed a playboy smile, and he lifted the water pistol prop he had kept from the stripper. Despite John Henry's and Ami's protests, he aimed the pistol at Lilibet's head and remembered a line from one of her last movies.

"But only in death does the pain end," said Cooper.

He squeezed the trigger, and a stream of liquor shot from the barrel of the pistol and soaked her stunned face, starting with her high penciled brows, then drenched her snakelike curls she had strategically placed to soften her chemically frozen forehead. The alcohol filtered through the long black tentacles of her fake eyelashes and rained down over her puffy cheeks, which widened with horror as her red-painted lips parted like a great white shark ready to scream or bite. With Lilibet, it was hard to know which to expect.

Ami lowered her phone, gasping behind her free hand clamped over her mouth. At the same time, Lilibet wiped the alcohol off her face, smearing her black eyeliner until she resembled a grotesque gothic grandma.

At that moment, Cooper experienced a wash of relief cleanse him of the years of guilt and fear. He had beat Lilibet at her game. He had stood up to her, declawed her. He had found and broken the invisible barrier that had long ago trapped them in a superficial web of poisonous codependency. The look of shock and vulnerability on Lilibet's face was something Cooper had never seen her genuinely express before, never thought she would be capable of displaying. He was sure it was a look that would be forever stored in his memory.

Cooper couldn't tell whether she was about to pass out from dizziness or if she was still in shock. He spaced his legs on the subfloor to balance himself, get good leverage to defend his damaged body if she attacked him. Lilibet's eyes remained unfocused but open, joined by a deepening crease on her brow ridge as if the plastic surgery that had held her brows so unnaturally high was a cord that had been severed. Her chest sank, and she swallowed before bending her head down.

"Wait, Ami. There's . . . there's one more thing . . . one more thing I want you to record," said Lilibet in a defeated, exhausted tone.

She waited until Ami's trembling arms again lifted the phone and punched the red record button. In turn, her eyes settled portentously on Cooper, then on Ami and John Henry before turning her back to them and walking to the right side of the upper floor; her high heels left an echoing thud on the weather-grayed plywood. Without uttering a word, she lifted her dress a few inches above her ankles, pivoted around just enough to blow a kiss for the camera, and then she jumped over the open edge.

Cooper felt his heart scurry into his churning gut.

He couldn't have accurately perceived what he thought he had just witnessed. It had to be a bad dream and nothing more—nothing more than watching Lilibet's countless awful film premiers, the ad-libbed, rush-production melodrama he had suffered through in second-rate movie theaters and warehouses since before their marriage. All the years Lilibet had faked or threatened suicide; she had cried wolf too many times for this to be real.

The screams coming from Ami and John Henry proved it was real. And in the very same spot Lilibet had killed her daughter years earlier. With the height of the second level, they were standing on and the extended hill below the bottom floor to the brick patio, there could be little hope that she could still be alive. Of course, she would end it this way, a trope Cooper had seen too often in crime films.

As though they had all become robots, moving due to some remote-controlled obligation or conscience, they walked, not ran, down the stairs, through the musty foyer, and out of the tomb of a house. When they cut through the overgrown vegetation and came around to the right side, Lilibet's twisted body was sprawled unnaturally on the brick patio, right beside a white gardenia bush in full bloom, both defying the weeds that surrounded it. John Henry reached down to check for a pulse, but his expression let Cooper know she had finally triumphed in ending her life. Cooper broke a stem full of gardenia blooms off the bush and placed them on top of her body. Her left hand bent above her head caught his attention last: All but her middle finger was folded down. She was shooting the bird at Cooper.

"Leave it to Lilibet to have the last word. She couldn't even die with dignity," he said, when the Mayfields also noticed the crude hand gesture smashed against the brick patio.

"I'm leaving here, and don't either of you try to stop me," said Ami, backing away from Lilibet's body before turning toward the concrete walkway, dragging her injured leg with every step.

John Henry grabbed handfuls of hair on both sides of his head and took a step back before he ran after her. "But, Ami, sweetie, where will you go? What'll you do? Our credit cards are maxed out, and we're all out of cash."

"I'll text one of my friends to come and get me—if they'll have anything to do with a destitute lesbian porn star who just recorded her lover's suicide. Otherwise, I'll hitchhike to the police station if I have to," Ami yelled, increasing her pace toward the lonely dead-end road.

Cooper hobbled toward Ami while reaching for his wallet. He pulled out the only cash he had on him, thirty-five dollars, which he tried to hand to Ami.

"I cannot take that from you," said Ami, over her shoulder. "I don't want the court or my attorney to think I received a dime's restitution from you. But I will receive restitution for what you did to me, and it'll be far more money than you can hold in that foul hand of yours."

Left standing there, holding a wad of cash in the air,

Cooper felt like the scum of the earth. He limped toward John Henry instead. "Please, take it. You can at least get a cab to the police station." He tried to stuff the cash in John's shirt pocket, but he shoved Cooper away from him, jarring his injured back.

"I know you were trying to repair my marriage to Ami, but it's too late. You had us all in terror for hours with that water pistol. I think we're done here, Cooper." John Henry kept his hands up defensively and gave Cooper the most hopeless, most disappointed look Cooper had ever seen a human face make, a look that he would remember in the grave. Then the boy ran as fast as he could and caught up with Ami halfway down the street.

Cooper collapsed on his knees in the weeds near the edge of the road. "No, it can't end this way. It can't," he said to himself, wheezing from fighting back anguished tears. Vanishing in the distance were the fleeing lives he had helped ruin. Behind him, bleeding out on the brick patio, was the corpse of his wife. Between the two was a void of disbelief. How had Cooper's life gone in this direction? Lilibet had been holding Cooper's secret over him for most of their marriage. She had manipulated him for all that secret was worth. But when he finally lost his fear and outed both of their secrets ahead of her, the fickle woman up and killed herself. She bloody killed herself and didn't say one word to make Cooper look bad—not. One. Disparaging. Word.

An old dark voice whispered in Cooper's brain. *Because she knew, old boy, she knew you had a conscience*

*left, and killing herself would be the ultimate revenge, a
permanent revenge.*

No, Cooper blocked that thought. He shouldn't
think so lowly of his poor dead wife. She had obviously
lived with the guilt of their daughter's death for too long.
And whether she wanted to talk about it or not, Cooper
should have pinned her down and assured her—scratch
that—he should've lied out of his ass that he didn't hold
her responsible for Misty's death in the least. Instead, he
had made the mistake of assuming time would let them
both forget and heal. That was when Lilibet started
toying with Cooper, bringing up his confession about
not getting a real diploma. Since the day of Misty's
funeral, she seemed to find her mission to make him hate
her. He had needed a weapon against Lilibet as well, a
secret he could threaten to share, so he had used her own
guilt against her. And this wasn't fair. This wasn't how
their years of suppressed secrets were supposed to turn
out. But then again, neither was Cooper's hairline which
had receded.

18

DEBT TO SOCIETY

Cooper was so exhausted he didn't think he would ever be able to pry himself out of his recliner in the den of his house. He still felt awful for ruining the lives of the Mayfields. If Hollywood ever created the Newlywed Annihilation Game, he would be the best host it could get. From the moment he had arrived back home in New Orleans, he had been busy settling lawsuits, paying for damages left and right, and then there was the matter of Lilibet's funeral, a stage production in itself. The funeral plans were typed out on paper, all scheduled out in her will.

1. Send a press release with the funeral announcement to every Hollywood movie producer and studio.

2. For keepsakes, have brochures and autographed photos of me for all the guests. I want seventy-two lily

arrangements surrounding my silver and gold open casket draped with strands of pearls. A floral arrangement for every film I have ever made and let that be known. Someone from the Kennedy Center Advisory Board will know the best announcer for that part. If my face is crushed, scarred, or unpresentable upon death, hire a body double who is my size—smaller preferably. To make sure the body double doesn't laugh while guests pay their last respects, sedate her if necessary. Make sure she doesn't snore, though!

3. Get the latest Oscar-winning hair, makeup, and wardrobe artists to make my body presentable for viewing. But make sure they don't have my body violating any more cultural appropriation rules. I'm still catching hell for that damned Egyptian-themed wedding you ruined. Do not expose your balls at my funeral, or I will haunt you forever, Cooper Pearmain.

4. If her vocal cords have healed enough, see if Adele will sing the list of my favorite songs; they are in the Cloud like I'll be, no doubt. Perhaps Sir Elton can be talked into rewriting Candle in the Wind a third time just for me, only have him perform it on a harp this time. I don't want there to be any more comparisons of me and Marilyn.

5. This is a must: get Cher to perform the eulogy if she's willing.

6. Under no circumstance allow that two-faced, has-been, Kansas-born, Scientology cow anywhere near my funeral. And you know damned well who I'm talking about.

7. I want eight of the top male models in loincloths to serve as pallbearers to carry my casket. That new Plath boy will do as long as he loses the platinum hair. A woman never wants any competition on her special day.

And that, the first page of the will, was only the beginning of Lilibet's funeral requirements. The reality that the funeral became included maybe fifteen guests, who showed up to hear an Elvis impersonator sing her favorite songs. They viewed Lilibet in a silver casket, which the funeral home director embellished the molded edges of with flat-gold nail polish. Instead of pearls, someone draped purple and green Mardi Gras beads over the casket, and a Cher-impersonating drag queen did Lilibet's hair and makeup and performed the eulogy in under two minutes. Cooper may have been mistaken, but the eulogy sounded like the beginning of a Prince song he remembered from the eighties. With no top male models willing or available, Cooper had to resort to crossing the Lavender Line of Bourbon Street to hire four male dancers with pierced nipples, and they agreed to change into four dollar-store Tarzan costumes and carry

the casket. They nearly dropped Lilibet, but the drag queen ended up grabbing the handle in time. And the guests almost peed themselves from laughter when she let out a string of curse words after breaking a "fuckin' fifty-dollah fingernail."

Cooper had been so wrapped up in red tape and finalities, he hadn't taken the time to open all his mail, which was now teetering like the Tower of Pisa in a stack on the small table beside his recliner. He pulled out, from what he was sure were more bills and lawsuit notices, a small package postmarked from San Antonio, Texas.

"The Alamo? I remember the Alamo." Cooper tore through the taped edges of the package and couldn't believe his eyes. In a transparent sealed bag was Lilibet's wedding ring with a note written on a restaurant napkin that she had rolled up and stuck inside the ring. A greasy fingerprint made the perfect seal for the note.

> Please, Wishing Well, please let Cooper forgive me for what I did to our child. I can make do with a man without buns. But all I want is to have the kind of relationship that the Mayfields have. And for this, I am giving up the one possession I hold most dear, my wedding ring.
> —Lilibet Bathroy Pearmain

Cooper dropped the note in his lap. A tsunami of guilt pinned him to the recliner. How much time had

passed? He didn't know. All he could do was gaze at the wedding photo of Lilibet and him in the frame on the fireplace. He wadded up the napkin wish and flung it at the photo.

"Damn you, Lilibet! You always had to have the last word, didn't you? You knew I would get this note. You always turned absolutely everything around on me to make me the guilty party."

He clutched the wedding ring he thought she had intentionally dropped in the water well so she could look single in Vegas. What if she had been sincere for once? Cooper would never know now, would he? And that was the way Lilibet always seemed to like it in her final days. She hadn't always been bitter and unbearable, not until Misty was killed. Before Misty was born, there had been a pleasant late-spring trip to Europe and a New York City stay for Christmas. The Tournament of Roses in Pasadena went well until Lilibet staggered into the street and tried to climb onto a traveling float covered in white lilies. She had dragged Cooper with her and demanded he give her a boost up into the float as though she were a nimble teen jumping on the stage to dance on American Bandstand. He pushed against her rear end as hard as he could, but she was dead drunken weight. The heel of her boot got caught in the float, and when Cooper fell, the float dragged her upside down for nearly two blocks before bringing the parade to a grinding stop. If that weren't bad enough, a gang of militant feminists thought Cooper had been trying to cop a feel of Lilibet, and they pinned him down on the road and began

kicking and punching him.

After several nights of restless sleep, dreaming about happier might-have-beens—if he and Lilibet had done things differently—if their baby girl had lived—if they had been more honest with one another—Cooper couldn't live with himself. He decided to use what money he had left, what money he hadn't spent paying for the funeral, emergency-crew assistance that he didn't need half of, a totaled limo, and a string of lawsuits, and take Lilibet on the European vacation she had wanted when he had retired. He could think of no other way to rid his plague of guilt for his role in Lilibet's suicide. Their marriage may have been a huge mistake from the beginning. There was no rescuing the Mayfields at this point, but Cooper's and Lilibet's time together couldn't end like this.

19

BON APPÉTIT

Still waiting for his food in the Paris restaurant, Cooper was again depressed from rehashing the recent events that had led up to Lilibet's suicide. But unlike the scripture about the Lord perceiving a thousand years as one day . . ., it was more the opposite for Cooper; one day with Lilibet seemed like a thousand-year prison sentence. Of course, he wouldn't say that to her now as he gazed across the dining table at her photo in the bejeweled frame. People continued to pass glances at him, the sad and lonely eccentric living in a fantasy that he was somehow making restitution.

"Don't wait on me. Your champagne is getting warm and your foie gras cold, honey dumplings," Cooper said to the photo of Lilibet.

He knew he would probably end up drinking her untouched champagne. Guilt was crushing him again, but this time about the young Mayfields. John Henry and Ami had divorced, and to avoid further embarrassments for all, Cooper had settled with them both out of court. Enough money to pay for the divorced couple to buy new homes and pay off their college tuitions. John Henry decided to become a civil rights attorney instead. Although John's family and friends dropped him over his new "out and proud" lifestyle, reports were that he seemed happier than ever.

Ami was a different story. She decided to finish school somewhere in the Northeast. Her family, most of her friends, and her pastor rallied around her, according to the neighborhood gossip anyway, which Cooper wouldn't be hearing anymore. He ended up selling his home in New Orleans and the unfinished home in California, as well.

It turns out Lilibet had one other fan of her work as a movie actress: A strange little man who had heard of her suicide at the deteriorating property on the LA news. He offered Cooper top dollar to buy and restore the property just as the Pearmains had envisioned it down to the blueprints. The stipulation for the purchase was that Cooper also had to sign over all movie rights, which Cooper reluctantly did, as he couldn't imagine anyone wanting to see a movie about Lilibet's life. Tour buses continued to stop in front of the property in the Bird Streets of the Hollywood Hills. But the locals started calling the dead-end street the "Bitter End" instead of Bittern Bend after a news tabloid had printed an article comparing the property to the Amityville Horror house. Cooper didn't think that was too farfetched of an equivalence.

And speaking of bitter, Cooper's brother was furious that he wouldn't be getting another dime from him.

"I know you sold the story about me and Lilibet to the tabloid," Cooper had confessed to Stan Pearmain. "I never asked you to burn the school down and cause injury to Professor Bowen. I'm done being manipulated and extorted by you or anyone. So, you will not be getting any more handouts from me."

"Some brother you turned out to be," Stan had said. "Our parents would roll over in their graves if they knew how you turned your back on family."

"You wanna know who else is rolling over in their grave? My wife, Lilibet. That story you sold to punish me is what led to her suicide, just so you know."

That was the last time Cooper had seen or spoken to Stan or Farrah. He took another sip of brandy when a woman walked past the table and then backed up to face him. She had shoulder-length straight hair that framed her heart-shaped face and deep-set eyes that many a man could become spellbound looking into.

"Excuse me, but are you from the US?" she asked.

"Yes, we are. How did you guess?" Cooper sat up straight and, with his napkin, wiped off any breadcrumbs that might be clinging around his lips.

"I recognized the woman in the photo. It's Lilibet Bathroy, the underground film actress from Hollywood. You must be a huge fan of hers to have an autographed picture." She placed her bare fingers over her collarbone. "I'm sorry; how presumptuous of me. Her being a celebrity and all, the restaurant must've put that there as a placeholder to reserve her table. She never settled for fashionably late; she wanted to be the Second Coming. You know, sound the trumpets and part the clouds late." The woman laughed, blushed, and looked away. "I'm sorry. You must think me terribly rude."

Cooper started to say that the only autograph he had from Lilibet was on their marriage certificate. But he didn't want Lilibet to hear him speak of her death on their vacation. Besides, he was curious how a pretty woman in France recognized her photo so easily.

"Not at all. I guess you could say I know the most there is to know about her, and I still find her a mystery. Are you a fan?"

The woman's smile shifted to the side as if trying to find delicate words.

"Not any longer. I auditioned for a role in one of the films she was in: *Tramp Train Gone off Track*. I didn't get the part, but Lilibet was brutally honest with me and told me I needed several years of acting lessons and a nose job if I was ever going to make it as a serious actress. I took it to heart and left Hollywood with a pretty low self-esteem. I always thought my nose was my only good feature."

"She could be quite curt." Cooper wiped his mouth with his napkin, trying to find anything wrong with her nose or any part of her body. The woman was a dish.

"'Curt' is an understatement if you ask me. Lilibet was known for mowing right over anyone to get ahead. That's why I've always wondered whatever happened to her. After all her efforts, she seemed to have disappeared.

The last time I saw her around Hollywood, she said she had met an attorney named Conner—no, 'Cooper,' I believe it was—said she couldn't stand to look at him, but he had the only thing a rising star needed . . . money and no backbone."

"Bon appétit!" said the waiter, after placing Cooper's food on his plate and walking away.

"Oh, look at me; I'm interrupting your dinner. The food's great here, by the way." Her hazel eyes sparkled, and her lips shifted awkwardly. "I won't keep you—I'll just take a stroll through the streets of Paris by myself and dream as they do here."

Cooper bolted up from the table. "I'm here single— I mean *alone*, too. Do you mind if I accompany you?"

"Are you sure? You haven't even had a chance to eat because of me." Her eyes suddenly seemed to catch the glow of every lit candle in the restaurant.

"I wasn't particularly hungry, anyway." Cooper placed on the table enough cash to pay for the food and a tip for the waiter. Instinctively, he started to grab the photo of Lilibet but decided she was where she needed to remain, with her bottle of alcohol and a straight-line view of the buns she preferred.

THE ~~BITTER~~ END

ABOUT THE
AUTHOR

Multi-Award-Winning Author Milan Sergent studied creative writing in college and began writing the novel series "Candlewicke 13" in 2007, a year after featuring some of the series' characters in his solo art exhibition, titled "Outsiders and Apparitions," near Rockefeller Center in New York City.

An artist and poet since adolescence, Sergent's poetic works also won an international book award. He lives with his wife of 31 years, Beatrice H. Crew, who is also an award-winning author.

To learn more about the author or his works, visit http://www.milansergent.com. While there, join the mailing list for important news updates and notifications about future novel releases.

ALSO AVAILABLE BY MILAN SERGENT

THE TWELFTH BOY

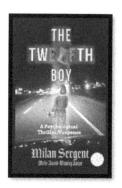

After years of waiting, Savannah Graysen finally finds love and has a miracle baby on Christmas Eve. The boy child, Noel, is a sign from the heavens that being a subservient wife and lover of Christmas has finally paid off until Noel, believed to be an abomination, ends up dead in a manger with a scripture carved on his little chest.

Savannah learns the hard way that some institutions cannot be touched, especially when they're ancient and sacred. Even God said so Himself: "Touch not mine anointed, and do my prophets no harm."

What starts as a mother seeking justice soon entangles her in a web of deceit so divided, so brainwashed, yet still so intent on its mission, that it cannot be reasoned with. If Savannah loses everything dear, will her bravery, she never knew she had, be enough of a reward in Hell?

Praise for *The Twelfth Boy*

"The Twelfth Boy by Milan Sergent is a fast-moving, page-turning novel that took my breath away. . . . I read this book in one sitting, glued to the pages, and I can't recommend it highly enough. It poses many questions about our perceptions of society and the ideas we are subjected to from our early years. A beautifully crafted book that deserves to do very well."

—Lucinda E Clarke for *Readers' Favorite*

Dang Near Royal

When the Gurneys receive a visit from a reality show producer, bringing news of a life-changing inheritance, they must choose to go down with their crumbling shack in rural Mississippi or try to pass themselves off as British aristocracy.

Will the dangerous conspiracy theories the elusive Gurneys cling to prove true when many try to convince them that they are victims of human trafficking being exploited in a snuff film?

Praise for *Dang Near Royal*

"[Dang Near Royal] is comedy at its finest. . . . This is all go right from the first page, a truly down-to-earth comedy with a touch of the bittersweet to it. Milan has written a story that you can only truly appreciate if you understand British humor. I do and I think this would go down a treat as a made-for-TV series in the UK."
—Anne-Marie Reynolds for *Readers' Favorite*

"One of the best comedy novels I have read for a long time. I found the clever play on words and the results of miscommunication throughout the plot absolutely hysterical. The characters each had unique personality traits which made for some incredibly humorous interactions. . . . This novel, however, is far more than a continuous stream of slapstick and hilarious situations; there are also wonderful relationship developments, and the bonds between the members of the Gurney family were completely endearing. The ending was a really good example of the importance of trusting your basic instinct when it comes to evaluating the goodness in people. I highly recommend this novel to anyone who loves well-thought-out and intelligent humour."
—Lesley Jones for *Readers' Favorite*

Outsiders and Apparitions

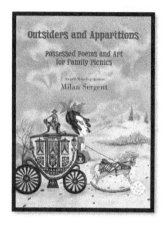

The Pitrick family picnic went off without a hitch until Patty drove the unwelcome wagon into a roadside ditch. Her daughter cried out with maddening dread while apparitions appeared high overhead. She didn't take it as a sign that Patty was dead, but that the crash had mashed her sauerkraut sandwich.

Outsiders and Apparitions: Possessed Poems and Art for Family Picnics by Milan Sergent is an eclectic book of poetry and art by an easily bored author and artist who broke free from gross boundary violations, conformity demands, and abandonment as a youth. The past now only apparitions: he is currently possessed with a mission to encourage expression without dull traditions, rules, or shackling expectations. The soul can be possessed, but the product it produces must be free to protest.

Praise for *Outsiders and Apparitions*
Possessed Poems and Art for Family Picnics

"This superb collection of poetry and art, Outsiders and Apparitions by Milan Sergent, cleverly confronts societal opinions on outward success, happiness, and inner fulfillment . . . . Each poem is illustrated with the most extraordinary and exceptional artwork. I was absolutely captivated by this collection. Milan is such an inspirational artist and writer. His talent for provoking thought and change in human behavior is superb . . . ."
—Lesley Jones for *Readers' Favorite*

Martyrs and Manifestations

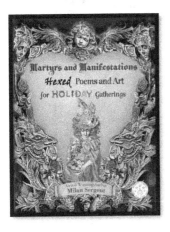

This is an eclectic book of poetry and art by an easily bored author and artist who broke free from gross boundary violations, conformity demands, and abandonment in his youth.

With oppressive forces still clawing from the grave, and people who try to shame or silence victims and embarrassing history, Sergent is currently on a mission to encourage expression without dull traditions, rules, or shackling expectations. Authoritarians can leave us feeling hexed, but you can break the spell.

"Engaging storytelling . . . bursts with odd, witty, playful incidents and characters. The narrative continually surprises . . . charming . . . laugh-out-loud funny."

— The BookLife Prize by *Publishers Weekly* for Book Two of the Candlewicke 13 Series.

"Whether you're a younger reader or just young at heart, this is a very immersive, high-quality fantasy series that never ceases to amaze me with its imaginative quality and new twists to the plot."

— K.C. Finn for *Readers' Favorite*

"Vibrant and funny. . . ."

— The Booklife Prize by *Publishers Weekly* for Book One of the Candlewicke 13 Series